OVERSIGHT

WITHDRAWN

OVERSIGHT

A NOVEL

DENNIS BATCHELDER

NetLeaves

OVERSIGHT Copyright © 2023 by Dennis Batchelder.

All rights reserved. Printed in the United States of America. No part of this book may be used or reproduced in any manner whatsoever without written permission, except in the case of brief quotations embodied in critical articles or reviews.

This is a work of fiction. Names, characters, organizations, places, events, and incidents are either the product of the author's imagination or are used fictitiously, and any resemblance to actual persons, living or dead, events, or locales is entirely coincidental.

The scanning, uploading, and distribution of this book via the Internet or via any other means without the permission of the copyright owner is illegal and punishable by law.

Published 2023 by NetLeaves

Paperback ISBN: 978-0-9798056-6-0
Ebook ISBN: 978-0-9798056-7-7

*For my three perfect grandchildren.
May you have lots of cousins.*

Prologue

Five Years in the Past

"Do people die in this story?" the girl with the curly brown hair asked in a whisper.

The white-haired man pondered her question. "It is about one's fear of dying too soon, Miss Zelly."

"I just hope there's a dragon in it," the boy said.

"I will be sure to include a dragon, Master Simon." He gazed at the three children standing in front of his chair and cleared his throat. "Once upon a time—"

"It's a fairy tale," Simon told the two girls. "They all start this way."

"Maybe in England, but not in Brazil," Zelly said.

The other girl, tall and slender, added, "Not in China, either. At least none that I've ever heard."

The old man smiled at each of them in turn. "Thank you, Miss Zelly. And you too, Miss Ying. Shall I continue?" When they nodded, he said, "There was a king, and he was very sad."

"Why would a king ever be sad?" Ying asked.

"He must have lost his dragon," Simon said.

"Can we let Mr. Morgan tell his story?" Zelly asked.

Mr. Morgan said, "The king's magic garden was dying, and he was running out of time to save it."

"A magic garden? Really?" Ying crossed her arms. "We were kidnapped. Our families were murdered. Sorry, Mr. Morgan, but we have no time for this."

"We can't change what already happened to us," Zelly said. "But hearing about a little bit of magic would be nice."

The old man polished his glasses and stared at them for a long minute. Then he told them this story.

Once upon a time there was a king, and he was very sad. The king's magic garden was dying, and he was running out of time to save it.

The garden was a very special place. It grew the most beautiful flowers, and it fed those in need with delicious fruits, nuts, and vegetables that were found nowhere else. People traveled from faraway lands to see this amazing garden and eat its magical food. This brought peace and prosperity to his people. The whole world was better because of the magic garden.

Only a few special people could care for the magic garden, for it wouldn't obey just anybody. All caretakers were born with very special eyes that could see what the garden needed. The king had these eyes, and he had been one of the garden's caretakers since he was a young man. He served the magic garden for most of his life, tilling and pruning and watering it to perfection. But the other caretakers grew old and died, and no new caretakers came. The king was the last one, and he also was dying. It had been foretold that the garden would disappear if it ever lost its caretakers, and that made him very sad.

The king suspected that a jealous rival was capturing the caretakers, so he sent out his dragon on a mission to rescue them. After searching far and wide with an orb that could spot a caretaker's special eyes, the dragon found the rival and freed the captives. The dragon returned to the king carrying the world's last three caretakers—a fourteen-year-old girl from the east, a twelve-year-old girl from the south, and a nine-year-old boy from the north.

The king knew these three could work together to care for the magic garden. But they were children, and their eyes needed time—more time than the king had left—to grow so they could see what the garden needed.

The king thought about how he might be able to stretch his remaining time. He realized there was only one way to save the magic garden. He arranged to be placed into an enchanted sleep, which would let him live long enough for the children's eyes to mature. He spoke with his assistant, and she agreed to rule in his name while he slept.

The king found tutors to teach the children the ways to care for the garden, so that in just a few years' time they would be ready to rule as the land's princesses and prince.

And when he was done with all his preparations, the king was no longer sad. He lay down on his bed and entered his enchanted sleep, knowing the magic garden and the world would live happily ever after.

When Mr. Morgan finished, he sat quietly, wiping the tears from the corners of his eyes. Then he said, "Today I must take my leave. My dearest wish is that my story will stay with you and help you understand."

He stood and pulled all three children into a tight embrace. Then, he took Simon by the hand and led him out through the door.

As they followed behind, Zelly whispered to Ying, "It's a metaphor. He's the king, and we're the new caretakers."

"We'll be overseers," Ying said. "Mr. Morgan has a tumor in his head. He told the doctors to take it out and keep him alive, knowing it will scramble his brains."

"Can he survive until we're all nineteen?"

"I'm the oldest," Ying said. "He only needs to live long enough for me."

One

Present Day

Ying wants me dead before I turn nineteen.

Her wishes and my wishes are not aligned, obviously. My need to stop her compels me to show up at our bootcamp classroom over an hour early. It's not even seven o'clock in the morning, which puts a real damper on my Brazilian spirit. But I need Val's help if I'm going to survive.

I pause at the classroom door and take stock. I have my essay, and I have my data. My power-red v-neck, contrasting with my morena clara, light brown, skin, sets the right fighting tone. The v-neck's letting too much cleavage show, and that won't win me points with Val. I tuck its back deep into my jeans. I pull on my hair, like somehow that's going to convince my curls to loosen up and cascade over my shoulders.

Val sits at the teacher's desk, typing on her laptop. She wears a summery green blouse, loose jeans, sandals, and a delicate silver necklace. Green, the traditional color worn by Soul Identity employees, looks great with her shoulder-length auburn hair and fair skin.

Val is Soul Identity's acting CEO. We're an ancient organization with our own vocabulary, and CEO is just her external title. We know her as the trustee for Soul Identity's last surviving overseer.

Our overseers run the world's oldest and richest bank, their hands on the trillions of dollars that our depositors have entrusted us to deliver to their future, reincarnated selves.

Piles of money can't just sit. They must be invested. You want to mine asteroids? End world hunger? Conquer, absorb, or just terrorize your country's neighbors? Just convince a Soul Identity overseer that your idea will have a big payoff at some point in the next few decades, and you'll get whatever funds you need to succeed.

Because we're so old, the general public confuses us with many of history's secret societies. But we're not part of the Illuminati, Knights Templar, Opus Dei, Freemasons, Rosicrucians, or even the World Economic Forum. Those guys were—and continue to be—some of our largest borrowers. We let the conspiracy theorists focus on them while we maintain our low profile.

Soul Identity's overseers approve every strategic investment decision. They drive the world's agenda with no one the wiser. And they answer to nobody but themselves. Being an overseer is the best job in the world, and I happen to belong to one of the thirty-five ancient overseer soul lines. I'll be able to take my rightful place in eighteen months, just as soon as I turn nineteen.

If Ying doesn't kill me first. She's turning nineteen tomorrow.

As I walk in, I check that it's just me and Val in the room. I hand her my essay. It's not just any essay. It's my final call for her to take immediate action.

"Can you read this before class?" I ask. "It'll only take a minute."

She glances at the first page. "What is it you want me to see, Zelly?" she asks in her light Russian accent.

"The last five paragraphs are the ones that really matter."

She skips to the end. I watch her eyes dart back and forth. Her brows rise, and she glances over the paper at me. She flips back a page.

She puts down the essay with a frown and gazes at me steadily. The same gaze she's used on me since Ying, Simon, and I arrived five years ago. The one that makes me squirm and tell her more than I want to.

I'll screw this up if I say the wrong thing, so, for once, I keep my mouth shut.

She clears her throat and reads aloud, "This requirement that we must be nineteen before we can serve is dumb. Our trustee claims she can't change it, but that's not true. She's not addressing the risk that the next overseer could eliminate her future peers."

I remain still and hope my essay is persuasive enough.

"We've been doing this dance all year," Val says. "You know I don't have the authority to make you an overseer early, and yet you keep asking me. How can you be so afraid of Ying?"

"She's going to block me and Simon. And then she'll probably kill us." I try to hide my exasperation, but I fail. "It's happened too many times in the past."

She glances at my essay, then back at me. "You treat Ying and Simon as your rivals, but I've spent the last five years putting the three of you through bootcamp, working on a collaborative culture, teaching you to be partners. Are you saying that I wasted my time?"

I don't want to say that. What I want to tell her is how Ying, when we're giving tours to the Soul Identity visitors who have no idea that we're their future overseers, never misses a chance to correct me and put me down. How every day I catch her staring at me with another inscrutable expression. How she tries to get Simon to align with her against me. And how she does none of these things when Val and Scott are around.

But I can't say any of that because it'll just sound petty.

I force myself to drop my arms to my sides. "You told me to talk to her, and I did."

Val folds her hands under her chin, elbows on her desk.

"I asked her for nothing more than a promise to not obstruct, but she won't even give me that," I say. "She's not my partner."

"She's practically your sister. She'd never hurt you. And in eighteen months you'll be serving alongside us."

I stare down at the floor and take two deep breaths before I look up.

"What happens if you're wrong?" I ask.

She crosses her arms. "I'm not wrong. Ying is good."

"But if she's not, how does Soul Identity recover? She'll be in charge, and all your work to change our culture . . ." I spread my fingers. "Poof."

She stands up and walks to the window, staring across the Puget Sound at the Olympic Mountains shining coldly in the summer morning sunshine. "This is crazy, Zelly."

"It's only crazy if you do nothing. You need to make all three of us overseers. Now."

I catch a glimmer of what I hope is hesitation brewing in her eyes. I say, "Do you really want me and Simon to get screwed out of our heritage?"

"Of course not. But I'm doing what Mr. Morgan wanted."

"Mr. Morgan wanted all three of us to run Soul Identity. Not just Ying."

"True," she says. "And he could have changed the age nineteen rule before his brain surgery. But he didn't."

Five years ago, right after terrible people kidnapped the three of us and assassinated every other current and future overseer, Archibald Morgan was diagnosed with an inoperable brain tumor. Realizing that he'd die before Ying, Simon, and I were old enough to take over, Mr. Morgan appointed Val as his trustee and forced the doctors to cut out the tumor, even though it sliced apart the thinking areas of his brain.

Mr. Morgan's sacrifice bought Soul Identity the time it needed for us to grow up. A heroic plan but a flawed one. Because it's essentially a license for Ying to commit murder.

"Simon and I had just as much training as Ying. We're just as ready," I say.

She sighs. "I'm sorry, Zelly. The answer is still no."

So far, our discussion hasn't strayed from familiar territory. But this time I'm going to reel her in with data.

"I want you to look at my latest analysis," I say. I pull out my phone and project its display onto the flatscreen hanging on the wall behind her.

She turns around to face the monitor as I bring up a timeline graph.

"This covers the past thousand years," I say. "Each line you see is an overseer's service dates."

Val stands up and walks to the monitor, examining it. "That's an interesting way to look at overseers."

"Thanks. Now I'm going to overlay the times when a new executive overseer was put in charge." I press my screen and drag another data table on top of the graphic. This causes blue dots to appear along the timeline.

She rests both hands on her hips. "That's a lot of executive overseers."

"Not really," I say. "Remember, it's ten centuries. Twenty-five executive overseers, each serving an average of forty years."

I drag another table onto the timeline. "One last piece of data. Check out what happens to the existing overseers."

Bright orange arrows appear, pointing to the end of each overseer line. I zoom in the screen. "Fun fact—after a new executive overseer is appointed, eighty percent of their peers die within the first year."

Val studies the chart for a long minute.

"Eighty percent," I say. "And that's not even counting those who never got to serve."

She rubs her chin, and I force myself to wait.

"Bootcamp is supposed to break this pattern," she says. "You three are different than your predecessors. I raised you to collaborate."

"Eighty percent," I say. "Are you willing to risk our lives on the hope that your training will override power's ability to corrupt?"

Both of us stare at the screen, saying nothing.

Then she sighs. "How sure are you about that eighty percent?"

"You know me with data," I say.

We both look out the window. A seal pokes its head above the surface of the water, its whiskers glistening. It snorts, coughs, and slides back under the waves.

She'd better not act like that seal. I need her to commit.

"Can you send me the raw numbers?"

I shake my head. "We can't wait for more analysis. It's time for you to act."

Her jaw tightens.

"Please, Val. Don't screw this up."

She stares at me, her eyes narrowing.

I hold her gaze, willing her to understand, hoping I didn't overdo it.

"For your sake, Zelly," she says in a measured tone, "I'm going to pretend you never stopped by."

"But—"

She hands me my essay. "Lose those final paragraphs and resubmit."

I don't blink, don't nod my head, and that holds back the tears long enough for me to give a "Yes, ma'am" and turn away.

I walk out of the classroom before I embarrass myself. I close the door and resist the urge to kick it.

Ying's trying to kill me, and Val won't help. I'm on my own.

Two

I head outside and inform the security guard that I'm going to the park. She nods, and I walk south, down Beach Drive.

We live across the country from Soul Identity's main headquarters, and since Val spends half her time here with me, Simon, and Ying, she needs full-time guards protecting her and the facility.

But very few people know who we are. I take my walks alone, my anonymity keeping me free from the guards' stifling presence.

Tomorrow the anonymity ends for Ying. And once she's outed, I expect most people will figure out that Simon and I are also overseers-in-waiting.

That's not until tomorrow. I can enjoy my freedom today.

Saturday summer mornings in West Seattle bring sidewalks crowded with runners, joggers, and dogwalkers, and I weave my way through them to reach the park.

I sit on my usual bench perched above the rocky beach. My gaze flits over the water. I avoid dwelling on my conversation with Val, and instead let my mind fall into the abyss of a memory from five years ago.

Mamãe had stuck her head in my bedroom door. "Come down and see your grandmother," she said to my twelve-year-old self. "She made pastéis just for you."

I answered her without even looking up from my keyboard. "After I fix this bug."

She stepped into the room, turned my chair around to face her, stared directly into my eyes. "Come down. Say hi to Vovó. Then go back to your bug."

"Ten minutes. That's all I need," I said, without seeing her, without savoring her.

She sighed, kissed the top of my head, and left.

I never got the chance to say goodbye to her. Or to Papai. Or to my Vovó.

A half hour later, after fending off increasingly sharp requests to come downstairs, a man in a mask crashed through my window and used what I now know is a soul identity reader to scan my eyes.

The man was on contract with an enemy organization—The Alert Foundation. He slapped a gag over my mouth and zipped ties onto my wrists and ankles. He dangled my writhing body out the window, where his accomplice reached up, hauled me to the street, and bundled me into the backseat of a waiting pickup truck.

As we drove away, my tranquil childhood ended as I witnessed my house and my family explode in a giant fire ball.

Back in the present, in the park overlooking the beach, I take a deep, cleansing breath, and I tuck that memory away.

Even though those bad guys got crushed in the aftermath of their failed attempt to take over Soul Identity, my family is gone. The best way I can honor my parents' memory and exact my revenge is to become an overseer and use my power to make sure these kinds of criminal groups are eradicated.

Meanwhile, Ying and I are on a collision course. Val might have been able to stop it, but she was too afraid of overstepping her role as trustee. If I survive the next year and a half, it won't be from relying on her.

My eyes follow a barge getting itself tugged toward Tacoma. The tugboat is a thousand yards in front, its cable dipping into the water. If you didn't see barges every day like I do, you wouldn't think the tug is in charge.

Some would say that having overseers in my past lives makes me lucky. But here's the real story. I'm just a barge. My past is a tugboat, pulling me wherever it wants. It robbed me of my family, and it robs me of my agency.

My past is a double-edged knife of both opportunity and obligation. I need to learn about it as much as I can, so I'm ready for wherever it pulls me.

Otherwise, I'm dead.

Three

I return to the classroom only eight minutes late.

Simon has stolen my seat, again. He knows it's mine, but at fourteen, he still thinks it's his job to teach me a lesson.

"You snooze, you lose, Zelly." His English accent still comes through, but fainter than it used to.

As I walk behind his chair, I reach up and tousle his blond hair. I straighten the bowtie he always wears to bootcamp.

He grabs my wrist. As he leans close to whisper in my ear, I catch a whiff of cologne.

"Your favorite teacher is coming."

I smile and pinch Simon's cheek. "You are my favorite. Nobody else."

I throw my backpack on the center desk and wave at Ying who sits, as usual, at her desk by the window. She doesn't notice because her nose is buried in a pocket-size, hardback copy of Machiavelli's *The Prince*.

Her infatuation over the past three months with that book is how I know she's got it in for me.

I raise the center desk to standing height and shove my chair underneath.

Val says, "Glad you could make it, Zelly."

"Sorry I'm late. I must have overslept," I say.

She shakes her head, but she plays along and doesn't mention our earlier encounter.

"What's happening in bootcamp today?" I ask.

"Scott's taking us out on a field trip," Val says. "He stumbled across an invention that he claims could change Soul Identity as we know it."

Scott Waverly is Val's boyfriend. They met twelve years ago at Soul Identity. The bad guys used his technology to locate us and kill our families, but Scott and Val rescued us. That makes him my hero.

"The 'as we know it' part sounds ominous," I say.

"Perhaps," she says. "I thought it presented a good teaching moment, so today we'll go see the company who owns the invention, and we can judge for ourselves."

"Changing Soul Identity is a good thing," Ying says. She's wearing a green pinstripe pantsuit, a white blouse, and low-heeled black pumps. The suit has big shoulder pads and flared legs to put shape into her slender frame. She's got her straight and shiny black hair pulled back into a tight bun.

She sure looks ready to be an overseer.

I ask her, "What's going to be the first thing you change tomorrow?"

She smiles at me. "I want to do something big, Zelly. Something that brings new energy to Soul Identity. It's been five long years since we've had an active overseer. We need it." She looks at Val. "I say this with all respect and no offense for our current trustee."

"No offense taken," Val says, with a smile that seems a little strained.

"Maybe this invention that Scott found could be that big thing you're looking for," I say to Ying.

She rubs her nose but doesn't reply.

"C'mon, girlie. It's only one more day. Are you excited?"

"You should stop calling me girlie, Giselle. Practice for tomorrow's new reality." Ying puts her book in her backpack and darts a glance at Val. "Becoming an overseer is a big responsibility. I hope I'm ready."

A typical Ying deflection with a huge dose of fake humility. She's so much better at it than I am.

"You've prepared for almost five years," Val says. "You're ready. Tomorrow you become our executive overseer, and I become your number one supporter."

Ying smiles. "I look forward to your assistance."

I want to throw up. But instead, I say, "And I look forward to a field trip with Scott. I'm hoping we see some cool technology."

Just like Val and Scott, and unlike Ying and Simon, I'm a full-fledged techie. Back in Rio, my parents bought me a PC for my tenth birthday, and before I was eleven, I had published my first Minecraft mod. If it's got silicon inside, I'm all over it.

"Scott should be here in half an hour," Val says. "We have time for a short lesson."

Simon groans, but Val keeps her eyes on me. "This is an important one," she says. "You need to pay close attention."

I stare back at her.

She gets to her feet. "Listen to this statement. We interpret our own actions based on our best intentions, yet we interpret other people's actions based on our worst suspicions." Val spends a minute looking at each of us. "Who can give me a real-life example of this discrepancy?"

I wonder if Val chose this lesson after our talk this morning and if she's sending me a message.

I raise my hand. "If I criticize Ying, I believe I'm helping her improve. But if Ying criticizes me, I think she's trying to look good by making me look bad."

"I look good because I put the effort into being the best," Ying says. "And besides, your flaws don't need any help from me to be noticed."

Ouch.

I ask, "Don't you sometimes assume that I'm trying to hurt you?"

"I would never admit to it."

"You don't have to admit to it," Val says. "Everybody assumes the worst in others at least some of the time. That's why today we're going to learn how apply MRI—Most Respectful Interpretation—to other people's actions."

Val indeed chose this topic because of me.

Val has us practice figuring out most respectful interpretations. Simon talks about his supervisor at the depositary. Of course, she doesn't know he's an overseer, and she acts super rude toward him—tossing around insults, ignoring important questions, telling jokes at his expense. We come up with this MRI: she's frustrated with her own terrible teenage kids, and she plays those frustrations out on Simon. This is way more respectful than Simon interpreting her actions as a cruel and incompetent manager.

Ying raises her hand and asks Val, "What could be the most respectful interpretation for Zelly begging you to promote her early?"

How does Ying know about this?

Val points at me. "I think you should answer this, Zelly."

Ying and Val must have talked after I left.

I throw on a fake smile. "I'm more interested in the most respectful interpretation of how Ying knows this."

After an uncomfortable silence, Simon says, "I just want to point out the irony that all three of you are acting without respect. During an MRI lesson."

Did Val anticipate that we'd turn MRI into a passive-aggressive weapon? She seems distracted, so it's hard to tell. Instead of mediating like she usually does, she says, "I'm going to bring Scott over. Be back soon." She shuts her laptop and leaves the room.

As soon as the door closes, Ying walks over to my desk. "Do you really think I want to kill you?"

I stare at her. "Serve-te carapuça?"

She raises her eyebrows.

"Does the hat fit?"

She sighs and throws me that inscrutable expression that she's so fond of. But then her face breaks into a bright smile.

"All I can say, Zelly, is thank you."

I shake my head.

"Now we know, once and for all, that you and Simon have to wait your turn."

"That's why you're thanking me?"

Ying's smile broadens. "Now we can move past this and figure out how to work together. You have nothing to fear from me."

Who smiles at their accuser?

Guilty people do. It's clear that she's lying. But before I can confront her, Scott and Val march into the classroom looking like they just had an argument.

Four

"Right before I brought you three to Seattle," Val says, "I promised Mr. Morgan that I'd involve you in our business and that I'd always try to explain the principles I used to make my decisions. But there's so much to learn, and we didn't get to cover everything," she says. "I wish I had spent more time showing you examples of companies who try to trick us with their fake soul line information."

Scott has been standing up against the front wall, his head down, his thumbs poking at his phone. He says, "You said you wouldn't do this."

"Do what?"

"Call it a trick. You don't know that's true." He says this while looking at his phone.

Val crosses her arms. "It's always a trick. The information is always fake."

Scott looks up. "It feels different this time."

Val says to us, "Many startups claim to have access to information about our members' soul line ancestors."

"They're trying to cash in on this huge, unmet demand coming from our members," Scott says. "And I get it. My only recorded soul line ancestor happened to be tight-lipped. But even if he had left me many letters, I would want even more."

"Too bad there's no way to satisfy that hunger," Val says.

"Perhaps there is."

She sighs. "I guess it's time for you to share."

Tech time.

Scott puts away his phone, steps forward, and shoves his hands into the back pockets of his jeans like he's reciting something from memory.

"One of my security buddies, Jeremy, called me up," he says. "Last year he was trying to use quantum entanglement as a way for people to communicate without anybody eavesdropping."

"Quantum what?" Simon asks.

"Entanglement. When two particles act in harmony with each other. But it doesn't matter. Jeremy convinced himself that it wasn't worth the effort."

Scott tells us that Jeremy was flirting online with an astrologist, and when he bragged about his cool project, she asked him if quantum entanglement could help her do past lives readings. This got Jeremy wondering if the soul identity remains entangled with its carriers across time. He told the astrologist that she might be on to something.

"Did she realize he was just trying to get into her pants?" I ask.

He grins. "She did if she was any good at her job. She dumped him for a wealthy Texas widower."

Scott says that Jeremy kept toying with the idea, and he came up with some technology that helps people to observe their soul line ancestral experiences through a process named after the Greek word for 'live again'—xanazo. He pronounces it as KSAH-nah-zoh and spells it out for us.

Scott says that Jeremy offered to sell us his company, and

that we should take this seriously. "Vicarious observations flesh out your past in ways our depositary cannot. His technology can totally disrupt our business."

"Hold up," I say. "Vicarious observation? Fleshing out your past?"

Scott rubs his hands together. "Imagine you're inside the head of one of your soul line ancestors. You can't change anything, but you see what they saw, hear what they heard, and feel pain and pleasure just like they did. A totally immersive experience. That's xanazo."

We have nothing like this—just dusty old journals and a few artifacts that require our customers to invest their imagination to even get a glimpse of their ancestors' lives.

But imagine they could follow their soul line ancestors around and experience them with all their senses. I would love to do that.

"Xanazo sounds like it could be gross," Simon says. "I don't want to feel anybody throwing up. Or going to the bathroom, or eating poisoned food, or getting hurt."

"You can experience winning a race," Ying says. "Or accomplishing something significant."

"Maybe," Simon says. "If you can choose who and what you observe."

"What are the chances it really works?" I ask.

Scott smiles. "We don't have to speculate. We're visiting Jeremy's lab, and you can experience xanazo for yourselves."

If I could vicariously observe my soul line ancestors, I could learn some tricks to defend myself. I'd be able to protect myself from Ying.

Then again, Ying could learn some tricks to attack me.

Val's biting her lip. She's probably thinking like me, realizing that we future overseers could use this xanazo technology in evil ways.

Overseers have that kind of history. It's a good reason to be worried.

Five

We have ten minutes before leaving, and Simon is in my room, helping me fix my glasses.

Before the kidnapping, my dream was to start a computer game company and pull my family up and out of middle class. That dream has since died. I'll never be seen as an overseer if I spend all day writing games. Yet another example of how my past dictates my future.

But I've dealt with the disappointment. I'm already going to be podre de rico, with plenty of money, and like it or not, my family is gone. These days I geek out on electronic gadgets that could help Soul Identity.

My current gadget is a pair of modded eyeglasses. If I were to look at Simon through them, two tiny cameras would scan his eyes. The difference between his two irises, what we call his soul identity, is unique only while Simon is alive. His soul line ancestors had it before he was born, and his soul line descendants will have it after he dies.

People get all kinds of mushy feelings about their soul line descendants. They go to great lengths to help them succeed, and that's why Soul Identity thrives. We've been around for 2,600 years, storing people's money and memories in our depositary, promising to pass it all to their soul line descendants. Not only do we have lots of money to invest; we also have a huge database of all the soul identities that we've collected over the ages.

Anyway, my code calculates the soul identity and retrieves the person's name and status from our database. If we know anything about them, the glasses project an information bubble onto its lenses, just like a heads-up display.

Scott says that once I'm done, he'll market my smart eyeglasses to his existing customers who use his Soul Identity apps. He thinks that both the soul seekers and the soul line recruiters will love them.

I'd like to show him my progress, but first I've got to squash the rest of my bugs. This one shows the information bubble right on top of people's faces, which makes it distracting when you're trying to talk to them. I wrote a fix last night and need to test it. I plug a cable between my laptop and the glasses, open the debugger, and transfer my updated code.

I put on the glasses and face Simon, who stares at me with his eyes wide.

"You don't have to do that anymore," I say. "I fixed that bug last night."

"Finally." He relaxes his face. "What are you working on now?"

"Getting the info bubble right." In just a second, a bubble with Simon's name and status icons pops up, but it still hides his face.

I scowl at my code, but it seems fine. I take off the glasses and check the mini heads-up display projector. It's loose and no longer calibrated. I use a jeweler's screwdriver to tighten it.

I put the glasses back on, and this time the info bubble floats over Simon's head, right where it belongs.

"I am such a genius," I tell him.

"You are, Zelly," he says as he looks at his phone. "But let's not be late for the field trip."

Scott's friend Jeremy lives on Vashon Island, the top of which sits almost five miles down and across the Puget Sound from our place. To get there, we need to take a ferry.

We climb into one of the company cars, and Val drives us to the Fauntleroy Terminal and onto the boat.

During the short ride across the sound, Scott and I stand at the side railing next to the car.

I close my eyes and enjoy the feel of the breeze and the ferry's motion over the waves. "We should do this more often," I say. "I love being on the water."

We watch three cormorants clustered together on a floating log, drying their wings. As the ferry intrudes into their space, they take to the air.

"Did you ride the ferry in Rio?" Scott asks.

"Most weekends. That was my favorite excursion."

After a few more minutes of watching the breeze blow the white foam off the peaks of the waves, I hand him my modded eyeglasses. "Check these out. I think I'm finally ready."

He runs his finger around the rims and over the cameras. "You got them working?"

"Put them on and see for yourself."

He obliges.

I try not to blink when he looks at me, though I know my software works better than that.

"Very cool," he says. "Your bubble says you are Giselle Oliveira, so nice job."

Scott walks over to the car and pokes his head inside. "And now I can see Valentina Nikolskaya and Ouyang Ying, even though they're in low light. And one more . . . There he is. Simon Green."

He takes off the glasses. "That's awesome work, Zelly. What comes next?"

I replay that awesome work statement a few times to myself.

"I want to get a hundred pairs built," I say. "Then we can beta test them on your customers."

"You'll need to choose a factory. I can help you ask for quotes."

We walk back to the railing, and he turns the glasses over in his hands. "I wonder if these could help me test our new reader access points."

Scott found a security vulnerability in the reader access points we recently installed inside our office buildings. They require both an ID badge and a matching soul identity to let you pass.

When he ordered them, Scott specified they needed to verify that a real human was using them by strobing a light into the eyes and checking if the pupils contracted. That way you couldn't get in by holding up a picture of an eye.

"That makes sense," I say. "What's the vulnerability?"

"I'll show you," he says. He pulls a reader access point out of his messenger bag. He flashes his ID badge across it, then holds the reader lenses up to his eyes. The lights blink green, allowing access like they're supposed to.

Then he uses a photo of his eyes and holds it up against the reader lenses. He flashes his badge, and the lights blink red, denying access.

"So far, so good," I say.

"But watch this." Scott uses his left eye, but just a photo of his right eye. The lights still blink green, allowing access.

"They only verify that the left eye is real?"

He nods. "It's a big vulnerability."

It sure is. If I wanted to pretend that I was Scott, I could just generate a fake right iris that, when combined with my own left iris, will generate his soul identity.

His new reader access points look high-tech, but to a sophisticated attacker, they're no more secure than plain old badge readers.

I think about what it would take to attack his access points with my eyeglasses. I'd have to calculate the fake right iris, and then I'd have to project it into the reader access point instead of onto the eyeglass lens.

This sounds like fun. "I'd love to build you a proof of concept."

"That would be awesome," he says. "Then I can show them that the access points need replacing."

"I'll write some code and try it out," I say. "It shouldn't take me long."

He hands me the device. "Let me know once you get it working."

Six

The ferry arrives at Vashon Island, and Scott directs Val down a tiny and bumpy road that follows the shoreline. She turns into a paved driveway and parks next to a silver conversion van.

The five of us stand in front of a tidy forest-green beach cottage. It has white trim and a bright red front door. A steep ramp climbs the left side to a balcony on the second floor. All the window blinds on this side of the house are pulled closed.

Scott walks up to the door and raps on it. I hear a click. He turns the handle, steps inside, and beckons us to follow.

"Sorry we're late," he calls out as the rest of us enter the house and into its kitchen. A living room area straight ahead boasts floor-to-ceiling views framing the Puget Sound.

Scott leads us through the kitchen and points at two couches in the living room. "Grab a seat while I check on Jeremy." He climbs up the stairs.

Ying and Simon sit, but I walk across the hardwood floor to the sliding doors. I open the middle one and step onto the patio.

Below me lies a narrow, rocky beach littered with washed-up driftwood. A seagull and a crow fight over a half-eaten crab. The seagull grabs it in its beak and flies off, and the crow chases and divebombs the seagull. When the seagull drops the crab, the crow snatches it out of the air and returns to the beach.

Val comes over and stands next to me. "Those birds will always find a way to fight with each other, no matter how much food is available."

"Like me and Ying," I say. "Though I'm not sure if I'm the seagull or the crow."

"Sometimes you're the crow. Sometimes, like today, you're the seagull. Just avoid being the crab."

Good advice.

I glance at her. "Can I ask you something?"

"Always."

"How can you already know the xanazo thing is fake?"

She sighs. "Every time somebody shows us this kind of stuff it turns out to be fake. And fake information leads to bad, even dangerous, actions. Our job is to shut these guys down before they hit the mainstream and make a mess."

This seems personal for Val. Maybe she's thinking how forty years ago, one of our members was tricked into believing that her dead husband was reincarnated as baby Val. They conned the poor lady into killing herself in the misguided hope that they'd be reunited.

"I'm afraid the technology will go viral before we can control it," she says.

"That would be fine if it works, right?"

"It won't work. These things never do."

We watch the crow pick at the crab.

"But even if it does work," she says, "we'll have to make sure it doesn't get abused."

I doubt she's worried about abuse. Val's probably afraid of

Soul Identity losing its monopoly on soul line information. That means Scott's insistence about interrupting bootcamp with today's field trip is to help Val deal with that change.

I hear somebody clear their throat, and I turn. Scott stands above us on the small balcony, shading his eyes from the sun.

"Jeremy's almost ready," he says. "Come on up."

The four of us climb the staircase, and it empties us into a room with a huge worktable dominating its center. Around the edges stand two 3-D printers, three workstation areas each with two huge screens, and a love seat facing the window.

My kind of place. But something's missing.

A toilet flushes in the back. A sink faucet runs, and a door twangs as it opens.

Jeremy is a handsome, brown-skinned man, no older than twenty-five, with a well-built chest and powerful shoulders popping through his shirt. He's got a huge smile outlined by a short-trimmed goatee, and he's pushing himself in a wheelchair.

"Welcome to Chez Jeremy," he says.

Chairs. That's what was missing.

After Scott introduces each of us, Jeremy has us stand around the worktable.

He rolls himself to the window side. "Y'all can enjoy the view this way."

"Thanks for seeing us on short notice," Scott says.

Jeremy waves him off, and he asks Simon, "You ready to vike, little man?"

"Vike?" I ask.

"It's hella better than calling it vicarious observation or even xanazo," he says. "And the word vike is both a noun and a verb. Versatile."

"It's not the name that we came to hear about, Jeremy," Scott says.

"A great name transforms a good product into a remarkable product," Jeremy says.

Scott pus his hand on Val's shoulder. "Convince this lady here that your technology is real."

"Riding the vike is as real as it gets. It's awesome. Maybe even better than sex."

Silence ensues and Jeremy grimaces. "Uh, my apologies. I don't get many young visitors. Who's ready to vike?"

I start to put up my hand, but then Scott says to Val, "You're the one who needs convincing. How about you go?"

Val squints at Jeremy. "You should show us more first," she tells him.

"Sure thing." Jeremy rolls his wheelchair over to a workstation. He reaches into a box and lifts out a black ski hat covered with blinking red Christmas lights.

"This beanie, my friends, is a portal to vike space," he says. "It's a self-contained brain computing interface."

Jeremy turns the beanie inside out and shows us the sensors and transmitters that press up against the back of the wearer's head. A fat rechargeable battery sits at the base of the neck.

"What's the beanie's job?" Val asks.

"You've used noise-canceling headphones before? This baby cancels your senses—all of them. The sensors read the signals heading into your brain, and the transmitters add anti-phase signals. Then we activate your PCC, and your brain generates the vike all on its own."

"What's a PCC?" Simon asks.

"I'll show you." We follow Jeremy to another of the workstations, where he grabs a life-sized, 3-D plastic model of a brain. He pulls it apart and points to a tiny, kidney-bean-shaped section deep in the middle. "Your posterior cingulate cortex is most active when you're daydreaming. It lets you relive your own memories."

"What's the magic part?" Val asks.

"Magic?" Jeremy asks.

"The part that makes your company special enough to purchase."

"Ah," he says. "The magic comes from you."

"Me?"

"Well, from Soul Identity. This might sound crazy, but if you picture yourself drawing Soul Identity's logo just before the beanie activates your PCC, you'll be able to access not your own memories, but the memories of your soul line ancestors."

"Our logo?" Ying asks.

He smiles at her. "Weird, huh?"

"How can this possibly work?" Val asks.

"Dang if I know. I'm pretty sure your logo is the key that activates a primitive part of our brains' default mode network, but I have no idea what comes next. Is it quantum resonance across time? Dark matter particles? A person's soul?" Jeremy raises his arms and lets them fall.

"You don't know how your invention works," Val says.

"I don't have the faintest idea," Jeremy says. "But once you ride the vike, you won't care that I can't explain it to you."

Ying asks Scott, "What happened when you viked?"

"I imagined the logo, and I found myself in a dark room filled with ribbons of light. Each ribbon was a timeline of memories of one of my soul line ancestors."

"That's what viking is?" Val asks. "Sitting in a dark room full of ribbons made out of light?"

"No, the vike started when I jumped onto one of the ribbons and I became Ned Callaghan."

"Ned Callaghan?"

"The opal miner," he says. "My soul line ancestor. Remember the skull we found in that Slovakian cave?"

She nods. "You became him?"

"And I was no longer me," he says. "The word observation is a misnomer. But really, Val, it's like you're asking me to describe a dream. Just vike, and you'll see for yourself."

She scrunches up her face like she's sucking on a maracujá azedo.

But I'm more than ready to put on that beanie and vike into one of my own soul line ancestors and finally feel what it's like to be an overseer. Before Val can snap out of her analysis paralysis, I raise my hand and say, "I'll go first."

Seven

"Way to dive right in, Zelly!" Jeremy says. He points at Ying and Simon. "You guys should pay attention, so you can go next."

He opens a manila folder and places it on the worktable in front of him. "There are just three things you need to remember. First, study the Soul Identity logo, so you can create your own mental image." He hands each of us a laminated sheet of paper emblazoned with our logo, triangles drawn around the right and left Eyes of Horus.

But it's not quite our logo. I use my phone to access our website. I compare its logo to the one on the paper. Where ours has both eyes on one triangle, Jeremy's logo splits the eyes so they're on two triangles that make up different sides of a pyramid.

"This isn't our logo," I say.

"Good catch," Jeremy says. "I'm using the original Psychen Euporos logo, from the earliest records I could find. Way back when Thales started things in Miletus." He points at my phone. "Your current logo won't let you vike. You need the real deal. Make sure you can imagine yourself drawing it with your eyes closed."

I study Jeremy's version. Its pyramid is more like a diamond with its base squashed almost flat and its top stretched out. I examine the eyebrows, the swirls and teardrops hanging from the eyelids, and the lines extending from the outer corners. I close my own eyes and imagine drawing the logo myself.

"Second thing," he says. "Remember Scott describing a dark room with ribbons of light? That's the vike space. You can get an idea of what's happening on the ribbon by brushing it with the back of your hand. Once you choose a spot, jump onto it with both feet, and hold on tight, because the ribbon's gonna buck and wriggle and try its best to toss you."

Ying points at Jeremy's wheelchair. "How are you able to jump on?"

"These duds work just fine in vike space," he says. "No paralysis, no wheelchairs. Nothing but the real me, standing tall."

Vike space sounds great.

"And one last thing. Never vike all the way to the end of a ribbon. That's when your soul line ancestor died, and you don't want to go there."

"What happens if you do?" Simon asks.

"Do you ever dream of falling off a cliff?" Jeremy asks him.

"Every now and then."

"Have you ever hit the ground?"

"Never."

Jeremy opens his eyes wide. "Because if you did, you'd die. Instantly."

"Nonsense," Ying says. "That's a myth."

"Okay, you won't die if you vike off the end of a ribbon. But you will suffer, because time is different." Jeremy points at my phone. "We'll set your timer for just one minute, and that gives you about a day in vike space. But if you run off the end of the ribbon before your PCC deactivates, you'll get stuck in a timeless zone."

He stares at me. "Lemme say it again. Timeless. Imagine being stuck in a place with no sensory input for what feels like forever."

Yikes.

Val turns to Scott. "You told me this was safe."

"It is." He looks at Jeremy. "Why are you scaring them?"

Jeremy says, "Don't worry. It's not gonna happen. And if even if it does, it won't kill them. It just won't be as fun. That's why I'm telling them."

Val turns to me. "You're sure you want to do this, Zelly?"

"I'm positive." I look at Jeremy. "Logo. Feet. And stay away from ribbon endings. I've got this."

But do I?

Jeremy directs me to sit in the loveseat facing the window with my feet up on a hassock. He rolls his wheelchair to face me. Under his guidance, I pull the beanie over my head. My curls stick out of the bottom.

He has me scooch down so my neck is supported by the back of the seat. He holds up a sheet of paper with a QR code on it and tells me to scan it with my phone. I follow the prompts to install an app. It asks for the beanie's ID, and Jeremy reads out a string of numbers.

"Now tap *Calibrate*," he says.

A series of pictures of various shapes and colors flash across the screen of my phone. I hear fragments of Tchaikovsky's 1812 Overture, and the phone vibrates with short and long pulses. A few seconds later, the app shows *Calibration Successful*.

"What about my other senses?" I ask.

"If we calibrate your vision, hearing, and sense of touch, we know enough to auto-calibrate your taste and sense of smell."

"Pretty impressive," I say.

"If you think that's impressive, this is gonna blow your mind. Tap on *Test Touch*."

I tap, and I can't feel the phone. I watch it slip out of my hands and onto my lap, but I don't feel it land. I can't even feel the couch under me. It's like I've gone weightless.

I concentrate and guide my numb left hand down to my lap. I use my fingers like a claw to pick up the phone. I rotate my wrist to view the screen. I bring up my right hand and force it to tap *Stop*.

"Did you have any sense of touch anywhere in your body?" he asks.

I run a mental inventory and shake my head. I try to stop myself from glancing at Jeremy's legs, but my eyes betray me.

Jeremy notices and grins. "Watching you try to pick up your phone reminds me of my early wheelchair days."

I can't imagine surviving without any sense of touch.

I tap *Test Hearing* while he's talking, and it's like I pressed a mute button. Jeremy's lips are moving, but I hear nothing. I try to say something, and I can't hear myself. All the background noises that I didn't even realize were there are gone, too.

Maybe there are benefits to having a mute button on life. But not for me. I'm happy tapping *Stop Test* and hearing the little things again. Like the muted sound of waves lapping the shore, birds chirping, Simon scratching his arm, Val whispering to herself, Scott adjusting his stance, Ying patting her leg, Jeremy breathing.

"Did it mute everything?" he asks.

"Dead silence."

"Great," Jeremy says. "The vision testing auto-stops after ten seconds."

I tap *Test Vision*, and it's like he's put a blindfold on me. I reach up to check if my eyes are still open, and they are. Scary.

After what feels like an hour, I can see again.

"That's it," Jeremy says. "You're ready to vike"

Scott asks Val, "Impressed yet?"

"I'm interested in only one thing," she says. "Whether any soul line information transfers."

"Noted," Jeremy says. "Let's get Zelly's vike going."

A shiver runs through me as I wonder what will happen when all my senses disappear. Will I freak out?

But I can't stop now, not with everybody watching me.

"Bring it on," I say.

"Don't forget to draw the logo," he says.

I hope I remember how to draw it.

"When you're ready, tap *Vike* and set the duration to one minute. It will start itself automatically once you confirm."

I tap, set, and confirm, and my world goes dark, silent, and weightless.

Eight

Nothingness. No sound, no light. No sense of up or down. I'm neither hot nor cold.

It's not as bad as I thought it would be. Losing every sense all at once has allowed my brain to adapt instead of to compensate.

Elated and empowered, I realize I need to envision myself drawing the Soul Identity logo. But with what should I draw? A pencil sounds boring. So does a paintbrush.

I arm myself with a sword. And with three quick cuts, I carve a large triangle into the blackness in front of me. Fiery lines of molten gold fill the gashes my sword leaves behind. With two more cuts I attach a second triangle.

My sword carves eyebrows on each side of the pyramid. Shining white light fills the grooves. I add both eyes, and I give them each a teardrop. I place a glowing blue iris into the centers. Did I miss anything? The swirls at the eye corners. I flick the tip of my sword to carve them in.

As soon as I finish the second swirl, the pyramid tilts and moves toward me. It accelerates, and I can't dodge it. I scream as the molten gold and the tip of the pyramid reach my chest.

But the pyramid disappears, along with my sword. I remain alone in a dark, cavernous space. And I start to wonder what I did wrong. Did I draw the wrong logo? Should I have not used a sword? Stuck to one color? Most importantly, am I trapped here? The time was for one minute, but didn't Jeremy say that it could feel like forever if I screwed it up?

Everybody knows I'm impulsive and rash. Why would they let me go first?

But wait.

On my left, ribbons of light glow in various colors. The warm air around me carries a whiff of fresh cinnamon. There is a faint but deep, melodic chanting in the background. I have a tangy taste in my mouth, and I feel a slight breeze on my arms.

That breeze tickles more than just my arms. I glance down and discover that my clothes didn't make it to—what did Jeremey call it? Vike space.

I am standing on a flat disc that's five feet wide. I can't see any kind of floor beneath it. I look to my left, and the disc swivels so I'm facing the ribbons.

There are at least fifty of them. Most are short, under ten feet in length. But a handful of the ribbons stretch out for miles. Scott said they represented timelines of soul line ancestors. This means only a few of my shared-identity predecessors were blessed with long lives.

I lean toward the ribbons, and the disc moves forward like it's a futuristic hoverboard. I test it by leaning in all directions. I can also go up and down by standing on my toes.

I want one of these hover discs at home, not just here in vike space. Too bad nobody's invented them. Yet.

I zip around the ribbons as I figure out what else I can do with the hover disc. I love how it can accelerate. It takes just a few seconds to reach the ends of the longest ones.

I return to where I first started, and I stare at the ribbons. Time to choose. I remember Jeremy's warning about avoiding the ends, so that eliminates all the short ribbons, leaving me a handful to choose from. I raise myself up so I can reach the one closest to me, and I slide down about a third of the distance to where it flows both thick and wide.

I'm ready for this. I reach out and let the back of my hand brush against a bright orange bend. I smell sulfur, and I hear guns firing and people screaming. I see uniformed soldiers running out of a trench and toward a bridge.

I don't want my first vike to be the experiences of a soldier during a war, so I pull back my hand. I tiptoe so the disc rises high enough to reach another long ribbon, guessing that this will take me back to an earlier soul line ancestor. Preferably before guns were invented.

I should aim for something more soothing. I find a spot that's placid, with more soft greens and blues and less oranges and reds. When my hand brushes this ribbon, I smell salt water, I hear seagulls, and I see ocean waves in front of the bow of a small ship, an island poking up in the distance.

I do love the sea, and a boating-based vike sounds perfect. I just need to figure out how to start. Jeremy said the ribbon would try to throw me off. I raise the disc until it's just a foot beneath the ribbon so if it tosses me, I won't fall too far.

The ribbon runs in front of me, left to right. I jump up and land with my legs spread. I find myself standing, swaying on the ribbon like I'm on a tightrope. But the ribbon writhes back and forth, and it gives a great up and down shake. I lose my balance and I land, butt first, on the disc.

Ouch. Do my feet need to be at the same point in time? I spin the disc until the ribbon of light runs on my left side, and I step my left leg over to straddle it.

I leap in the air and bring my feet together, making sure they're parallel with the ribbon. I stick out my arms to help balance, and I land so that the balls of my feet are touching the ribbon. I flex my knees to keep from falling off.

This time the movements aren't as sudden. My feet sink into the light like they would into sand on the edge of a beach. I watch the light climb up my shins. When it gets to my knees, I realize that my feet haven't hit the disc—somehow the light has absorbed them, and my legs, and now my waist. I hold up my arms as the light creeps up my chest, my neck, and my eyes, which are overwhelmed with a blinding glare. I try—

Nine

"— Eat it," you say with a snarl. "Now."

The woman crosses her arms over the large tear in her blouse. She kicks the clay bowl. Rancid bits of meat and vegetables spill out as the bowl skitters across the floor and out of the cell.

You dodge the splash and come back to the wooden bars. "Captain says he'll whip me if anything happens to you."

Her smile shows mostly gums. A few yellow teeth remain. "Doesn't matter anyway, silly girl. They're coming for me. They're coming for him. He's dead already. Just too dumb to know it."

It's hot, and the cell smells like piss.

"Whatever. Starve yourself for all I care." You leave and climb the steep ladder to the main deck. Back topside, you wind your scarf around your forehead and shade your eyes from the blazing sun.

"She eat anything?" asks a man wearing nothing but a loincloth. His chest and arms are covered in crude tattoos. He hawks and spits over the railing into the azure water below.

You shake your head. "She says she'll be rescued."

The man gestures back behind him. "See anybody coming?"

You look across two or three miles of open water at the great stone mountain rearing up in the middle of the island. "Nobody."

"Probably thanking their gods I took her off their hands. Drunken all that wine, beaten each other up. Now they must be snoring it up on the beach."

"Probably," you say. "But a breeze would get us gone. Before they wake up and notice."

"It'll come tonight," the man says. "In the meantime, them fish need gutting."

You shuffle to the stern next to a pile of flopping fish. You pick up a stout stick and prod one free. The fish is at least two feet long. You club it over the head, pull a knife out of your belt, and kneel on the deck. With quick slices, you remove the fins, slice open the belly, and gut it. You separate the roe from the gills and entrails and cut off the head and tail. You toss the slippery guts, fins, head, and tail over the railing and into the water. You place the fish meat and the roe in the basket, and you do this again and again, until you exhaust the pile of fish and fill the basket.

You groan as you stand up, your knees cracking. You wipe your hands on your robe and brush the scales off your arms. The seagulls are divebombing the entrails, and you pause to watch the shark fins circling the few remaining heads. You pick up the basket and carry it over to the rear ladder. You climb down while holding the basket in one hand, your bare feet slipping in an oily puddle at the bottom.

"What took so long, wench?" The man's large belly strains against his dirty tunic. He flicks back his greasy ponytail and points at a table. "Leave them and get out of my galley."

You climb back up the ladder and walk to the bow, where the man in the loincloth frowns at the blue sky.

"Fish gutted?" he asks.

You nod.

"Try feeding her again."

"Just gonna waste it," you say.

"Do what I tell you."

You climb below to the galley.

"Captain wants her to eat," you say.

The cook slices off five pieces of raw fish and places them in a clay bowl. A splash of vinegar and he hands it to you.

You walk belowdecks to the cell, stooping low to avoid the crossbeams. On the way, you pop two of the slices into your mouth. The vinegar bites into your tongue.

The woman lies on the rags, facing the wall.

"You hungry yet?" you ask. "I brought fish. Fresh."

No response.

You sigh, set down the bowl, and reach down the front of your robe. You grab the key that dangles between your breasts. You unlock the door, pick up the bowl, and squat next to her.

"Hey," you say. "You alive?"

No answer.

You reach out with your left hand and shake her shoulder.

In an instant, she grabs your wrist and pulls on it as she flips over to face you. She yanks your hand up to her mouth and bites down on your little finger.

You scream as she twists her head back and forth, her teeth tearing through your skin and grinding into your pinky's bones. The pain dashes up your hand, shoots into your arm, and lands deep in your chest. You club her in the ear with the bowl, and she pulls away after one final bite, blood dripping down her chin.

You hold up your hand. The top two thirds of your pinky are gone. Gooey strands of blood and saliva dangle from the red flesh.

"You're a monster!"

She glares at you as she chews once, twice, and a third time. You hear the bone crunch. She swallows and grimaces. "There, I ate. Happy now?"

You let out a howl and struggle to your feet, clutching the stump of your pinky with your other hand. You lock the door, kick it, and stumble back to the galley.

"She bit my finger off!"

"Let me see." The cook's examination brings tears to your eyes. "Doesn't look bad. You still have a stub."

"That savage ate it. Stared right at me while she chewed and swallowed."

"She's feisty, all right. Exactly what the captain needs." He grabs a rag, twists it, and ties it tight to the stump of your pinky. "Go topside and wash your hand in the sea. Scrub it clean. And watch for sharks."

The captain waits at the top of the ladder. "What's with the hollering? Did you feed her?"

You show him your missing pinky. "I brought her fish, but she ate my finger instead."

The captain roars with laughter, and he cuffs the side of your head. "Teaches you to stay suspicious."

You walk back to the stern. A small rowboat floats next to the rudder, and you climb down the rope ladder and step into it. You lean over the gunwale and dangle your bloody pinky stump in the water. Pain jolts up your arm, and you gasp. You squeeze the stump and poke at the wound. You stare at the trail of blood streaming away in the clear water, and you pull out your hand when a shark fin appears.

You clamber up to the deck, and you hear the captain laughing belowdecks. You walk to the bow and sit with your legs dangling over the side. The sun begins to sink, the sky glows in pink and orange, and you pull out a harpa de boca and play melodies as the sun vanishes and the throbbing in your hand subsides.

When darkness falls, you stand, cursing as you bang your pinky on the railing. You walk to the stern and—

Ten

I jerk awake, my heart pounding. I need to sterilize my pinky before it gets infected. I grab for my left hand, and my phone drops to the floor with a clatter.

"Zelly," Scott says.

"I need antibiotics."

"Zelly," he says again.

I stare at him and then at Jeremy in his wheelchair. When did they board the boat?

"Give her a moment," Jeremy says. "Zelly, you okay?"

Jumbled sensations flood me. I remember the calibration, the logo, the vike space, and jumping to my soul line ancestor's timeline.

"I . . . I was on a ship, somewhere warm. The captain kidnapped a woman and locked her up." I hold up my left hand. "My job was to feed her, but she bit off my pinky and ate it."

Simon grins. "Zelly got eaten by a cannibal."

Ying sits next to me on the loveseat. She asks, "What was vike space like?"

"Just as Scott said—ribbons of light. I was on a hoverboard that let me float close enough to reach them."

"How many ribbons?" she asks.

"At least fifty. Most of them were short. I'm guessing these were my soul line ancestors who didn't live long."

She asks, "Did you know what was going to happen before you viked?"

I nod. "I touched a couple of the ribbons with the back of my hand to help me choose."

"Like watching previews?" Simon asks.

"Sort of. But these previews let me smell and feel."

Ying says to Jeremy, "I'd like to go next."

"Hey, I want to go," Simon says.

"I can do you both at the same time," Jeremy says.

Simon takes my place on the loveseat, next to Ying, who unwinds the bun in her hair to fit the beanie's sensors.

While the two install the app and calibrate, I think about my vike experience.

I don't recall anything about sailing in my soul line ancestors' public records. I'll have to research and try to identify who, when, and even where, I viked. I can even try to track down which overseer, if she was an overseer, was missing most of her left pinky.

How much of my initial confusion was caused by a lack of context? If I had known more about her before the vike, would I have been able to better follow what she was doing?

I have no clue about who the captive woman was, why the captain wanted her, how my soul line ancestor was there—or even when and where "there" happened to be.

Come to think about it, the chances are slim the woman and the crew spoke either English or Portuguese. So why could I understand what they said? The vike must be replaying perceptions and not just the raw sense signals.

Lots to explore later.

I walk over to the window, and Val follows me.

"Did you discover anything new?" she asks.

"Everything was new."

"I mean, information that wouldn't be in your soul line collection."

"I was a servant on a boat. That was new to me." I raise my eyebrows. "You know I can't access my soul line collection yet."

"Just vike yourself, Val," Scott says. "You have no known soul line ancestors, so any information is new."

"That tells me nothing," she says. "I can't verify any soul line ancestor. The information could just be made-up crap and I'd never know."

"I see," he says. "You want information that's tied to one of our known soul line ancestors, but isn't in our soul line collections, so there's no way we'd know about it beforehand."

"And that can be independently verified," Val says. "Zelly?"

Maybe the archives have recorded if one of my overseers was missing her pinky. Maybe they won't mention she worked on a ship and then maybe I could find proof elsewhere that she did.

But that's a lot of maybes. I shake my head.

"Me neither," Scott says. "I viked to Ned fighting at Gallipoli, but I already knew he had been there."

Jeremy helps Ying and Simon start their vikes. Their beanies' lights change from red to blue. They both sit forward, eyes half open and unfocused. Every now and then one of them gives their limbs a shake.

"Did I twitch like that?" I ask Jeremy.

"Everybody twitches and yelps like they're dogs dreaming," he says. "You gave a loud holler after you started."

That must have been when I thought my carved logo was going to pierce my chest.

"I'll only get worried if they stop twitching," Jeremy says. "That would indicate they've viked off the end of a ribbon."

Simon's beanie lights turn red. He jerks and sits up and stares wide-eyed at us.

"Your vike is over, Sy," I say. "Welcome back."

Simon stares right through me for at least a minute. He reaches up with both hands and rubs his eyes.

"Is he okay?" I ask.

"Re-entry experiences vary," Jeremy says. "He'll be fine."

"Sy, can you hear me?"

"I hear you," he says. Then he smiles. "That was awesome."

"Where did you vike?"

"I flew an airplane! Alone. I inspected the plane and took off, and I flew over a city, and the countryside, and a high mountain range."

"Do you know where you were?" I ask.

"Somewhere in Asia. I saw pagodas when I soared over the towns. And dragons, too."

"Real dragons?" I ask.

"Statues of dragons."

I glance at Ying. Her beanie lights shine blue, and she's still twitching.

"Why isn't she back yet?" I ask Jeremy.

He wheels his chair closer to her. He takes the phone from between her fingers and opens his eyes wide.

"Problem?" I ask.

"She changed her vike time." He bites his bottom lip. "To six hours."

"We can't wait here that long," Val says. "Please bring her out now."

Jeremy scrunches up his face. "The thing is," he says, "I can't stop a vike in the middle."

"Won't taking that beanie off her head stop everything?" I ask.

"No, all the beanie's doing now is keeping her senses canceled. Taking it off will mix her viked senses with real-life. I highly recommend we don't do that."

"Then stop the vike," I say. "Deactivate—what was it? The PCC?"

"That's the issue. I only know how to activate it."

Val says to Scott, "You told me this was safe."

"If you can't stop a vike, it's downright dangerous," Scott says. "You'd think that would be something you'd tell people before they started."

"Now hold on," Jeremy says. "I have a standard set of warnings that I go through. I tell everybody to vike for one minute, and that's the default setting. Ying would have had to change it herself, say she was sure, and then she'd have to confirm again. She knew she was increasing her vike time."

"If she didn't know the consequences, it doesn't matter how many times you got her approval," Scott says.

Jeremy looks like he's about to argue, but instead he sighs. "That's an excellent point."

Scott motions to Val, and they walk over to the window and whisper to each other. I ask Simon to get up, and I take his place next to Ying.

I wonder why Ying changed the time, anyway. Was she trying to out-compete me and Simon? Or mine her overseer past to find ways to get rid of us?

Either way, we're stuck here until she's awake. That's not very considerate, and it sure doesn't bode well for the culture of Soul Identity under her leadership.

"Is she just going to lie there for six hours?" I ask Jeremy.

"Pretty much." He wheels over to a cabinet and rummages around inside of it. "She needs a diaper, just in case. Would you mind putting it on her?"

"Simon and I didn't need diapers."

"Viking is like sleeping. Your body controls itself, usually. But let's say you didn't go to the bathroom before you went to bed. You may have to get up in the middle of the night."

"And Ying can't get up while she's in a vike."

"Right," he says. "One time I viked for only two hours, and when I came out of it, I had wet my pants."

He hands me an elastic waist, pull-on adult diaper that looks like the ones I used to help my great-grandmother wear.

He says, "I use these during long vikes. Saves me from cleaning up afterward."

"What's your longest vike?"

"Six hours because that's what my phone app limits it to."

Jeremy brings me a blanket, and I drape it over Ying's waist. I reach underneath to take off her boots, pants, and underwear, and I slide the diaper up her legs. I pull her pants back up and slip on her boots. I fold Ying's underwear and place them in her suit jacket pocket.

"How long will the battery last?" Val asks.

"At least twenty-four hours of continuous use."

"Let's bring her home," I say.

Val nods, and says to Jeremy, "We can get the beanie back to you after she wakes."

"Hold up," Jeremy says. "That vike portal is my intellectual property. You can't take it with you."

Nobody says anything for a minute.

"You see, Jeremy, Soul Identity is all about taking it with you," Scott says. "We're not going to wait here. We're taking Ying home."

Eleven

Jeremy glares at Scott but eventually he says, "Fine, but I want my vike portal back by tomorrow."

"Deal." Scott scoops Ying into his arms and carries her down the staircase.

By the time we walk out the front door, Jeremy has rolled himself down the outside ramp. He intercepts us at the conversion van.

"When she comes out of her vike," he says, "make sure you feed her. An active PCC consumes a lot of energy. She'll lose at least two pounds in the next six hours."

Nobody says anything on the way back to the ferry terminal. Once we drive onboard and the ferry starts to cross, Scott gets out of the car. He beckons me to join him.

"I'd rather not," I say. "I've always been a bit nervous on boats."

He gives me a funny look. "Did you just say you were nervous?"

"Yeah. Ever since I can remember."

"On the way over here, you said how much you loved taking the ferry."

"Why would I say that?"

"I must have misunderstood. No big deal."

He walks away, and I get out and chase after him, keeping away from the railing.

"What exactly did I say this morning?" I ask.

He tells me that I talked about taking the ferry when I was a child in Rio and how much I enjoyed it.

When Scott heads back to the car, I gaze over the water, even though my heart pounds and I want to hide in the car.

I force myself to think about Rio and the ferries I took. I close my eyes and remember times I spent on a fishing boat with my grandfather, just off the Ipanema and Copacabana beaches. I recall the ferry ride over here this morning.

I wait until the pounding in my chest subsides. I'm still afraid to look straight down, but I should be fine after another few hours of practice.

―――

When we get back home, Scott carries Ying up to her room and sets her on the bed. I prop two pillows behind her head and shoulders.

"I'll keep an eye on her and let you know when she's up," I say.

"Thanks. See you guys at dinner."

Scott leaves, and I look at Ying, wondering again why she changed her timer to six hours.

Maybe Ying felt she needed a quick way to gain a year's worth of experience. I should have done that myself.

I set an alarm for when her vike will end. For the next two hours, I sit at her desk and work on my modded eyeglasses.

Scott's idea to use my glasses to trick a reader access point sounds fun. It takes me an hour to write the code. Now, if I press the reset button, the very next person's eyes I look at will be used to generate a fake right iris image that, when combined with my own left iris, matches their soul identity. Then, once I'm in front of a reader access point, I'll press the button twice to fool it.

Ying's still viking, so she makes the perfect test subject. I put on the eyeglasses, press its reset button, and use my fingers to open her eyes so I can build my "I am Ying" right iris image. Then I grab her ID badge from her purse.

I hold up the reader access point Scott gave me and wave Ying's badge at it. I press the eyeglass reset button twice as I look into the reader lenses.

Unfortunately, the lights blink red.

I think for a minute. The reader must have gotten confused by seeing both my right eye and the crafted image.

I try again, this time closing my own right eye.

The lights blink green. The reader access point thinks I'm Ying.

It works! Scott's going to love this proof of concept.

An hour later, I'm still in Ying's room, eyeing the beanie on her head.

I want to see Jeremy's code.

Most embedded systems prototype boards, like the one in my eyeglasses, let the developer update and debug through their charging ports. I find a USB-C port next to the beanie's battery.

I can plug in my computer's interface cable and take a peek.

The problem with these ports is that systems stop executing and drop you into a debugger if you plug in a cable. If that happens when I attach, the beanie will stop blocking Ying's senses. That might mess up Ying's vike.

But now that I've found the port, my brain can't go anywhere else. I try to distract myself with my eyeglass code, but that black beanie on Ying's head is a SIREN calling out my name.

If Jeremy's vike portal does go into debug mode, I can just restart it. That would take me no more than five seconds. I do the math. Five seconds of real time is about two hours in vike space.

Is the need to satisfy my curiosity worth two hours of confusion for Ying?

This is the kind of ethical dilemma that I wish Val had reviewed with us in bootcamp.

I build my own moral equation. Ying's unilateral decision to vike for a longer period has cost me six hours of babysitting time, whereas my impact to her would be at most only two hours of confusion.

Sounds like a fair trade to me. In fact, Ying should thank me for going so easy on her.

Val would be impressed with my ethical decision-making skills.

I still want to limit Ying's confusion, so I decide to do what I can to block her senses. I go to my room and grab my noise-canceling headphones and my napping blindfold. I put them on Ying, and I stuff her nose with tissues.

I plug in the cable. The beanie's lights turn red, and the debugger pops up on my screen. I get the code running again in less than two seconds.

Ying suffered around a half hour of sensory confusion during her vike. She can thank me later, when I get around to telling her.

I poke around and discover that Jeremy programmed the vike portal in Python, a scripting language, giving me access to his source code. I download it to my laptop, unplug the cable, and start digging in.

Jeremy's code is clean with lots of comments. It's broken into three modules. Housekeeping talks to the phone app and manages power, sense-blocking figures out the canceling signals, and activation send commands to the PCC.

I ignore the boring housekeeping stuff and read through the sense-blocking module. The beanie has paired sensors and transmitters for each sense—sight, hearing, taste, touch, and smell. The canceling routines read the sensor data at the edge of the brain, calculate its inverse, broadcast it through the transmitters, and doublecheck the result for continuous calibration.

I geek out on reading code, and Jeremy's is beautiful. Most of it.

His ugly code is what he wrote for the activation module. He passes in the duration to keep the PCC activated, collects some sensor data, and runs a complicated formula to create the activation command.

I try to crack open the formula. It has a cryptic comment at the start. It says, "# TODO insert refs once GJ shares."

GJ, whoever or whatever that is, wrote this formula that activates the PCC.

I'm still trying to understand it when my alarm goes off, the beanie lights turn red, and Ying begins to moan. Not in pain, but more how I sound when I take that first bite of passionfruit cheesecake.

Twelve

Ying does more than moan. She thrusts her hips up and down in a way that convinces me her vike involved activities much more carnal than eating cheesecake.

I pull the tissues out of her nose, lift off the noise-canceling headphones, and remove the blindfold. I take off her beanie and tuck it into my backpack.

After a few seconds, Ying opens her eyes and looks around. "Why are you in my bedroom?" she asks.

"Welcome back," I say. "When we saw you changed your vike time to six hours, we brought you home."

"My vike time? Wait, I remember. We went to Vashon Island."

"Do you remember where you viked to?"

"A long time ago. I was an overseer . . . They had an amazing amount of power. They got so much done."

"From what you were doing when you woke up, it seems they also made time for fun."

She smiles, but she doesn't say anything. Classic Ying.

"Which overseer was it?" I ask.

She frowns. "It might be best if our vike experiences remain private."

Why would she say that? What did she learn? And why won't she share?

Ying reaches down to her waist and slips her fingers under her pants. Her eyebrows go up. "Why am I wearing a diaper?"

"Jeremy had me put that on you, so you wouldn't wet yourself. I put your panties in your pocket."

Instead of thanking me, she frowns. And that just gets me thinking that if she's not going to share, there's little sense in hanging out with her. I grab my backpack, remind her that it's almost time for dinner, and leave, resisting the urge to slam the door behind me.

Before I go downstairs, I poke my head into Simon's room. "Ready to eat?" I ask.

"Yup. How's Ying?"

"She's fine. But she wouldn't share anything from her vike."

"She's acting normal then. That's good news."

I lean my head against his doorframe. "I guess I was hoping that she'd change."

"In what way?"

I shrug. "Now that she's sure we're not joining her as overseers until later, she'd ally with me."

"Fat chance," he says. "You did call her a killer."

I sigh. "Why can't she talk to me about this?"

His eyes go wide. "Seriously? Do you realize how intimidating you are to your peers, Zelly?"

I shake my head. "Me?"

"You ace every exam. You have to run every group project. Both Scott and Val take your suggestions for most every dilemma. Then you have this amazing coding gift. You're super intimidating to both me and Ying."

I put what I hope is an encouraging look on my face. "You guys are awesome, too."

He snorts. "You take up all the oxygen in the room, Zelly, and you know it."

"Are you suggesting that I change?"

He shakes his head. "No. But you may consider cutting Ying a break for wanting to show everybody that she's capable on her own."

I nod and smile to Simon, but I'm thinking that the more I can intimidate Ying, the less the likely that she'd dare kill me.

Simon and I cross the patio to the dining hall, on the ground floor of Soul Identity's Seattle guest house.

George and Sue give us cheery welcomes. Once upon a time, they ran the guest house at headquarters. Later they worked in our physical security division. In fact, they ran Scott's operation that rescued the three of us.

Now they're semi-retired, spending their summers in Seattle running the dining hall. This is great for me because George is a gadget lover.

While Simon walks back to the kitchen with Sue, I show George my modded eyeglasses. He puts them on and utters many oohs and ahhs.

"These are fantastic, Zelly. Or should I now call you Giselle Oliveira?"

"Zelly is perfect."

"Seriously, these are nifty. You should sell them to old people like me so we can remember everybody's names."

George gives me cool ideas, too.

He takes off the glasses and hands them to me. "When can I get a pair?"

"How about you take these?"

"For real?"

These eyeglasses contain the hack I did for Scott's reader access points, but George won't be able to use it since I hard coded it to just my eyes.

If I give the glasses to George, everybody benefits when he can keep track of who we are. Scott can wait to see my hack once I build another pair.

"They're all yours," I say.

He puts them on. "Sue, come see what Zelly built this time!"

"I'm busy, my love," she calls. "Do you want your meal to burn?"

George winks at me. "Someday I should just say yes and throw her for a loop."

"I double dare you."

His fakes a shiver. "My wife is an ex-intelligence officer." He drops his voice to a theatric whisper. "Did I ever tell you how she saved me from being killed by neo-Nazis?"

"Almost every day."

"The benefits of getting old. I always have new stories to tell you kids."

As I show George how to use the charging case, Scott and Val walk in.

"Did Ying have any problems waking up?" Val asks me.

"She was a little confused, but no more than we were."

I omit the detail about interfering with her vike just so I could get to the beanie's source code.

When Ying opens the door a few minutes later, George walks over and peers at her through the modded eyeglasses. "Good evening, Ouyang Ying."

Ying pats his shoulder. She walks over to Val and stands straight, her hands clasped behind her back.

"I'm very sorry, Val. I created an inconvenience for you."

It feels rich that Ying is apologizing to Val when I'm the one who had to diaper and babysit her. But that's Ying.

"I promise it won't happen again," Ying says.

"I was worried for you," Val says. "How are you feeling?"

Ying crosses her arms. "Everything is fine."

"Why did you change your vike time to six hours?" Scott asks her.

Great question.

"Because that was the longest it would go. I expected Jeremy to wake me up as soon as you wanted to leave."

"Uh, that's the problem," I say. "You assumed that Jeremy could stop a vike. He can't."

Ying gasps. "That's insane!"

"And it's dangerous," Val says. "The first thing we'll do is fix the safety issues. Before somebody gets killed."

The first thing we'll do?

"Wait a minute. Are you acquiring Jeremy's company?" I ask.

"As fast as we can," Scott says. "All the vicarious observation tech will belong to Soul Identity by midnight."

Apparently, Val no longer believes that Jeremy's company is fake.

"What's the rush?" I ask.

"We have to get his company off the market before others discover its potential," Val says. "I'm seizing this opportunity for Soul Identity."

It does seem like a great opportunity. I can't wait to vike again.

But I see Val acting scared on her very last day of being the only one in charge of Soul Identity.

Maybe she's scared about potential competition. Or after Ying's six-hour vike, she's scared of Ying's ability to make good decisions.

Ying says, "I think buying Jeremy's company is a great idea."

Val smiles. "I was sure you'd agree. I'll send you my first cut at an integration plan tomorrow right after the ceremony."

"I look forward to it," Ying says.

I highly doubt that. Knowing Ying, she's probably forming a plan to sideline Val.

But enough of this speculation. I turn to Ying and say, "Tell them about your vike experience. You went back to an overseer, right?"

Ying frowns at me, and I hold up my hands and walk away. But I stay close enough so I can eavesdrop.

I hear Scott ask, "Do you know where you went?"

Ying says something, but I can't make it out.

"Cool," Scott says. "What was Egypt like?"

I still can't hear Ying's answer. And before they say anything else, Sue and Simon come out of the kitchen carrying large serving dishes.

"Who's hungry?" Sue asks.

"I am," George says. "What's for dinner?"

"Kale salad, a vegan meatloaf, and roasted Brussels sprouts for you."

"Lucky me."

"And we have broiled salmon and mac and cheese for everybody else," Simon says.

George sighs.

Ying and I go to the kitchen. She grabs the tableware and I get the other serving dishes.

"Why do you think Val bought Jeremy's company so quickly?" I ask.

"It's a blocking move," she says. "She's thwarting any potential competitors."

"Is this good for us?"

"Of course. Think about it," she says. "In just six hours I earned more than a year's worth of knowledge and climbed a tall mountain of wisdom. Imagine if I could experience every moment of my previous lives."

"We would be the best overseers ever," I say.

She uses her hip to push open the swinging door to the dining hall. "I don't know if I'd be the best," she says. "But I'm sure I would be extraordinary."

Thirteen

George and Sue want us to hang out in the dining hall and play board games, but soon I go back to my room. It's already eight o'clock, and I want to dig into Jeremy's code before we fly to Sterling.

Soul Identity will be the new owners of Jeremy's vike technology, and I want to understand how the beanie's PCC activation works. I can try to solve how to interrupt a vike. That sounds fun, and that contribution might remind Val that I'm ready to be an overseer.

And that would give me time to take a second vike. I'm eager to revisit the lady on the ship. Does my soul line ancestor become an overseer or a pirate? Or both? Does she fall in love or live a life of solitude?

So much to discover. I can't wait for more.

Time is short, though. We need to reach the airfield by four-thirty tomorrow morning. I doubt that I'll go to bed. But just in case I fall asleep, I set my alarm for three-thirty.

As I settle into dissecting the activation formula code, my mind keeps replaying the conversation I had with Ying in the dining hall when she said what a better overseer she would be if she could experience every moment of her previous lives.

I feel the same way. It would be beneficial to tap into the experiences of our soul line ancestors, especially the ones who were overseers.

But something bothers me, and I'm not sure what.

I bring my attention back to the activation formula. It's beginning to make sense. The LEC, or lateral entorhinal cortex region of the brain, produces timestamps that get attached to memories. Jeremy's code reads a timestamp, reads it again a second later, and predicts what the timestamp will be when the requested duration has passed. It tells this to the PCC, so it knows when to fall asleep.

Doesn't that feel backward? It's like having to decide in the morning what time you will go to bed. That's great, unless your evening plans happen to change, and you end up slumped over your late dinner, face planted in your vegan meatloaf. All because you picked the wrong time to fall asleep.

It feels backward because it's a hack to the PCC. And hacks are never pretty.

Hack or not, that's how the activation code works. Now I'm back to thinking about my conversation with Ying. I realize that I'm bothered not by what she did say, but by what she didn't. When I told her that *we* had the chance to become the best overseers ever, all she said was that *she* would be extraordinary.

She's going to keep any knowledge she gains from viking to herself.

But I could be overreacting. I should practice what Val taught us this morning and figure out the most respectful interpretation of Ying's behavior. I message Simon and ask him to come to my room.

Five minutes later, he's sitting on my bed, already in his pajamas.

"Remember Val's lesson this morning?" I ask.

"Of course."

I recount my conversations with Ying, including her comment about overseer power, her refusal to share what happened during her vike, and how she wouldn't acknowledge that we'd all benefit. I also mention how Ying's vike ended in the middle of a sexual encounter.

When he's done giggling, he asks, "You want to figure out the most respectful interpretation?"

"That's why I asked you here."

"Ying's afraid that if she tells us about her sexy vike, she won't be allowed to go back for more."

"Come on. Who would stop her?"

"Good point," he says. "So how about this? Ying is embarrassed at the way her overseer ancestor behaved, which is much worse than what we know from history, and she doesn't want anybody to find out."

I think about that. "I guess that's possible," I say. "But it's not resonating with me."

We're both quiet for a moment.

"I'm out of ideas," he says. "You should tell me your not-so-respectful interpretation."

I might as well put it out there.

"Ying wants Soul Identity all to herself," I say. "To be the only overseer."

"By getting rid of you and me?" Simon scratches his head. "I suppose she could do it. But she'd also have to get rid of Val."

"Val's a trustee only while Mr. Morgan is alive. And he'd be an easy target."

His eyes open wide. "That's definitely not respectful."

"No, I suppose not," I say. "But if it's true?"

"We could just ask Ying what she meant."

"And if she lies?"

He sighs. "We're going in circles. How about we figure out which overseer she viked into?"

I knew it was worth asking Simon to come.

I use my laptop to pull up an interactive overseer timeline that I built for last year's capstone project. It overlays a map of the world with all thirty-five overseer soul lines.

I click on Ying's image from a dropdown containing the last known people from each line. That reduces our list to nine—Ying plus eight of her soul line ancestors.

"Did she tell you where she viked?" Simon asks.

"No, but I overheard Scott talking to her, and he said Egypt." I check when Soul Identity was headquartered there, and I add a time filter to include just 321 BC until 231 AD. That shrinks our list down to two overseers in Ying's soul line: Philo and Origen.

We read about these ancient overseers by clicking their profiles and running internet searches. It takes some time to convert the dates shown in the Soul Identity profiles, which are written as the year of the corresponding Roman Emperor, to the dates on the internet, which use the modern calendar. But soon the two men's stories emerge.

Philo was a Jewish thinker who lived in Alexandria around the time of Christ. He doesn't stand out in the Soul Identity archives. He becomes an overseer when he's forty-five. Fifteen years later, in 40 AD, Philo serves as an ambassador for the Alexandrian Jews on a trip to Rome, where he loses a dispute between the Greeks and Jews in front of Caligula. He dies the next year.

Origen was a Christian scholar and one of three overseers under Demetrius, both the Bishop of Alexandria and executive overseer. In 231 AD, a plague kills his two peers, leaving just him and Demetrius. Weeks later, Origen becomes executive overseer and shifts the headquarters from Alexandria to Caesarea in Palestine. Demetrius stays behind in Alexandria and dies the next year at the ripe old age of 105. Origen lives in Caesarea for many years and dies at age 69.

I can't see Ying getting excited about Philo's life as a thinker and failed diplomat. Origen seems more like her kind of guy.

"It's got to be Origen," I say. "Two overseers die, one retires, and he moves our headquarters to another country. Tell me he wasn't doing something shady."

Simon sits, brooding, tapping the desk with his fingertips.

"I hope it's Philo and that you're wrong about Ying," he says.

There's no way it's Philo.

Just like I picked up a new fear of boating in a one-minute vike, Ying's brain might have rewired her moral compass after her six-hour vike into Origen. And that could leave me and Simon, not to mention Mr. Morgan, in even more danger.

We need to talk to Ying.

Fourteen

As I tell Simon how I inherited a fear of boats from my one-minute vike, my phone buzzes with an incoming message.

"Ying's coming over in five minutes," I say.

"Good. We can get this cleared up."

"I'll bet she wants another vike. Should I give her the beanie?"

"You might as well. She's in charge tomorrow anyway."

I pick up the beanie and stare at it, wondering if I should erase the code on it so Ying can't use it tonight.

Or not erase it. I could modify it. I pull up the activation module and add two lines of code. The first line checks if the duration requested is for exactly six hours. The second line, an evil line of code, will get called if that answer is yes.

"What are you doing?" Simon asks.

"Oh, just fixing a bug."

What I don't tell him is that the bug I'm trying to fix resides in Ying. Better that he doesn't know.

I upload the new code into the beanie and disconnect just as the door opens.

"Hi, Zelly. Oh. Hi, Simon," Ying says. "What are you guys doing?"

"We're talking about our vikes," I say. "Come and join us."

She gets a serious look on her face. "We're better off treating our vikes as private."

"Why is that?" Simon asks. "Did something bad happen to you?"

Ying looks at him but doesn't say anything. Instead, she points at the beanie on my desk. "I was hoping you had that with you."

"I need to give it back to Jeremy," I say. "He's coming at midnight."

"He's selling his company to us. He doesn't need it back."

"Then I should bring it to Val."

She puts her hands on her hips. "I need to use it again. Tonight."

"It's not safe," Simon says. "We don't know how to break out of a vike."

"It's safe enough. The three of us viked this afternoon, and we're fine."

"Well, not quite," I say. I tell her how I developed a fear of boats. "We don't really know the consequences that come from viking."

"You must have picked up new insights," she says. "That makes it well worth the risk."

She strides across the room and sits on my bed, and Simon and I both spin our chairs to face her.

She says, "I need to be a great executive overseer. If I can vike again tonight, I'll get more experience, and I can avoid making rookie mistakes."

I pick up the beanie and say, "I wanted to vike tonight."

Something sparks in her eyes. "I'm the one who needs it."

I set the beanie back on my desk. "Well, you'll be the boss tomorrow. Then you can vike as much as you want."

"Zelly," she says, "I really need to do this."

I stare at her. "If you want to vike tonight, you have to tell us what happened in your last one."

She frowns. "Our vike experiences should remain private."

I stay silent, keeping my eyes on the beanie.

At last, she sighs. "What is it you want to know?"

I shrug. "Nothing in particular. Just share who you viked into and something cool they did."

She nods. "That's easy enough. I spent almost two years as Philo. When he was an overseer in Alexandria."

Did she really vike to Philo and not to Origen?

"And you wanted something cool," she says. "I climbed up the Alexandria lighthouse, one of the seven ancient wonders of the world."

"Wow," Simon says.

"Which year were you there?" I ask.

"I don't know."

"In those days, they based the years on the emperor," Simon says. "Who was it?"

"Augustus," she says.

Simon throws a glance at me. We both know Ying is lying, because Philo became an overseer eleven years after Augustus died. When Tiberius was the emperor.

"Is that enough sharing?" Ying asks. "Can I please have the vike portal?"

I hand her the beanie, and she stands up.

"It's all charged," I say. "I was playing with it, so remember to calibrate."

She glances at her watch. "What time do we leave for the airport?"

"Four o'clock sharp," Simon says.

"Great. That's plenty of time."

I should at least warn her about my code change.

"Wait," I say. "I've been going through the code. Don't vike for six hours. It's not safe to do that much in one day."

"How would you know the safety limits for viking?" she asks.

"Just trust me on this. Limit yourself to no more than three more hours tonight. It's much safer. And you'll make your flight."

Ying gives me one of her enigmatic smiles and departs, beanie in hand.

Fifteen

Simon leaves soon after Ying. I didn't tell him how I modified the beanie's code.

I lie down and try to sleep, but now it's almost midnight, and I'm still wide awake.

At least I warned Ying. That's what I kept repeating to myself as I think about the code change that I made.

If Ying chooses to vike for the full six hours, my code will instruct her PCC to stay active all the way until midnight on my nineteenth birthday. Ying will remain on her vike for the next year and a half until I also become an overseer.

Did she heed my warning?

Schrödinger scoffed at quantum entanglement in his thought experiment with Einstein. His theoretical cat was both alive and dead until Schrödinger observed and became entangled with it.

He may have mocked the idea, but I can relate to it. Until I go to her room and observe her, Ying is both awake and asleep, both powerful and helpless, both trusted and untrusted.

My alarm goes off at three-thirty. It's time for me to check if Schrödinger's cat survived.

And I need to do is remove my code from that beanie, so I don't get caught.

I knock on Ying's door, but she doesn't answer. It's unlocked, so I let myself in.

Ying is dressed in a blouse and skirt. She lies on her bed, her head back on her pillow, her phone in her hands pressed against her chest.

She's wearing the beanie, and its steady blue lights indicate her vike is active. However, her phone shows the vike ended five minutes ago.

Ying ignored my warning, my evil code change worked, and Ying is only six hours and five minutes of her way through an eighteen-month-long marathon vike.

First things first. I plug my laptop cable into her beanie, override the debug session, and replace my changed code with the original.

When my evil code is gone, I sit next to Ying, watching her body twitch, thinking about the last time I sat on her bed.

Back when I was fourteen, I had walked by Ying's door. She was curled around her pillow, her eyes puffy and red. Next to her lay a book, open wide but face-down so I could see the cover. It was Greene's *The 48 Laws of Power*.

I sat next to her. "What's wrong?"

She flipped over and faced the wall. "I'm fine."

But it wasn't convincing, so I stayed while she sniffled for a few more minutes. I picked up the book and leafed through it.

I said, "In Brazil we have this word called saudades. It's the sadness you get when you know that something from your past won't ever happen again."

Ying swiveled her head toward me. "Why are you telling me this?"

I placed my hand on her back. "I get the saudades, too, Ying."

She moved it off. "We're not friends, Zelly. Stop trying to act like we are."

"You're my friend. You're probably even my best friend."

"We may be friendly to each other," she said, "but we'll never be friends. Can't you see that? We're overseers, and that puts us at odds with each other. We don't have a choice."

"We don't have to act like our soul line ancestors, do we?"

She rolled her eyes. "That's so naïve. We have twenty-six centuries of history that teaches us how to behave."

"Don't you want to at least try to be friends? For as long as we can?"

"We'll never be more than frenemies. Just deal with it." She took the book from me and turned back to the wall. "And close the door when you leave."

Three years later and here I am, back in her room, Ying lying in her bed not talking to me. Almost like before, except that now I've embraced my past and accepted the limits to our relationship.

"You left me no choice, girlie." I reach out my hand and stroke her cheek. "But I wish you had listened to my warning."

I take a quick shower, wrap a scrunchie around my wet curls, and slip into black yoga pants and an oversized teal sweatshirt. I grab my roll-on and my backpack and make it downstairs two minutes late.

Scott, Val, and Simon are standing by the front door with their luggage.

"Where's Ying?" Scott asks.

Like I'm going to tell him. I shrug, hoping he can't tell how nervous I am.

"Did she start another vike?" Simon asks.

"She better not have," I say.

"Why would she be viking now?" Val asks.

"I had the beanie, but she came last night and took it."

"Didn't she vike enough yesterday?"

"She said she wanted more experience before becoming an overseer."

Simon says, "Zelly said she planned to vike, but Ying said she wanted some extra learning before today."

Scott and Val exchange glances.

"Let's check on her." Scott says.

When they walk upstairs, Simon grabs my arm. "I found something interesting. Did you know that one of your soul line ancestors served with Origen?"

I shake my head. "We would have seen it last night."

"You filtered her out by choosing just the Egypt dates. She joined later, after he moved the headquarters to Caesarea."

"Zelly, can you hear me?" Scott hollers from upstairs. "Could you bring your laptop up here?"

They found Ying.

I run up the stairs with my backpack, Simon right behind me. Val stands in the hallway, talking on her phone.

I enter Ying's room.

Scott waves Ying's phone at me. "The app says the vike has completed, but the beanie lights are blue. Jeremy wants to walk us through a debug."

"Let me get set up." I pull out my laptop and a USB cable.

Val comes in and puts her phone on speaker. "Go ahead, Jeremy. We're ready."

"Right on," Jeremy says. "Who's got the debugger?"

"Zelly's here," Scott says.

"Hey, Zelly," he says. "Okay, here's what you need to do. Open your IDE and start a debug session."

Good thing I practiced this earlier.

"Done," I say. "What's next?"

"You're gonna plug a USB-C cable from your laptop into the beanie. But before you do it, listen to me. That's gonna drop the beanie into the debugger, which makes things confusing for Ying. You must be quick."

I plug in the cable and send the break sequence in less than a second. Much faster than last time, but I can't tell them that.

"Okay, I'm plugged in."

"Great. Now, Zelly, I need you to grab the activity log."

Porra! Activity log? Jeremy's going to know what I did.

My stomach tightens up like it's about to cramp. I breathe in through the nose, out through the mouth so I can look like I don't care.

Jeremy explains where to find the log, and I download the file to my computer. I open it, and Scott scoots closer to me.

"What am I looking for?" I ask Jeremy, keeping my voice steady.

"Go to the end and find a line starting with the word *PCCSLEEPTIME*. We can see how long her PCC was told to sleep."

I find the line. Scott reads it and says, "There's no number, Jeremy. Just the word *Overflow* encased in brackets."

The cramp is gone. Talk about dodging a bullet. The log doesn't show my code change.

But then Simon opens his big mouth and says, "Zelly, you did warn Ying not to vike for so long."

My stomach thinks Simon needs to stop talking, now. I throw a glare at him.

"You said you saw something in the code," he says.

Porra dupla!

"You saw the code, Zelly?" Scott asks.

"I went through it after dinner." And before dinner too, but that's irrelevant.

I need a way out before I get caught. Good thing I'm Brazilian. I've had lots of practice with finding what we call jeitinho, the little way through rules and convention.

I'm going with diversion.

"Jeremy, I was reading the PCC activation function," I say. "That code is super tricky. Who is this GJ that I saw mentioned in the comments?"

"GJ? What are you talking about?"

"Pull it up," Scott tells me.

I open the original version of the code.

"I see it, Jeremy," Scott says. "It's a TODO line. It says to insert refs once GJ shares."

"Is GJ somebody who worked on this project?" Val asks.

"No," Jeremy says. Then, after a minute, he adds, "Well, not really."

"What does that mean?" Val asks. "Did you disclose this GJ in our purchase agreement?"

A long pause. "GJ helped with the PCC activation function," Jeremey says. "And no, he's not disclosed."

Val taps her phone. "He's on mute," she says. "Scott, if we don't have all the inventors signing off, we may have a problem with the purchase."

"Let's figure out how to wake up Ying before we tell him that," Scott says.

Val unmutes. "Jeremy, how do we get Ying out of her vike?"

"I'd better come to your offices and see what we can do."

When Val disconnects, she says to Scott, "I need to tell Sterling to reschedule today's ceremony. I'll also call the lawyers to see what options we have. Can you work with Jeremy to get Ying out of her vike?"

"Of course," Scott says. "Simon, I'm betting that George has adult diapers. Could you bring one for Ying?"

After Simon returns, I kick him and Scott out of Ying's room. I put the diaper on her, and I take her hand.

I may be upset that Ying lied to me and scared that she's busy learning new ways to hurt me and Simon, but I'm not proud that I stuck her in a vike for the next eighteen months.

As I sit there, I reach the conclusion that I have two almost impossible challenges ahead of me.

First, I need a solid plan to survive Ying's attempts to block my overseer future. Not my usual seat-of-the-pants approach but something bullet-proof.

Second, I must get Ying out of her vike and not wait eighteen months. Because although I've justified what I did, I don't want to be the kind of overseer who needs force to get her way.

But not yet. She needs to stay in her vike until I have a survival plan. First things first.

Sixteen

Jeremy arrives before six in the morning. We don't have an elevator for him and his wheelchair, so Scott carries Ying downstairs to the main level and lays her on the couch. I stick a pillow under her head and straighten her skirt.

"I'm concerned about the overflow message in the activity log," Jeremy tells Scott. "I want to dump the memory and see what that value was."

"Will it affect Ying?" Scott asks.

"For the ten seconds it takes to dump its core," Jeremy says.

The PCC wakeup time is set to my birthday. If they see that, they'll never trust me again.

"Hold on," I say. "You're about to give Ying a confusing five hours."

Scott nods at me. He asks Jeremy, "How important is this?"

"If you want to wake her up, I need more information."

"You're saying there's no other way."

"I don't know of one."

They're going to find out what I did, but I can't stop this dump without it looking like I don't care about Ying.

The thing is, I do care about Ying.

"If we need to do this," I say, "we should block her other senses." I go upstairs and bring back the same blindfold and noise-canceling headphones I used on her earlier.

Jeremy fires up his laptop. He plugs the cable into the beanie and taps on his keyboard. Ten seconds later, he exits the debugger.

I take the headphones and the blindfold off Ying. Meanwhile, Jeremy starts reading through his memory dump.

I start wondering what I'll say once they catch me.

Two minutes of pins and needles later, Jeremy lets out a sigh.

"Find anything?" Scott asks.

"Nothing," he says. "The memory was garbage collected."

I put on a sad face even though I'm dancing inside.

Jeremy closes his laptop. "I'll keep digging, but she's gonna need a feeding tube and something more long-term than diapers. Do you guys have a doctor you trust?"

"We do." Scott taps on his phone. "Somebody will come shortly."

I ask Jeremy, "What's the longest time you've viked?"

"I once did two six-hour vikes in a day," Jeremy says.

"Any side effects?" Scott asks.

"None that I noticed," he says. "But the vike time isn't what's bothering me. It's what happens when she falls off the end of her ribbon."

"Viking past the time of death," I say.

"Exactly. That will seriously mess anybody up."

I ask, "How messed up are you talking about?"

"I went off the end for less than a minute," he says. "I don't ever want to go through that torture again. When I got back, I passed out. Took me a week to recover, and I still get nightmares from it."

"All from one minute?" Scott asks.

Jeremy says, "Nobody could survive for five minutes."

"That's not what you told us at your house," I say, thinking that I won't forgive myself if Ying dies from her vike.

Jeremy sighs. "I never anticipated anything like this happening."

He never anticipated somebody like me changing his code.

"We need to figure out how much time we have before she reaches the end of the ribbon," I say.

Scott nods.

Simon asks me, "Do you think she went back to Origen?"

"Ying always likes to master a subject before she moves on," I say. "I'm sure she did."

"How do you know where she went?" Scott asks.

"From what she said, her first vike was around the year 231," Simon says.

Scott nods.

I use my phone to look up Origen again.

"Wikipedia says he died around 253," I say. "Her last vike lasted six hours, which Jeremy says is a year of ribbon time."

"At least one," Jeremy says. "Depending on sensory input. It could be closer to two years."

"That means her last vike ended no later than 233," I say. "And if she went back to where she left off, she's got twenty years left."

"That's a conservative sixty hours," Scott says. "How long has it been?"

"Since nine forty-seven last night," Jeremy says. "Almost nine hours ago."

"That means she's got fifty-one hours left," Scott says. "Give or take."

Nossa Senhora! I just wanted to stop Ying, but if we can't wake her up in the next two days, I'll become her murderer.

I put a countdown timer on my phone. And I set up a shared messaging channel for us. Scott, Jeremy, and Simon pull out their phones and accept its invitation.

And then we stare at each other.

Simon speaks first. "You guys are the techies. Can't you just somehow run the beanie in reverse?"

"Doesn't work like that," Jeremy says.

"We need to dig into the code," I say. "We've been treating the activation routine like it's a magic spell."

"That's because it is a magic spell," Jeremy says.

"No, it's code," Scott says.

"We should talk about this GJ dude," I say.

Jeremy stiffens. "There's nothing to talk about."

"Did GJ do the PCC research?" Scott asks.

Jeremy just stares back at Scott.

Scott pulls out his phone and makes a call. "Val, Jeremy is here. We're at a dead end, and I need some help. Did you talk to the lawyers? . . . Are you sure? . . . Hold on a sec."

He points at Jeremy. "Val says if your warranties and representations are fraudulent, she can do a claw back on everything we paid you."

Jeremy stays silent.

Scott listens to his phone and hangs up. He walks over to the window and pulls the curtain aside. "Furthermore," he says as he gazes outside, "imagine you weren't truthful about the ownership of the IP. You'd be in breach, and Ying's situation says we can sue you for damages."

Jeremy closes his eyes and balls his hands into fists. "I've done nothing fraudulent."

Scott faces him. "Were you truthful about who wrote that activation code?"

"Not exactly."

Scott leans forward. "Tell us about GJ before it's too late."

Seventeen

"Giovanni Judd," Jeremy says.

"Who's that?" I ask.

"The GJ that's mentioned in my code. That's his name."

"Does he work for you?" Scott asks.

"No. He's his own man. A long time ago he might've worked for DARPA, but not anymore."

"Why'd you keep him a secret?" I ask.

"Because he's a kook! A conspiracy theorist. He may be bright, but I was trying to sell. The dude would've messed everything up."

"And yet it was you who messed everything up," Scott says. "Dude."

I'm the messing-up dude, but I keep quiet. Just like Jeremy kept quiet about GJ. He only spilled the beans after Scott threatened to take his money away. What kind of threat would make me admit what I did to Ying?

"How can we talk with this Giovanni?" I ask.

"I can secure message him," Jeremey says. "He typically answers in a few hours."

"Does he live around here?"

"No, he's in a compound in northern Idaho. He'll probably do a video call with us."

"Probably?" Scott asks. "What does his doing a video call depend on?"

"What he might have read online," Jeremy says. "Or his assessment of current worldwide security. God knows what sets him off. But even if he won't join a video call, we can go to his place and talk to him in person. He'd love to meet with peeps from Soul Identity."

Jeremy types a message into his phone and promises to let us know as soon as he hears anything.

"I should update Val," Scott says.

"Simon and I will start with some internet research," I tell him.

"Researching what?"

"Whatever we can find that would help us deactivate Ying's PCC."

We agree to meet at noon.

Simon taps on my open door. He's standing there with his backpack.

"I'm scared, Zelly."

"Me, too."

Does he realize that we're scared about different things?

He sets his laptop next to mine and sits down. "What are we researching?"

"What Ying was going to do to us, so we can come up with a survival plan."

He stares at me. "She's going to die in two days."

Oops. I need to tread carefully so I don't lose his trust.

"I am sure that between Scott, Jeremy, and this kooky Giovanni Judd, they can solve how to end Ying's vike," I say. "They're smart."

"And what if they can't?"

Then Ying will die. I try that on, but I can't make it fit.

"You're right," I say. "Ying is our priority."

He shakes his head. "Wow, Zelly, you had me worried for a minute."

If he knew what I did, he'd be terrified.

"We need our own vike portal to play with," I say. "So we can experiment with waking up from a vike."

And so I can vike back and figure out what Ying was up to.

"That sounds dangerous," he says. "Can't we just research?"

"You want to save her, right?"

"Yes, but where do we get one of Jeremy's beanies?"

"Let's ask for one," I say.

I post a message to the channel, requesting a vike portal for Simon and me.

Scott writes back in less than a minute. "Val says it's too dangerous. She doesn't want anybody else viking until we figure out what happened to Ying."

I write, "Fifty-one hours. We don't have time to figure it out first."

"She still says no."

"Sy, we need that vike portal," I say. "Can you jump in?"

He sends, "Don't sacrifice Ying because you're scared about us getting hurt. Please, reconsider."

After a long three minutes of waiting, Scott writes, "Val refuses to risk the lives of the two of you. You are too important. And I agree with her."

Without viking, how can I figure out Ying's plans to hurt us? I glance at Simon and wonder if I should tell him how I changed the code. We're out of ideas, and maybe I should come clean before they figure it out.

But before I can confess, I receive a direct message from Jeremy. He writes, "I have enough spare parts to build another vike portal."

Eighteen

I show Jeremy's message to Simon.

"I'll go to him alone," I say. "I should be the only viker. Just in case there's a problem."

Even though I know there won't be a problem with the vike.

"What if you also get stuck?" he asks. "I don't want to be the only overseer."

"Hmm. If only Ying felt that same way."

"I'm serious, Zelly. Don't do anything rash."

I grab his shoulder. "I won't."

And I mean it. There's no need for anything rash. I can vike a few times to figure out how to exit early, and I can use those vikes to learn as much as I can about Origen. Matar dois coelhos com uma cajadada só—kill two birds with one stone.

"While you're constructing a new vike portal, what can I do?" he asks.

"Internet digging on Giovanni Judd. The more we understand him, the better chance we have of convincing him to help us."

He nods, then hoists his backpack onto his shoulder. "See you at noon."

Once he's gone, I get online and search for as many paintings and portraits of Origen as I can find. I want to be able to recognize him in my ribbons of light the next time I vike.

Most of the images I find depict Origen with a long face and a flowing beard. But these were paintings from the Middle Ages, more than a thousand years after he died. There's no way they're accurate.

I do find a few images of Origen as a young man, beardless, wielding a knife, his pants pulled down and his private parts in hand. There is a tale that he castrated himself due to his misinterpretation of scripture.

With no reliable portrait of Origen, I search for information on Caesarea. Herod the Great built the city on the ruins of an old Phoenician settlement and named it to get in good with Caesar Augustus. The city had the world's largest artificial harbor, a long double aqueduct, a theatre, and a hippodrome. I study photos of the ruins and try to imagine what they looked like during their heyday. Once I have a general idea, I walk downstairs.

Jeremy sits next to Ying's couch, his attention directed at the computer in his lap. He's taken off his hoodie, and I try not to stare at the muscles that give a great shape to his t-shirt.

"Give me a sec to wrap this up," he says.

He can take his time.

The doorbell rings, and I answer it. A middle-aged lady dressed in white, a nurse's cap on her head and a black bag in her hand, has her finger on the button.

"Olga Ivanova reporting for duty, ma'am," she says.

"Duty?"

"I have a patient." She reaches into her bag and retrieves an index card-sized piece of paper. "Ying Ouyang, nineteen years old."

I lead her to the front room and point to Ying lying on the couch. "Olga, meet Ying."

"First business is to take that thing off her head," Olga says. "Hats inside of houses bring bad luck."

"Don't touch that!" Jeremy says. "She'll die if you do."

Olga listens to Jeremy's explanation of the danger of removing the beanie.

"I see," she says. "Now I must insert a feeding tube. Please, leave me alone with her."

I would hate to be showcased where anybody could walk by and gawk at me. "Let's bring her upstairs to her bed," I say.

Olga looks at her papers. "Not in my work order."

"I'll do it," I say.

I carry Ying up the stairs. She's not heavy, but I'm still almost out of breath by the time I reach her room. Olga follows and watches as I lay Ying down.

I use a cable to plug Ying's beanie into a wall charger. I show Olga the bathroom, and I point her to the extra towels. I give her Simon's phone number in case she has any emergencies.

Downstairs, Jeremy is still pounding on his keyboard.

"Any progress?" I ask.

"I just finished searching all the free memory to see if the garbage-collected activation code was still lying around."

Yikes.

"You find anything?"

"Yeah. Something weird," he says.

I do my best to maintain a face of wood.

"What was it?"

Jeremy holds my gaze while my heart hammers away.

He says, "You know something, Zelly."

Jeremy is jogando verde, just fishing, to see if I will admit to anything. Fortunately, he's not without his own problems.

"I do know something," I say. "I know you didn't write that code."

His eyes break contact with mine. "It's fine. I don't need to know. Let's just get Ying woken up."

Jeremy and I will be able to work together just fine.

I tell him that I want him to experiment on me while I'm viking.

"It's not gonna work," he says. "The only way I can send a command to your PCC is after you imagine drawing your logo."

"So, let's do that. Instead of canceling my visual senses, let's transform them into a big, fat, flaming Soul Identity logo."

"But imagine your confusion when that logo pops up in the middle of your vike."

"I'll be observing," I say. "Who cares if it's confusing? Let's see if we can do it."

Even though it's a great idea, it takes me some time to convince him.

Eventually, he rests his elbow on his wheelchair arm, fist under his chin. "Let's build that vike portal and give it a try."

Nineteen

I follow Jeremy outside to his conversion van. He uses his key fob as a remote to open the side door and extend a ramp. He wheels inside, gesturing for me to follow.

The front has a passenger seat and a space in front of the controls where Jeremy's wheelchair must lock into place when he's driving. The back of the van has a small kitchen, a raised bed, and cabinets.

"Does it have a bathroom, too?" I ask.

"Of course. And a shower. Even satellite internet." He points to a cabinet on the right built into a countertop under a long, tinted window. "Open that up and grab me the plastic bin that looks like a milk crate."

I drag out a transparent, red plastic cube about eighteen inches long. I set it on the countertop and get out of his way.

Jeremy pulls out a soldering iron, a multimeter, a black tool bag, a snarl of wire leads, and a quart-sized baggie filled with chips and sensors. He arranges these items in a neat row.

"Do you have a beanie we can use?" he asks.

"Will a baseball cap work?"

"Yup. Your noise-canceling headphones, too, because I don't have enough sensors. And a sewing kit."

I go to my room to retrieve the baseball cap and earphones. Then I walk next door and borrow Sue's sewing basket. I bring everything back to the van.

Jeremy has me search online for a brain diagram to help us place the sensors and transmitters for vision and touch.

He hands me one final pair of sensors, this set twice as large as the others. "Put these up by the temples. They're for talking with the PCC."

I spend the next hour researching placement, soldering longer leads onto the sensors and transmitters, and sewing them into my baseball cap.

Meanwhile, Jeremy inserts the leads into the right spots on the microcontroller board and plugs in a USB cable. He disables the code controlling the lights, the battery charging, and the smell, hearing, and taste canceling. Then he uploads the new code.

I open my phone's app, plug in the new pairing code, and once it connects, I put the baseball cap on my head, careful not to twist the power cable. I tap *Calibrate*, but it fails, because we forgot to disable the hearing calibration code.

Jeremy uploads a fix, and this time the calibration passes. We're ready to try it out.

"You can't vike standing up," he tells me. "You'll just get hurt. Lie down on the bed."

I climb up on the mattress. The USB cable is short, so I keep my head next to the countertop.

We run through the tests for vision and touch, which blind me and make me feel like I'm floating, just like they did yesterday.

We have a working vike portal.

Before Jeremy says anything, I slip on the noise-canceling headphones, stuff tissues up my nose, and set the vike time to a minute. When everything goes blank and I feel like I'm floating, I imagine my sword carving the Psychen Euporos logo into the space in front of me. The pyramid tries to stab me again, but I find myself standing naked on a hovering disc.

Just like last time, a warm breeze stirs the air, and I catch a whiff of cinnamon. I hear faint chanting. The wide ribbons stacked up on my left side start to glow.

I'm back in vike space.

I need to find the city of Caesarea in one of these ribbons of light. And so, just like last time, I ignore all the short ribbons and focus on the remaining handful.

I maneuver my disc to the top-most long ribbon and touch the back of my hand just a foot or so after it starts. I see a transparent image of a tiny foot, and I hear a baby crying. A putrid smell bursts into my nose.

I slide a few feet down the ribbon and touch again. A forest surrounds a river, and birds cry in the background.

The third touch is dark and silent, like my soul line ancestor is stuck in a cave. Or hiding from somebody.

I lean into my disc to make it go faster, and I let the back of my hand bounce in and out of the ribbon of light. Instead of taking tiny sips, I'm drinking from a fire hydrant of sensations. I speed through many images of forests and rivers. Once a huge, tusked beast, but not much else. I reach the end of this ribbon without seeing many other people. No villages, no cities, and no Caesarea.

I maneuver my disc to the beginning of another long ribbon and use my back-of-hand trolling method to zip through it. This ribbon is full of horses and scenes of violence with bows and arrows, with long stretches of riding across deserts and mountains covered in snow. Nothing looks like Caesarea.

The third ribbon has a lot more people, and I catch glimpses of pyramids, cities, and even cats and donkeys. And some beast that looks like a camel, but I am moving too fast to be sure.

The fourth ribbon is the one I viked into yesterday at Jeremy's place. A coastal village, ships, and many scenes with nothing but ocean. I glimpse the woman in the cell who bit off my pinky, and I feel a twinge of pain in my own hand.

And there, further down that same ribbon, I catch a glimpse of a Roman city that might be Caesarea. I'm moving fast, so I bring my disc back around to see it again.

It is Caesarea, on the same ribbon I viked into yesterday. The lady who lost her pinky.

What are the odds?

I don't ponder this for long. I move my disc under the ribbon, and I jump in.

Twenty

"— *You'll be squashed if you don't move now!*" The solider rides high in a horse-pulled chariot, and he holds a tall iron staff topped with an eagle. "Stay off the road, lady!"

The man next to you grabs your arm and yanks you onto the footpath. "We have to be careful," he says. "They don't know who you are."

The man wears a white tunic. He has curly black hair, sharp eyes, and a clean-shaven face covered in acne scars.

"Thank you, Junius," you say.

A chariot, followed by four long columns of foot soldiers, passes by. You look back at the ship. Porters hefting large crates stream out of the holding area and onto the dock. A lady in a white robe, sandals, and a silver ribbon in her hair avoids them as she steps off the gangplank.

"What's so important that they need soldiers?" you ask.

"It's a Sabbatical year, so they're dealing with a famine," Junius says. "The soldiers are probably protecting the wheat and the wine. But a whole century of them seems excessive. Let me find out."

While he interrupts the hurried steps of a tiny, toga-clad man, you step over to the edge of the wharf, holding back a shiver. The gulls circle overhead in a cloudless blue sky. The water is still, and it's clear enough to see to the bottom. You close your eyes and feel the phantom rocking of the ship.

Junius returns. "We need to be careful. There's bad news from Persia. The boy emperor is dead."

"Already?"

He shrugs. "He lost the battle to King Shapur. Now Philip the Arab has declared himself emperor, and he's marching home to Rome. The local governor thinks we'll have another crazy year of competing emperors. He's locked down the port and the mint to be safe."

"How far away is Psychen Euporos?" you ask.

Junius points to a building to the left, on the far side of an open platform. "It's close. Just on top of that warehouse."

You follow Junius across the crowded street and past screaming vendors and pleading beggars. You hold up the hem of your robe to ascend a long flight of stone steps, and you pause at the top in the coolness of a small building's shadow.

Junius directs three porters to place bags and boxes in a pile on the inside of the gateway to the building's yard. High on the wall, just above the open door, is a tile mosaic of a pyramid emblazoned with the Egyptian Eyes of Horus.

"This is it," Junius says. "Welcome to the headquarters of Psychen Euporos. I'll get you introduced and settled before I go."

Junius instructs the porters to stay with the baggage, and he walks through the doorway. He motions to you, and you step into a dimly lit foyer.

Two young ladies lead you and Junius to reclining couches, and you sit back while they remove your sandals and wash your feet. The water is cool, and you accept the offered towel, dip it in the water, and wipe your face and forearms. You wash your hands and spend a minute getting the dirt out from under your nine fingernails.

The ladies take your towels, and they bow and leave through a curtain on the back wall. You detect a hint of incense in the air. One lady returns with two half-filled goblets and a full pitcher.

Junius lifts the pitcher and tops off each goblet with its clear liquid. He hands a goblet to you.

"Careful," he says. "I diluted the wine as much as I could, but it's still going to be strong."

You take a sip, and you make a face as a salt-and-sour taste bites your tongue.

"They use seawater here," Junius says. "Barbarians."

You drink deeply and set your empty goblet on the floor. You rest your head on your outstretched arm, close your eyes, and feel the waves . . .

. . . Junius speaks in a whisper. "Yes, from the Delphi office a week ago. We sailed out of Paphos yesterday."

"How long have you known?" a deep voice asks.

"Almost a month now."

You open your eyes enough to peek through your eyelashes. A middle-aged man in a green robe is crouching next to Junius. His full head of hair is racked with finger-sized curls, gray streaked with white.

"She's the real thing," Junius says. "She came for the Oracle, and we read her while she was waiting. We tripled checked. She's definitely an overseer."

"That's for the match committee to decide, not you. How much of this does she understand?"

"It was a pretty big deal for us in Delphi, as you might imagine. We held a parade and a feast in her honor."

The man snorts. "That's awfully presumptuous."

"She knows she'll be richer than Croesus and that she'll live here. And just so you're aware, we sent scrolls to both Rome and Alexandria. If anything happens to her, it will be on you."

The man in the green robe jumps to his feet, his face red.

Junius stands up and moves so close that his nose touches the other man's.

"It's time, Origen," he says. "Release those bad memories. The Oracle says nobody lives forever. You should keep this one alive."

Origen glares back.

Junius hands him a leather folio. "And Delphi needs this commission."

Origen stalks out of the room.

Junius lets out a sigh and sits down on his couch.

"Did you hear any of that?" he asks.

"Just the end," you say. "You should stick around for another few days."

"I know when I am not welcome. But Origen knows what's good for him. You, Lillia of Cagliari, will be recognized as an overseer before nightfall."

"He's a jerk," you say. "How can anybody work with him?"

"He needs you. Learn what you can, as quickly as you can. We're counting on you."

The ladies return and help you with your sandals. They lead you out the doorway, where you see two old women and one young man standing in the courtyard, blinking in the bright sun.

"Please allow us to examine your eyes, madame," one woman says.

They sit you on a stool and face you toward the sun. The young man holds up a scroll that shows paintings of two light brown irises side by side. Underneath the eyes is a diagram containing a scattering of arcs, lines, and triangles.

The old women and young man take turns stepping close to you, laying their hands on your cheeks, peering into your eyes. They glance at the scroll that they hold, then back at you.

"The paintings match perfectly," the young man says to the old women as they step away. "They are her eyes. Without question."

After the three of them whisper to each other, they all face you.

"We welcome you, Overseer Lillia of Cagliari," the young man says.

You bow your head.

A voice stabs out from behind you. "So, you have confirmed it."

Origen walks up, still in his green robe, a scowl on his face.

"Yes, Overseer," says the young man. "Congratulations. You are no longer serving alone."

"You three may go," Origen says.

The young man rolls up the scroll, and the three of them leave through the gate.

Junius walks through the doorway. "With that good news," he says, "I shall be on my way. Congratulations, Lillia."

"Thank you for your instruction and your kind words, Junius," you say.

"It was my pleasure." Junius steps in front of Origen, no more than a foot away. He holds out his hand.

Origen sighs and hands him the leather portfolio. "The treasury has been notified."

Junius slaps Origen on the shoulder. He calls to the porters, and they leave through the gate.

Origen heads back into the building. "Follow me, Lillia," he says. "Don't keep me waiting."

You walk back through the doorway just as he disappears behind the curtain—

Twenty-one

I expect an old Middle Eastern man, but instead a cute Black guy in a wheelchair stares at me. His lips move, but I only hear a quiet murmur.

He's Jeremy, not Origen. I'm Zelly, not Lillia of Cagliari.

Jeremy removes the noise-canceling headphones that cover my ears. "Can you hear me?"

"Now I can." I pull the tissues out of my nose.

"Did it work? Did you vike? Where'd you go?"

I'm not going to tell him that I'm tracking Origen.

"It worked perfectly," I say. "I viked into the same girl as last time, later in her life. I got off a ship and walked around a port city. Crazy."

He smiles. "Did the cannibals eat any more of your fingers?"

"Very funny," I say. "I drank a glass of salty wine, and I fell asleep."

He nods. "And you woke up immediately."

"How would you know this?"

"That's how it works," he says. "Your girl's senses powered down while she slept. Time flies when nothing's going on."

I guess that's better than getting stuck with nothing to observe.

It seems that a vike is like having a vivid dream that you can't control. Because it's just sense coming through, what that dream means to you is based on your own ability to reflect and empathize. That ability comes from your experience.

Maybe it's good that Ying is stuck for so long in her vike. She'll get to experience more of Origen's life, and when she wakes up and processes what she observed, she might realize that a trust culture, not a competitive culture, is best.

That would be a great outcome. But it's going to depend on what kind of person Origen turned out to be. If his later years were filled with successful partnerships with Lillia, Ying will conclude that working together is the answer. But if Origen spent his life never admitting he was wrong, just doubling down on his mistakes and fighting with Lillia, Simon and I are screwed.

I need to learn what happens between Lillia and Origen. I want to vike back there right now.

But Jeremy still thinks I'm here to come up with a way to pop Ying out of her vike and I'm not going to tell him otherwise, because I'd have to admit that I'm the one who put her in danger.

We must keep figuring out how to end her vike. Just not too soon.

I take off the baseball cap and hop down from the bed.

Jeremy and I review the vision-canceling code together and mark what needs to change. While he gets it ready, I find a notepad and a pencil, and I re-calibrate the baseball cap.

While I wait for Jeremy to finish, I search for references to Lillia of Cagliari. I find nothing on the internet, but she's in our archives. Born in Sardinia, she served as an overseer from 244 until 270 AD.

Lillia came to Caesarea thirteen years after Origen, then overlapped with him for nine years before he died. This means she survived Origen's attempts to kill her. That's good news for me and Simon, but only if I can figure out his dirty tricks.

Junius seems to know how Origen got rid of his peers. Maybe he even explains it to Lillia during their trip to Caesarea. I could go back and vike into that voyage to find out.

If that doesn't work, maybe Origen either confides in or confesses to Lillia as he grows older. I could vike through the nine years they served together as overseers.

It's nice to have both a plan and a vike portal. I'm a lot more confident that I'll figure out how to protect myself and Simon from Ying.

Jeremy interrupts my thoughts. "I'm ready to capture," he says.

I put on the vike portal. While his new code is reading my brain's visual sense data, I draw our logo. I make sure I stay focused on the image. As I draw the two sides of the pyramid and the two Eyes of Horus, I remember the logo in the mosaic I saw above the doorway in Caesarea. I wonder if it's still there.

I double-check my drawing, and when I'm satisfied, I put down the pencil.

"Got it," Jeremy says. "All thirteen seconds' worth."

For the next hour, Jeremy updates his sense-canceling code so this thirteen-second video will get transmitted back to my brain. I backseat drive to make sure he does it right.

"Let's try it out," he says.

I tap *Test Vision* on my phone. Instead of going blind like before, I watch my hand drawing the logo. No matter where I turn my eyes, it's all I can see.

"It's creepy, but it works," I say. "Let's try it in another vike."

Before I can start, Jeremy's phone buzzes with a message from Giovanni.

"He's willing to help us," Jeremy says. "But he claims video calls can be hacked. We need to bring Ying to Idaho."

I glance at my phone. It's noon and time for us to meet with everybody.

"Let's go tell them," I say. "I can vike after lunch."

Twenty-two

"We're not bringing Ying to Idaho," Val says, again. "It's irresponsible."

We're deep into this discussion, but we've gotten nowhere.

Simon takes a deep breath and unclenches his fists. "We have to get Ying out of her vike."

Scott says to Jeremy, "Can you read Giovanni's reply one more time? We must have misunderstood something."

Jeremy hands him his phone. "Read it yourself. Apparently y'all don't believe me when I do it."

Scott reads aloud. "Jeremy wrote, 'I gotta get SI girl unstuck from xanazo. Can you show me how in vid call? 911!' And Giovanni replied, 'I can. But no vid calls. They're listening. Bring her here.'"

"Who's listening?" Val asks.

"Beats me," Jeremy says. "That's Giovanni acting all conspiracy theorist."

"Can't he send you instructions?" Val asks.

"I'll ask him," Jeremy says.

We await Giovanni's answer as we sit at the big table in the dining hall. The only sounds are George and Sue clattering in the kitchen and Simon tapping his fingernails on the table.

Jeremy's phone vibrates. He reads his message and says, "Special equipment is required, and we need to come to Idaho."

"Can he bring his equipment here?" Scott says.

Jeremy checks and the answer is swift. "No, he cannot."

"We have forty-seven hours left," I say to Val. "We could try to wake Ying up ourselves, and if it doesn't work, we can go to Idaho tomorrow."

Simon pounds his fist on the table. "Ying's on a bloody feeding tube, and she needs to be unviked ASAP. Not tomorrow. Not forty-seven hours from now."

I reach out and squeeze Simon's hand. "Dude."

"I'm sorry, Zelly. But you guys talk about her like we can wait, but we cannot. She's one of us. She needs us to help her now."

That shuts us all up. But it doesn't matter. Val's not going to let us take any risks.

If Val knew why Ying was stuck, she'd be more than happy to risk my life to wake her up.

"If we're not going to Idaho, let's at least hear what everybody found out," I say.

"I can go first," Simon says. "I spent my morning researching Giovanni Judd. Jeremy was right about DARPA. They fired him back in the nineties when he tried to fund research into witchcraft."

"And then, ten years later, the rest of the world went wizard crazy," Scott says.

"There's more," Simon says. "After he was fired, he dug for three years on an archaeological site in the Valley of the Kings. Then another dig in Miletus. He snuck into Iraq and dug in Babylon until the invasion. Over the next decade, he ran digs in Alexandria, Caesarea, and Istanbul. Maybe Bratislava, too, but I couldn't find anything about that."

"He's digging at old Soul Identity sites," I say. "Why don't we know about him?"

"Is Giovanni a member?" Val asks.

Simon shrugs.

"I can check," Scott says. He pulls out his phone. "Do you have a photo of him?"

Simon holds up his phone, and it displays a picture of a middle-aged man with early signs of balding. He wears a black dress shirt, open at the neck, gray chest hair spilling out under a wooden bead necklace. Large, thick-framed glasses make his eyes huge.

"Let me do it with my glasses," I say as I rummage in my backpack. "Zoom in on his face."

Simon pinches out, and I remember I gave George the eyeglasses.

"Give me a sec." I run to the back and into the kitchen.

George is sitting on a stool at the center island, watching Sue stir a pot on the stove. He's wearing the glasses.

"Good afternoon, Giselle Oliveira," he says.

"Can I borrow those eyeglasses for a sec?"

"Sure thing."

I put them on and go back to the table and stare at Giovanni's irises on Simon's phone. The info bubble pops up right where it's supposed to.

"He's a member," I say. "We know him as Giovanni Judd."

"I'm done," Simon says when I return from bringing the eyeglasses back to George.

"I'll go next," I say. "I've been thinking through ways we can send a message to Ying's PCC. I have an idea I want to try out, but we need to test it with a vike portal."

I glance at Jeremy. He better not blab how we already built one ourselves.

Val purses her lips. "No viking for now, Zelly. We can't risk losing you."

"My plan isn't dangerous," I say.

"Nobody thought Ying's vike was dangerous," she says.

I'm about to argue, but Scott jumps in. "What if Zelly runs her tests on me?"

Scott thinks he's helping, but if he's the one who vikes, I won't be able to uncover Origen's schemes.

She shakes her head. "You and I need to wrap up that analysis."

Good. But lest Val get suspicious at me giving up so easily, I say, "Not viking is a mistake and you know it."

"These aren't easy decisions, Zelly," she says. "But Giovanni's messages give me hope that we can wake up Ying without you viking."

"You'll never send Ying to Idaho, and you're shutting down my attempt," I say. "Are you happy Ying is trapped in a vike?"

I pushed her a little too much. Again.

She raises her eyebrows. "Maybe you'll understand how unhappy I am once you hear about the analysis Scott and I started this morning."

"Did you figure something out?" Simon asks.

"Almost," Scott says. "We're so close."

"Scott and I tore apart Jeremy's code," Val says. "We focused on what could have produced those overflow values that we saw in the logfile. There's only one place it could happen."

I try to uncross my arms without drawing attention to myself.

"What's the scenario?" Jeremy asks.

"It had to happen after the routine verified the wakeup time and before it was used. The log says overflow because it was set to more than 255 days in the future."

"I realize I am the only non-geek here," Simon says. "But I have no idea what you just said."

"Somebody changed the code that runs on the beanie," Scott says. "They reset Ying's vike time to be more than eight months out."

I'm getting a sense of impending doom.

"Are you sure it was rogue code? Not my mistake?" Jeremy asks.

"We're positive," Val says. "This part of your code is beyond reproach."

Jeremy raises both of his clenched hands. "Thank God."

"Thank us," Scott says. "You're off the hook because we dug through your code, line by line. Now we need to figure out who changed the code that ran on Ying's beanie."

I will my breath and my voice to remain calm and measured. "Just download the code from Ying's beanie and find out what the change was." I hope that I did a good job cleaning up.

"The one who changed the code wasn't that sloppy," Scott says.

Simon raises his hand. "I'm getting lost again."

Val says, "The code on Ying's beanie is identical to Jeremy's source code."

"Well, there you go." I struggle to not scratch my suddenly itchy nose. "Nobody changed it."

"Somebody changed it before Ying viked," Scott says. "And they cleverly changed it back after the vike started, in an attempt to cover their tracks."

Are they just fishing around, like Jeremy was earlier?

"How do you know this?" Simon asks.

"Because we're clever, too," Scott says. "We looked at the memory dump that Jeremy took this morning."

"I already checked that dump. The values were overwritten," Jeremy says.

"You were checking the data section. We went through the code section, and we found an extra two lines that had been inserted."

"What were they?" I ask, hoping they can't hear the tremor in my voice.

"They changed the vike time if it was set to six hours."

"Changed it to what?" Jeremy asks.

"We don't know," Val says. "The data section got overwritten."

All four of them stare at me.

Val speaks first. "Zelly, what did you do?"

Twenty-three

Last fall I dreamed that I had finally turned nineteen, and it was my first day as a Soul Identity overseer. In my dream, I went to my initiation ceremony and gave my acceptance speech. I met with the various department heads, I joined a strategy meeting, and I sat through cool demonstrations put together by the advanced research teams.

A dream I'd had before, except for one little detail. This time in my dream, I spent my entire first day on the job wearing not a single stitch of clothing. Not even a Brazilian biquíni fio dental.

When I woke up, I wondered how my dream-self could last the entire day without clothes. I searched online and discovered that many people have similar naked dreams and that it could mean one of two things. Either I was ashamed and hiding something or I was proud with nothing to hide.

I'm going to have that dream again tonight.

I can guess how Lillia of Cagliari would have handled this mess. She'd say that o peixe morre pela boca, fish die by the mouth. She'd keep quiet.

But I can't keep quiet and let Ying die while she's stuck in her vike.

Four sets of accusing eyes stare at me.

Simon's lip trembles. "Did you hurt Ying, Zelly?"

Jeremy shakes his head. "I can't believe I helped you construct another vike portal."

"She viked again?" Val asks.

"For a minute, while we were testing if it worked."

Val opens her mouth, but Scott says, "Let's give Zelly a chance to explain herself."

I face Val. "I did change the code."

Just as I'm about to confess everything I did, I see Val glance at Scott. That makes me pause.

"Go on, Zelly," Val says.

"What was that look?" I ask.

"What look?"

"The one you just gave Scott."

"Ah." She narrows her eyes. "That's my told-you-so look. Scott didn't want to believe you sabotaged the code."

Val thinks I'm a terrorist. She couldn't care less that I'm just trying to stay alive.

I'd be stupid to confirm her bias against me with a confession.

"I didn't sabotage the code," I say. "I was trying to figure out why Jeremy had put in a six-hour maximum."

"It's there for safety," Jeremy says. "Viking is hard on the body."

"That's what you claimed," I say. "I was playing with increasing the time. I uploaded it to the vike portal to test it out, but then Ying came by to borrow it."

I point to Simon. "You remember, Sy, that I told Ying I had been working on the code, and that it wasn't safe to vike for six hours. You heard me warn her."

"I did." He crosses his arms. "But you didn't tell her why it wasn't safe."

"Didn't you just say you're not a geek? Neither is Ying."

"But afterward," Val says. "Why didn't you tell us then?"

"I panicked," I say. "I went to her room, and that's when I realized she ignored me and got herself stuck. I put Jeremy's original code back in place and returned to my room to pack."

"And you pretended to know nothing when I found her," Scott says.

I hang my head and keep my mouth shut.

"When is the wake-up time?" he asks.

"Midnight on my birthday."

"That's only six months from now," Val says. "We wouldn't have gotten the overflow message."

"My nineteenth birthday."

Silence.

"Jeez, Zelly," Simon finally says. "You froze Ying until you also become an overseer?"

Leave it to Simon to find the significance in my actions. I try to make my eyes watery, but I'm not that good of an actor.

I tell another lie because I don't know what else to do. "I didn't mean any harm to Ying."

They stare at me, and I try not to squirm.

Eventually, Scott clears his throat. "I suggest we focus on ending Ying's vike," he says. "We can deal with what Zelly did later."

Great idea.

"You probably don't want to hear it," I say, "but Jeremy and I made good progress this morning. We're chasing something promising, and we need to continue."

Val sighs. "It appears we don't need more code analysis. Scott, can you please supervise these two? Zelly is not allowed to wear any vike portal."

"Of course," Scott says.

"Meanwhile, I'm going to arrange transportation to Idaho for all of us," Val says. "In case you don't succeed."

I want to argue with her, but she's right. My plan has a slim chance of working, and we need a backup.

Then Val stares at me, her eyes wide. "There will be consequences for what you did. I'm disturbed that instead of coming clean right away, you dug yourself a deeper hole."

I bow my head and try to look contrite.

At least she hasn't realized that I'm still digging.

Twenty-four

"What's your big idea?" Scott asks me once the three of us are squeezed around the tiny countertop in Jeremy's van.

"Jeremy captured the vision data of me drawing the Soul Identity logo. We can pipe that data down to Ying, trigger her PCC, and tell it to go to sleep."

Scott tilts his head to the side. "You're using the sense-canceling code to project your own vision data?"

"Right on," Jeremy says. "Zelly was about to test it in a vike."

"Zelly doesn't get to vike anymore," Scott says. "Test it on me."

Jeremy hands him the baseball cap and helps him pair his phone app with it.

"Test the vision," I say.

Scott presses the test button. "What should I be seeing?"

"Me drawing the logo."

"It's just a bunch of static. Like an untuned television back in the day."

"We messed something up," I say. "Let me try it."

"Val said no vike portals," Scott says.

"She meant no viking, and I won't."

Scott glances at Jeremy, who shrugs. He sighs and hands me the baseball cap, taking care not to twist the USB cable.

I put on the cap, Scott calibrates, and we test. I can see the mini video of my hand drawing the Soul Identity logo.

"It works just fine," I say.

"Huh," Scott says. "I guess each brain has its own unique vision processing."

"Let me try it," Jeremy says. "We can see if it's just Scott with the crazy brain."

But it's not just Scott. Our experiments show that each person has unique vision signals. We try to see if there's a way to normalize, but the data is well-encrypted. Even simple visual patterns are unique to each of us.

Bottom line, we can't trigger Ying's PCC with somebody else's vision data.

My idea bombed, and I need another one. I stare at the code and think about the command that gets sent to the PCC. It says to go to sleep at a specific time.

"What if we change Ying's clock?" I ask. "Convince her brain that it's already my nineteenth birthday. That could force her PCC to go to sleep."

"That won't work," Jeremy says. "Her clock is deep in the center of her brain. Our transmitters are too small to reach it."

"Can we get a bigger transmitter?" Scott asks.

"That's like using a steam roller to kill an ant. Lots of other things in her brain would get smushed."

"We could insert tiny wires directly into her brain's clock," I say.

They both stare at me.

"You don't really want to perform brain surgery on Ying, do you?" Scott asks.

I shake my head. "Just brainstorming."

I gaze out the van's window, past the driveway and between our two houses. I can catch a tiny slice of a view of the Puget Sound and Blake Island. Kind of like a vike slice. Just a tiny piece with little context. A container ship is heading down to Tacoma. I know where it's going only because I happen to know that Tacoma is the last port south of us.

If Scott and Jeremy looked out the window, they'd see the same slice of Puget Sound, but their context would make their stories different than mine. Jeremy's story might be about what's in the containers. Scott's could be about how long before the waves from the ship's wake reach our shoreline.

If we want to end up telling the same story, we'd have to collaborate and align on which context to apply to that tiny slice of Puget Sound. We could speak and write and even touch, smell, and taste our way to alignment.

But if our contexts start out so different, is there any way for us to align with Ying? I doubt it. Only one person can align with Ying when she's in the middle of her vike. Only Ying herself.

And just like that, a glorious idea comes to me. It's so simple and clean that it makes me giggle. By the time Scott and Jeremy look up, I'm laughing so hard and feeling so relieved that tears are running down my face.

"Has she gone crazy?" Jeremy asks Scott in a whisper.

This makes me laugh even harder.

"I'm not crazy. I know how to wake up Ying."

Twenty-five

We test my simple, clean idea on Scott, and we pop him out of a one-minute test vike on our first try. We do the same for Jeremy.

"I wish I could try, too." I try to sound like I'm disgruntled, but it's a half-hearted effort.

"I'm only following Val's orders," Scott says.

"But she's going to love this, Zelly," Jeremy says. "And not just because of Ying. You've solved that big safety issue she was worrying over."

Scott sends Val a message, and we climb out of Jeremy's van and head to the dining hall to meet her.

When she arrives, she hands Scott a beanie. "Show me with this vike portal."

Scott puts on the beanie, pairs with it, calibrates, and tests. He starts a five-minute vike. Time for me to show off to Val and earn a few redemption points.

"We were relying on tech to solve this," I tell her. "That was a mistake."

While Jeremy plugs the USB cable into Scott's beanie and uploads our new code, I place a blank piece of paper and a pencil in front of Scott.

"First, we shut off the beanie's vision sense-canceling routines," I say.

"Won't that mess up his vike?" Val asks.

"Our goal is to mess up his vike, so it's fine."

Jeremy types on the laptop. "It's off, Zelly."

"Great. Next, we make sure Scott is staring at the paper."

Jeremy grabs Scott's head from behind and maneuvers it until Scott looks at the paper.

"Now comes the cool part," I say. "Watch this."

I put the pencil into Scott's hand, and I guide it to draw the two sides of the pyramid, its base, and each Eye of Horus.

Once I'm done, Jeremy lets go of Scott's head and moves back to the laptop.

"Finally, we override our previous time by telling his PCC to activate for exactly one second," I say.

Jeremy presses enter. An instant later, Scott lifts his head and takes off the beanie, handing it to me.

"Wow," Val says. "You did it!"

"It was all Zelly," Jeremy says. "She's pretty amazing."

Val closes her eyes for a moment. Then she reaches out and squeezes my shoulder. "Thank you, Zelly."

I hand our new vike portal to her. "You're welcome. And you owe me a new hat."

"Let's go and bring Ying back," Scott says.

As we walk across the patio, Val pulls me aside. "Jeremy is almost right. You could be amazing, Zelly. But you won't be until you learn to control your impulses. To look before you leap."

Leave it to Val to twist my success into a critique.

I suppose Val thinks she has a lot to teach me about risk management. But in my eyes, she's shackled to her fear of failure, and that's not going to help me survive for the next eighteen months. With Ying about to wake up and me not viking, I remain in considerable danger.

We climb upstairs. Scott directs the nurse to pull out Ying's feeding tube before we move her downstairs. When that's done, I walk to Simon's room.

Simon glances into the hallway, then asks me, "Are you going tell Val that we've become suspicious of Ying?"

"No way. You'd better not, either."

He leans away from me and crosses his arms. "Why's that?"

"Because Val will tell Ying, and she'll know we're watching. We'll never figure out how she's planning to hurt us."

"But what if Ying isn't trying to hurt us? What if we're just being paranoid?"

"You saw how she was acting."

"And I see how *you're* acting. Something happened to you during your vike yesterday."

I can't deny that things have changed. I gained a fear of boats. I used to think Val was amazing. And I'm almost ready to kill Ying to guarantee my own survival.

Could the vike do this to me? Did something go wrong?

"You said somebody bit off your finger and ate it," he says. "Maybe that triggered some kind of paranoia."

"Hold on, Sy," I say. "I might be paranoid, but you're forgetting that we asked Ying a simple question and she lied. Who knows what else she's hiding from us?"

"You're right. She did lie. I just don't want to believe it." Simon is silent for a minute. "The most important thing is to wake up Ying. If you can do that, I won't tell Val about our suspicions."

"Will you help me figure out how Ying's going to hurt us?"

"I will."

The two of us walk downstairs. Ying is propped up on the couch, leaning forward. Her feeding tube is gone.

"Let's do this," Scott says.

I plug Ying's USB cord into my computer and upload our new code.

"I'll draw," I say.

Scott takes my laptop. "I'll drive."

I kneel in front of Ying, set a book on her lap, and place a sheet of paper on top of the book. I slide a pencil into her right hand.

"Ying is left-handed," Val says. "Will that matter?"

"It might." I move the pencil to her left hand. "Simon, make sure Ying's eyes are open and focused on the paper."

Simon adjusts Ying's head. Scott turns off Ying's vision canceling. I draw the logo. Scott sends the command to her PCC, and Ying's eyes flutter open.

Ying's gaze wanders around the living room, making its way back to me. She swallows.

"My throat hurts," she says with a hoarse voice.

"You had a feeding tube," Simon says. "It went up your nose."

I grab her hand. "Ying."

Her eyes open wide, and she pulls her hand away. "What went wrong?"

"Remember I told you not to vike for six hours?"

She bites her lip.

"That's because I modded that code to vike for longer. A lot longer. You've been viking for almost eighteen hours."

"You would have been stuck for a year and a half," Simon says. "They had to figure out how to wake you up."

Ying looks at Val. "What about my overseer ceremony?"

"I pushed it back a week," Val says. "I'm sorry, but we weren't sure how long it would take to get you back."

Ying glares at me, but she doesn't say anything.

"Zelly is the one who figured it out," Simon says. "If it wasn't for her, you'd still be viking."

"If it wasn't for Zelly," Ying says, "we'd be in Sterling, and I'd be an overseer."

Twenty-six

Ying took almost an entire week to recover from her long vike. And now that she has slept a lot and regained her weight, we're on the company jet on our way from Seattle to Sterling, so she can be instated as the executive overseer. Only six days behind schedule.

We're an hour out from landing. I'm sitting across from Ying. I've been pisando em ovos, walking on eggshells, with her all week long. She knows that I changed the vike portal code and got her stuck, and she knows that I'm the one who figured out how to fix it. She's told me nothing about her vike and nothing about her plans once she becomes an overseer.

She's not telling anybody anything. She's worn headphones and hasn't stopped reading Sun Tzu's *The Art of War* for the entire flight.

She's at war with me.

Knowing nothing about Ying's plans has kept me and Simon busy researching all we can about what Origen did in Egypt, so we can anticipate how Ying will try to get rid of us. But the ancient records are sparse, and Val still won't let us vike. All we've got hangs on a thin set of facts. In 231, two overseers died from sickness, Demetrius relinquished his role as executive overseer to Origen, and Origen moved the organization from Egypt to Palestine.

We need more context. We can get it if I vike back to Lillia of Cagliari and figure out what happened and how she survived.

A week ago, I didn't even know what xanazo was. Now I can't live without it.

Yesterday, in the hopes of building another vike portal, I went online and ordered a bunch of sensors and transmitters. But they won't arrive for four more days.

I tap the side of Ying's foot with mine.

She gives me a fake smile and goes back to reading.

I tap her again, and I mime removing her headphones.

She puts down her book and slides the headphones off her ears. "Yes, Zelly?"

"I wanted to talk before you become a high and mighty overseer. While we're still equals."

She darts a glance across the aisle at Val.

"Are you excited or scared?" I ask.

"Both. I can't believe today has finally come."

"I'm so jealous." I lean forward. "What are you going to do with all of your new power?"

She is quiet for a moment. Then she asks, "What would you do?"

I've been thinking about just that question all week long.

"I'd make the vike technology public," I say. "That could double, even triple, our members and deposits in just the first year."

"But what if we discover that viking has long-term side effects?"

"You've viked the longest, so you would know. Do you think you were harmed?"

"I doubt I'd be able to tell." She pauses. "I have noticed that I deal with conflict differently than I did before."

I raise my eyebrows.

"Like before my vikes," she says. "When people seemed threatening, I would just avoid them."

I bite my lower lip. "And now?"

She balls her hand into a fist and shakes it at me. "Now I've learned to strike back. Harder."

I sit back and try not to let her see me shiver. I remember what Simon said about me sucking up all the oxygen, and I wonder if my plan to increase my intimidation has backfired.

When I can trust my voice to not come out shaky, I ask, "This was how your overseer dealt with issues?"

She nods. "And it works. When he fought back and escalated against the bullies and jerks, all the infighting faded away."

From what little I've gleaned, Ying is rewriting history because Origen himself was the bully. He eliminated the other overseers and took over the organization. Only then the infighting stopped.

But I don't say this.

"Is anybody threatening you now?" I ask.

She doesn't hesitate. Just tilts her head at me and narrows her eyes. "Last week you were the threat," she says. "You trapped me in that eighteen-month vike."

She's decided to go there. I'm in trouble.

"Just a minute," I say, extending my arm toward her. "I didn't hurt you on purpose. And I warned you it was dangerous."

She bats at my hand. "Your warning was bogus. You should have told me you changed the code. But you didn't, and I could have died."

I stare out the airplane window as I wonder how I can respond without letting on that I know she's trying to kill me. And that all I wanted was to buy some time as I scrambled to protect myself.

I should just skip the excuses.

"You're absolutely right," I say. "I should have told you about the code change. I'm sorry."

We stare at each other for a minute. Then she sighs. "I'm scared, Zelly. It's fine for now when I'm the new overseer, but once you get here, everyone's going to realize how weak I really am."

Is Ying telling me that Simon and I are her real threats? That she can't allow us to become her peers?

"You're going to be great, girlie," I say. "You have an eighteen-month head start on me. I'll never be able to catch up."

She shakes her head. "I wish so much that what you say is true." After a minute, she asks, "What are your plans until you're nineteen?"

She wants to hear that I'll keep a low profile.

"I'm going to stay in school, go to bootcamp, help Simon, and hang out with George and Sue when they come to visit. Plus, of course, whatever you want me to do."

She smiles.

I bought myself time.

Before I can stop myself, I open my fat mouth. "And since we're being honest with each other, I want you to know that I will do whatever I must to make sure I do become an overseer."

What is wrong with me?

Ying narrows her eyes. And after a long moment of dead silence, she says, "I wish you good luck. You're going to need it."

She slips her headphones back over her ears and picks up her book, leaving me with our dreadful conversation looping in my head for the rest of the flight.

Twenty-seven

The next night, we're still in Sterling, at the end of Ying's overseer oath-taking ceremony. Simon, Scott, and I remain seated, all dressed up, in the front row of Soul Identity's auditorium. It's late in the evening, and we, along with a hundred or so local employees, wait for Ying's acceptance speech, a tradition that started in our Babylon years.

I wonder when I'll be able to vike into Lillia of Cagliari's acceptance speech way back in Caesarea, almost eighteen hundred years ago. I'll need a working vike portal for this, but I've solved for that. Even if Val and Ying never let me use theirs, my sensors and transmitters will arrive soon, and I'll just build my own.

And then I'll need to find a safe place to vike, as I've realized that's when I'll be most vulnerable.

I'd love to discuss these kinds of survival strategies with Simon, but he's upset about my last conversation with Ying. I challenged him to find the most respectful interpretation of her threat to me, but all I got back was crickets.

The plan is for Scott to fly home with me and Simon, leaving Val and Ying here to start their joint rule. I don't expect it to stay joint for long. We paid our respects to Archibald Morgan last night, and he just lay in his bed, staring at the ceiling, not moving. I think he'll bater as botas and die before long. That would put Val out of her job as his trustee.

I'm scared of Ying and even more scared that she'll become the only overseer. Especially after her two long vikes back to Origen. I need to know how Lillia outlived and outlasted him. I need to vike.

Val steps onto the dais. She looks classy, her red hair shining, her dark green pinstripe skirt suit offset by a silk, cream blouse. A leader anybody would follow and trust. She gives a little wave, and the whole room lets out a collective sigh.

Val speaks about the privilege of serving as Mr. Morgan's trustee and how it's been almost five years since Ying, Simon, and I were rescued. She says a few nice words about each of those who helped care for us—Scott, his parents, George and Sue, and various others. She introduces Ying, says more nice things about her, and sits down on the far left side of the stage.

Ying steps up to the podium to our standing ovation. She's dressed in a forest-green office suit with big silver buttons, a black scoop t-shirt, and black booties with a four-inch heel.

She leans into the microphone once the applause fades and we sit down.

"Thank you, Val. And thank you, everyone here and online," she says. "Over the past five years, I have learned that Soul Identity is a vital, relevant, and positive force in all of our members' lives."

That brings a big round of applause.

Ying holds out her hand toward Val. "For the past five years, our organization has been maintained by a fabulous trustee. Val has increased membership and refocused our value proposition. We've become a well-run and responsible corporate entity."

The audience applauds. Ying, though, wears a grim expression, and that makes me throw a glance over at Simon. But his eyes are glued to her, our new executive overseer, and he doesn't see my worried look.

Ying continues. "As Val mentioned earlier, five years ago, my entire family was murdered, and I was kidnapped."

This happened to me and Simon as well, but I guess this is Ying's moment.

"I am left with the inescapable conclusion that if it wasn't for Soul Identity losing its way and not doing its job, my family would still be alive."

Silence in the auditorium. And a lot of confused looks. Back on the stage, Val's wearing a slight frown.

Ying regards the audience. "I've spent time researching our organizational history. Really digging into it, back to the times when we were still known as Psychen Euporos."

Calling her vikes research is a bit of a stretch. But to be fair, last week Ying did spend the equivalent of several years in Egypt and Palestine.

"Back in those days," Ying says, "Psychen Euporos acted as the world's investment bankers. We were the de facto power behind every government, and we were agile enough to move from Babylon to Alexandria, Caesarea, Istanbul, and Bratislava to stay that way. We were ruthless, and we were unstoppable. Nobody dared challenge us. Nobody dared hurt our family members."

She holds up a finger. "But then in 1752, we migrated to the New World and changed our name to Soul Identity. We shifted to a pure business focus, and it wasn't for the better. Instead of shaping the world's collective history, instead of driving the world's best decisions, instead of funding the world's greatest initiatives, we took a backseat. We let the power we wielded slip away. Conspiracy theories about who actually ran the world abounded. Meanwhile, we grew weak. And we let others grow strong."

Ying points at Val. "These days, it's only gotten worse. Now we focus our efforts on building our profits and maximizing our value, when we should be building our power and maximizing our influence.

"Yes, we have grown. But what a waste."

Simon's eyes are wide. I want to flash him a told-you-so expression, but I'm distracted by my thoughts about how he and I are going to survive the next few years.

"Please, don't think this is all Val's fault," Ying says. "She's just the trustee at the end of two and a half centuries of the weakest and most ineffective overseers ever."

She puts both forearms on the podium. "But today is a new day. Years from now, when we look back, we will remember today as the start of a brave, new, and proud Soul Identity. Because this is when we started reclaiming what is ours. When we began to restore our old glory and we planted the seeds to regain our influence. Soul Identity will once again shape the world and its political landscape through our strategic investments. Soul Identity will once again be seen as the ones behind every successful conquest and overthrow by any world power. And it's because for the first time in a long time, we will have the right kind of overseer in charge."

Ying's arms have been slowly rising. She now stands with both fists in the air, and she pounds them down on the podium, staring fiercely at a subdued audience.

After a moment she whirls around and exits the stage by the rear door on the right. A few seconds later, Val stands up, casts a worried glance at Scott, and follows her out. Leaving the rest of us, in the auditorium and online, sitting in a stunned silence.

Twenty-eight

Simon and I spin in our seats and watch the Soul Identity employees leave the auditorium through the main doors on the right and out the exit up the stairs in the back. Most of them carry troubled expressions.

"What the heck happened to Ying?" Simon asks.

"It's what I've been warning you about," I say. "Let's get out of here."

Scott thumbs his phone. "Not yet. We need to time this right."

"Time what right?"

"Our exit." He puts his phone in his pocket. "If you go out those main doors, you'll be detained."

"Who would detain us?"

"I don't know. But you can see them waiting over there." He uses his chin to point.

I catch a glimpse of four security guards in gray uniforms standing at the doors, straining their necks as they peer at us through the gaps between the employees.

"Aren't they here to protect us?" Simon asks.

"They don't look like protection to me," Scott says. "You guys ready to go?"

"Do you have a plan?" I ask.

"I do. Try to keep up." He jumps to his feet, hustles to the stairs on the left side of the stage, and beckons to us.

Simon and I scramble after Scott as he climbs onto the stage and knocks on a side door.

I check the entrance. The security guards have made it through the main exit doors and around the crowd. Three of them climb onto the stage, and the fourth stays below, walking along the front row.

"What are we waiting for? Let's go," I say.

"The door's still locked," Scott says. "Give it a second."

As the three guards reach the middle of the stage, they spread out. The fourth waits at the bottom of the stairs we just climbed.

We edge closer to Scott. I wonder if we can jump off the stage and make it to the back door, but then I see two more guards up there, watching us.

We have nowhere to run.

Scott knocks again, and the door pushes open. Simon and I rush through, and Scott slams it shut before the guards can follow.

Val stands in front of us, breathing hard.

"Took you long enough," Scott says to her.

"It got messy," she says. "Follow me. Hurry!"

We're in a dark hallway, illuminated by safety lights. Val leads us to an emergency exit.

"We're going to walk out," she says. "One at a time. Go straight to the back of the guest house. And keep your heads down."

"Why the guest house?" I ask.

"We need to get Archie," Scott says. "Before they do."

He pushes open the door and grimaces at the alarm. Simon follows him. Then it's my turn, and then Val's.

The four of us keep within fifty feet of each other as we skirt around the edges of the bright parking lot. We clamber over a small stone wall, walk through a dark field, and gather outside the guest house's back door.

"Who's picking us up?" Scott asks Val.

She glances at her phone. "Uber. They're two minutes out."

"You've been running one of the world's largest organizations, and you're calling Uber?" Simon asks.

"I don't know who to trust right now, Simon," she says. "Do you have a better idea?"

"Uber it is," he says. "But there will be five of us."

"I got an XL. It's going to be a white Escalade. The driver's name is Boubacar."

"I'll bring Archie downstairs," Scott says. "You guys find his medicine. Meet you out front in two minutes."

He opens the back door and slips inside. Val pulls out a pistol-shaped black and yellow Taser from her pocket. She flips off the safety and walks through the doorway.

A minute later, Simon and I run inside and up the back staircase. Val is in the hallway, standing over a man on the ground. He's wearing a gray security guard uniform. The Taser's wires lead to his neck, and he's twitching on the floor.

"I've always wanted to Taser somebody," she says.

I walk into Mr. Morgan's room with Simon right behind me. We nearly bump into Scott, who's coming out the door, the old man leaning on his arm.

I stop in the bathroom and take all the medicine bottles I can find. Simon grabs the rest from the nightstand, and we rush back to the hallway.

Val kneels next to the security guard, who's now facedown and wearing handcuffs. The three of us run downstairs and out the front door.

Scott stands with Mr. Morgan at the bottom of the driveway. "Where the heck's that Uber?"

Val pulls out her phone. "Almost here."

A few seconds later, a white SUV pulls up. The driver rolls down his window. His deep black skin glows almost blue in the streetlight. "Valentina?"

"Boubacar?"

He opens the side door. Scott buckles Mr. Morgan into the seat right behind the driver, directs me and Simon to the back row, and climbs over Mr. Morgan to sit next to him.

Val hops in the front, and Boubacar slides behind the wheel and backs out of the driveway.

As we head toward the main gate, two police cars, lights flashing, drive toward us. Boubacar pulls over, and they speed by. I watch through the back window as they turn into the guesthouse driveway.

Val says to Scott, "We cut that a little too close."

He nods. "And we're still not out of the woods."

Twenty-nine

Boubacar taps on his phone. "Worcester Regional Airport is your destination?" he asks.

"Yes, please," Val says.

"It is my pleasure."

Boubacar looks in the rearview mirror at Mr. Morgan and Scott. "My friend," he says, "is that gentleman going to live?"

"Not forever," Scott says.

"Nobody is allowed to die in my Cadillac."

"He should be fine," Val says.

"I hope so," he says. "One time I picked up this very old lady at a nursing home, and I was sure she was going to die on me. The director put her in my car and told me to drive her home. Said there was nothing more he could do. I drove her all the way to Manchester."

"Huh," Scott says. "Did she make it?"

"I told you, my friend. Nobody is allowed to die in my Cadillac. Her daughter had me take her right back to the nursing home. Wouldn't even let her mother out of my car. We made it with nobody dying."

"Nobody's dying this time either," Scott says.

"Good," Boubacar says. "This is a short trip, my friend. If the gentleman does choose to meet his maker, please don't tell me. Just take him with you."

"Deal," Scott says.

I tap Scott's shoulder. "Don't you think they know about the jet?"

"I'm sure they do," he says. "That's why we're heading to the airport."

I look at Simon, then back at Scott. "Are you trying to get us caught?"

"No, we're trying to escape."

I shake my head. "I'm not getting it."

"Let them think they've outsmarted us," he says. "They'll converge on where they think we're going."

I want to tell Scott and Val that I warned them about Ying and we could have avoided an escape plan altogether if they had just listened. But right now isn't the appropriate time to bring that up.

Instead, I say to Scott, "You must have a plan."

"We do," he says. "Val and I did a bunch of threat modeling and contingency planning over the past week. So far we've been spot on."

"So far we've been lucky," Val says.

"Right. We need to get off the grid before we're spotted." Scott pulls a paper bag out of an inner pocket of his suit and removes five pairs of plastic sunglasses. "Put these on and keep them on, even though it's nighttime. Assume that my eye reading system is compromised."

Scott's company has hacked into most municipal and private webcams. He reads the irises, calculates the soul identities, and collects the coordinates. He used this tech to rescue us, and these days he shares with Soul Identity so they can help members find soul line descendants of the people who were important to them in their previous lives.

"Ninety seconds," Val says. "Boubacar, we have a slight change of plans."

"Anything you need, ma'am. Just tell me."

"We're going to hop out at the upcoming traffic light, but we still want you to drive to the airport. Keep the trip running until you get there."

Boubacar raises his eyebrows. "Do you want me to stop the trip once I arrive?"

"Yes, at the public departures drop-off."

"Yes, ma'am."

She holds out her hand toward us. "Pass up your phones."

We pass them up, and she places them on the console. She shows Boubacar a large USPS Priority envelope. "Once you stop the trip, power down all four phones, put them in this envelope, and drop it into a mailbox."

She sets the envelope on the dashboard, and she lays five one-hundred-dollar bills on top. "This is for your inconvenience."

"Thank you, ma'am." Boubacar points out the windshield. "Is this where you hop out?"

"It is."

Boubacar pulls to a stop at the red blinking light, and Val and Scott open their doors. Simon and I clamber over the seat and grab the medicine while Scott runs around the car, opens Mr. Morgan's door, and helps him out.

"Thank you, Boubacar," Val says. "As requested, nobody died in your Cadillac."

"Nobody." He grins and drives off.

We make our way to the side of the road. The intersection is empty and dark. A lake stretches out on our left, a narrow bridge in front of us.

"It's going to suck walking with these sunglasses," I say.

"You won't have to walk," Scott says.

A minivan pulls up to the intersection on our left, and we cross the street to meet it. The side passenger door slides open, and Simon and I climb in the back. Scott helps Mr. Morgan sit behind the driver, and he scrambles over the old man, just like he did before. But this time he sits in the middle seat, next to Val.

That's because another man already occupies the passenger seat next to the lady driving the minivan. They both wear sunglasses, but I recognize them easily. Mr. and Mrs. Waverly, Scott's parents.

Why would Scott call his parents, his now-retired business partners, to Massachusetts?

Thirty

We're still on the highway in the middle of the night. I'm not sure when, because Val gave our phones to Boubacar, and the dashboard clock in the front of the van is both too dim and too far away for me to read.

Everybody appears to be asleep except for me and Mrs. Waverly, who has hummed the same chorus to an unknown song so many times that I could just about do the harmony. She's got a heavy foot, and she barrels down the left-hand lane of the interstate, flashing her high beams at those in her way. Not a single car has passed us.

I haven't seen Scott's parents since Christmas when they came to visit him in Seattle. They had returned from a Miami-to-Los-Angeles cruise. Scott's dad couldn't stop talking about going through the Panama Canal. He called it the world's greatest shortcut. Scott's mom told us about the monkeys she saw on a canoe trip they took through the mangroves in Colombia. Scott once told me that he was worried his parents would be bored when they decided to retire from the security business that the three of them ran. But once they started cruising, they wished they had quit ten years earlier.

Sitting here in the dark, with everybody else asleep, I think about how Ying said in bootcamp that she wanted to do something big. I go over our conversation on the jet when she called me out for hurting her and wished me luck at ever becoming an overseer.

My thoughts move on to what she said in her acceptance speech about using Soul Identity to drive world events. Here I was scared about her thinking up a directed attack against me, and she went so much bigger.

How did Ying get organized so quickly? We just landed the day before in Sterling. How could she convince the security forces to turn on Val and force us all to run?

What bothers me is that I'm the one who armed her. I left her stuck in the vike, giving her extra time to observe Origen's sneaky ways.

I need to go back and vike through more of Lillia of Cagliari's life, so I can learn what other tricks Ying picked up from Origen. I might even spot a vulnerability.

But do we even have a vike portal with us? If so, Val should let me use it, now the tables have turned against us.

I should have stopped researching history and spent more time last week convincing Val that I needed to vike. Ying is several steps ahead of us, and we're stuck playing catch-up. This is what happens when you don't take risks. I've grinded through enough strategy games to know that over-focusing on defense leads to your demise.

The rays from the sunrise hit the back of my head and wake me up.

We're still on the road. Scott's mom is napping in the passenger seat while his dad drives. He's in the right lane, and we're moving at half the speed we maintained when his wife was behind the wheel.

Mr. Morgan is awake, eyes focused on nothing as usual, his seat reclined. Right behind him, next to me, Simon lies on his back, his bent legs taking up the extra seat between us. He's wearing his sunglasses, snoring. The ends of his unknotted bowtie drape across his chest.

Scott's head rests on Val's shoulder. I lean over Simon's legs to peek at Val, and she gives me a brief smile.

"Any idea where we are?" I ask her.

"We just crossed into Ohio."

"Aha, somebody's awake back there," Scott's dad says. "Who needs a rest stop?"

Simon tucks his legs under Mr. Morgan's reclined seat and sits up, yawning. "Yes, please."

Mr. Waverly pulls into the Ohio Welcome Center, and Scott raises his head. "Remember to put on your sunglasses," he says.

We climb out of the minivan, stretch, and trundle to the bathrooms. When we get back, Scott's mom has the rear door open. She gives each of us a bottle of water, two granola bars, and an apple.

"Scott said we can't stop at restaurants, so this is your breakfast," she says. "Eat it now before we drive on."

We must make quite a sight for the other travelers. Scott, Val, Simon, and I wearing wrinkled, formal clothes. Mr. Morgan in his pajamas and slippers. Scott's parents clad in shorts, sandals, and polo shirts. And all seven of us sporting identical sunglasses and chewing on granola bars.

"How much fuel do we have?" Scott asks his mom.

"Almost a full tank," she says. "I filled up in Erie while everybody slept."

"Did you wear your sunglasses?"

"Have you forgotten that your father and I were your partners in a security business?"

"It's unforgettable," he says. "Did you pay in cash?"

"What do you think?"

"Speaking of cash..."

"It's in the glove compartment. Stacks of it."

Stacks of money? What are they planning? And why aren't they telling us? We pile into the minivan and get back on the highway.

"What's our destination?" I ask.

"Toledo," Scott's dad says. "Four hours to go."

"Two and a half," Scott's mom says. "Now that I'm driving again."

An hour later, Simon nudges me. "This is a nightmare, Zelly."

I nod.

"It's time we come clean and tell them all the suspicions we've had about Ying."

"And let them know we lied to them? Are you crazy?"

"No, Ying is the crazy one." He juts his chin at Scott and Val. "Tell them now. Or I will."

It's time to engolir sapos. And even though I hate swallowing frogs, Simon's right. We need their help, and they need to know what we know.

I clear my throat. "Scott? Val? Simon and I have something to tell you."

"What's up, Zelly?" Scott asks.

"We've been scared of Ying ever since she woke up from that first vike."

"Her first vike? Did she say something?" Scott asks.

"Yeah, some weird stuff to Zelly," Simon says. "Like how doing more vikes would make her the best overseer in the world. She didn't mention us, even when prompted."

"That got us worried that she wanted to be the only overseer," I say. "And that she'd find a way to stop us."

Scott and Val eye each other.

"Then we researched the Egyptian soul line ancestor she viked into," I say. "His name was Origen, and he was a real bad dude. Somehow all his overseer peers just happened to die from the plague. He moved the whole organization out of Egypt and over to Palestine. We were afraid that she was planning to do the same to us."

"You were afraid she'd kill you?" Scott asks.

Simon and I both nod.

"In my last vike," I say, "I went back to Palestine to my soul line ancestor, Lillia of Cagliari. I met Origen. And I know that he's the one who killed the Alexandria overseers."

Another long look between Scott and Val.

"We spent this last week trying to find out all we could about what Origen did," I say. "We wanted to be ready for anything Ying threw at us."

"Does Ying know you suspect her?" Val says.

"She knows," Simon says. "Zelly warned her on the flight to Sterling that she wouldn't let Ying block her from becoming an overseer."

Val says, "Thanks, you two, for telling us this. But at this point, we trust Ying, and we don't think any of this business with the guards was her doing."

I try to keep the astonishment off my face, but I doubt I succeed.

"You don't think Ying's involved?" I ask. "Were you not paying attention to her acceptance speech?"

"Oh, I was paying attention," Val says. "Believe me, I paid attention to every word of Ying's acceptance speech. But just because Ying flexed her muscles about driving a new culture and redirecting the conspiracy theorists, it doesn't mean she's trying to kill you. Ying is also a victim."

I am about to reply, but Simon reaches out his hand, below the seat line and out of view of Scott and Val. He grabs my leg just above my ankle and squeezes. And when I glance at him, his head makes a subtle shake.

"You don't think Ying is part of whoever was trying to grab us and Mr. Morgan?" I ask Scott evenly.

He frowns and shakes his head. "I don't. I'm sorry, Zelly, but you misunderstood what Ying said after her vike. And now you've conflated that misunderstanding with her excitement in her acceptance speech. Ying's in trouble, and as soon as you are all safe in Toledo, I'm going back to rescue her."

How did Ying pull the wool over their eyes?

"This is crazy!" I say. "Just listen to yourselves. You're giving Ying excuses, and you're telling me it's my lack of understanding. That's gaslighting, and it won't work. I remember exactly what Ying said."

"It's been a long night, Zelly," Val says. "We should take a break. Can we talk more once we reach Toledo?"

"That's an excellent idea," Simon says, his grip still on my shin. "Let's take a break, Zelly."

I do want to find my cool again, so I force my face into a smile.

But I'm still screaming inside.

Thirty-one

As I stew in the back of the minivan, I reach the unfortunate conclusion that Scott and Val won't ever be able to see that Ying has gone bad. Their mentorship has got them thinking they're more like our parents.

I'll bet that the parents of the worst criminals in the world think their child is good at heart and just hangs out with the wrong friends.

Simon and I can see that Ying turned to the dark side after her vikes, but Scott and Val cannot. They're too close.

All that is understandable. What gets me upset is that instead of listening to my perspective, they're telling me that I'm crazy.

It must be because they're trapped, and they can't find a way to admit that they screwed up by not noticing how Ying had changed.

Now I'm feeling sorry for Scott and Val. Kind of. They still shouldn't try to make me think I'm the crazy one.

We arrive in Toledo, and Scott's parents navigate us past downtown and up Cherry Street. Scott's dad points to a sprawling two-story white house on the left. Its front porch is almost blocked from view by a single far-reaching tree.

"This is it," he says.

"Didn't you guys move to Colorado?" I ask.

"We did," Scott's mom says. "This house belongs to cruise buddies of ours. Mike and Monica Miller." She takes the next left and parks in the alley behind the house. "They've exchanged places with us."

"They're now in your house?" Simon asks.

"No, they're in the Caribbean, less than a week into our twenty-day cruise, living it up in our upgraded balcony suite," Scott's dad says. "While we're busy saving you from mayhem and destruction."

"Mike and Monica booked a last-minute, overnight trip to Puerto Rico," Scott's mom says. "We met them at the old fort and swapped passports, tickets, phones, and clothes. They waltzed onto the ship, we spent the night in their cheap hotel room, and we flew back, as them, to Detroit."

"We picked up their minivan from extended parking and drove straight to Massachusetts," Scott's dad says. "You know what happened next."

"Hopefully, they think you're still on your cruise," Scott says. "I'm glad it all worked out."

"Just like the good old days," Scott's mom says. "I've been missing this."

We get inside the house and allocate the bedrooms. Simon and I raid the pantry and snoop through the Millers' belongings. We join Scott and Val on the porch while Scott's parents and Mr. Morgan take naps.

"Okay, Simon and I believe Ying is working with the bad guys," I say. "Can you tell us why you disagree?"

"After the speech," Val says, "I followed Ying out the stage's back door. As soon as I got inside, I saw four of those gray-uniformed security guards walking her down the hall."

"See? She's with them," I say.

Val shakes her head. "Let me finish. They're not our security guards. And Ying was gagged and handcuffed, Zelly."

Why didn't she mention that before?

Hands on my hips, I ask her, "If that is true, how did you get away?"

"They didn't see me. Another guard was at the door, but I saw him first. He grabbed for my wrist, and when he turned, I landed a forearm strike on his neck. He stepped back. I moved in with a groin kick, and he went down. Just like they taught us in self-defense."

"Ouch," Simon says.

"That Taser I had at the guest house? I took it from that guard's holster," Val says. "I sent Scott a message to bring you two to the door, but another guard was patrolling the hallway, and I had to stash my guy and wait for him to leave."

"Meanwhile I was pounding on the door," Scott says.

She takes Scott's hand. "I came as quickly as I could."

"Okay, they grabbed Ying," I say. "If they're not our guards, then whose are they?"

"We think they might be from whatever is left of The Alert Foundation," Scott says. "Ying becoming executive overseer yesterday was their big chance to grab her and take over Soul Identity. But they screwed up. Even though they got Ying, they missed both Val and Archie."

I try and fail to stop a shudder.

"I thought you put those guys out of business after you rescued us," Simon says.

"I thought we did, too," Scott says. "It might not be them. Whoever they are, we have Zelly to thank for us discovering them."

"Me?"

"We only stumbled on these guys because Ying's ceremony got postponed, and they had already deployed their scouts onto our campus. We saw them, and that's what tipped us off and gave us a week to prepare."

"Even with the prep time, we still failed," Val says. "They have Ying, and the rest of us barely escaped."

"How can you be sure that she didn't stage her capture just to fool you?" I ask.

Scott and Val look at each other for a minute.

"I suppose that's possible," Scott says. "Honestly, I didn't even consider that because—"

"Because it doesn't make any sense," Val says. "Zelly, you have confirmation bias. You're twisting everything you see into evidence that Ying is bad."

Is it confirmation bias? Am I just too suspicious? Or am I merely using my unique knowledge that I gained from my vikes?

"I might be biased, but I've seen Origen myself," I say. "Besides, you mentored Ying. How can that not be clouding your judgment?"

Val crosses her arms. "Ying is a decent person."

"That doesn't explain the way she talked to me or what she said in her speech," I say. "You expect me to take your word that she's been captured, yet you ignore what I say."

"Zelly has a point," Simon says.

"We're going in circles," Scott says. "We need to figure out clothes and toiletries, find an anonymous way to get online, and plan for Ying's rescue. How about we talk again this evening?"

"Fine," I say.

But what's the use of talking about it again? Scott and Val can't see what's right in front of them.

Thirty-two

I borrow clothes from Monica's closet. I choose a huge sweatshirt and a pair of yoga pants that hang loose, but I wear my own heels, as Monica's sneakers are clown shoes on my feet.

None of Mike's clothes come close to fitting Simon. He takes off his jacket, cummerbund, and bowtie, removes the button studs, and rolls up the sleeves of his white dress shirt.

The four of us put on our sunglasses and take the minivan to the closest Target, which is fifteen minutes away. We load up our carts with clothes, toiletries, underwear, and shoes. Scott selects four prepaid mobile phones, and Val empties the rack of every Visa gift card they have. Simon and I grab bags of chips, nuts, and candy.

We wheel our shopping carts to the checkout.

"You guys just move here?" the checkout lady asks us.

"What gave us away?" Scott asks.

"Your family is shopping like you're on the first day of a witness protection program."

He smiles at her.

"Sorry they put you guys in Toledo. You must've not had enough evidence to be big shots."

"Ain't that the truth," Scott says. "Everybody is short on evidence these days."

"Wait, you guys really are hiding out?" the lady asks. "I was just joshing you."

Scott brings his finger to his lips. "Don't tell anybody we were here."

She mimes zipping her mouth shut.

When she has run everything through the scanner and bagged it, she says, "Your total is almost four thousand dollars. That's my largest ring-up ever."

Scott counts out forty crisp hundred-dollar bills. The lady grabs a highlighter out of her cash register drawer and checks each of them. When she's done, she gives him the change, and we exit into the parking lot.

We load our purchases into the back of the minivan.

"Way to go with the low profile," Val says.

"We might as well play along with her fantasies," Scott says. "That's better than her getting suspicious and calling the police."

When we get back to the Millers' house, I take a long shower with my new soap and shampoo, shave with my new razor, dry off with my new towel, make myself presentable with my new brushes and makeup, and dress in my new clothes.

"We're like brand-new people," I say to Simon.

"I hope not for long."

I give him a hug and a pat on the back. "Let's explore the neighborhood. Just the two of us."

We put on our sunglasses and walk up Cherry Street. After a few blocks, we come to an elementary school, and since it's the summer, the playground is empty.

The sunlight fades and the shadows stretch long. We sit on the lone swing set, giving ourselves tiny pushes by scuffing our feet in the gravel below.

Simon spins in circles, and as he untwirls, he asks, "What did you think about Scott and Val's story?"

"About Ying being a victim and not the instigator? I wish it was true."

He stops spinning. "Me, too."

"But it's so hard for me to believe. Something happened to Ying during her vikes."

He reaches out and grabs the chain on my swing, turning me to face him.

"Even if Ying is bad, she's still a victim," he says. "No way she'd team up with the guys who killed her family. She needs to be rescued."

"We don't even know who the bad guys are."

"But it doesn't matter who they are. It doesn't matter if we're afraid of Ying. If she's in trouble, we have to help her."

Darn it. He's right.

I look him in the eye. "Then let's rescue her."

"I was hoping you'd say that."

We walk back to the Millers' house and tell Scott and Val we're ready to talk.

While I'm waiting, I stare at the family photos on the walls. Mike and Monica have twin sons, now grown, and they show up in Toledo at Christmas for an annual holiday pajama photo. Forty of these shots chronicle the growth of the boys and the rise and fall of Mike's beer belly.

Forty years of family happiness, at least at Christmas. Imagine if my past could have stayed quiet for that long.

Who am I kidding? Those photos show forty years of a forced Christmas obligation, decades of listening to the twins' spouses and kids complaining about missed opportunities of holidays in the sun.

Mike and Monica Miller brought the tyranny of their past upon their whole family.

When Scott and Val come downstairs, we walk to the porch.

"Zelly and I discussed this," Simon says. "It doesn't matter if Ying is bad or good. She needs to be rescued as soon as possible."

"We agree," Val says. "And as we save her, we can't risk losing the power we have over the bad guys."

"What power?" I ask. "They already have Ying. What else do they need?"

"Overseers only do so much without each other's consent. By ourselves we have limited authority."

"That means you and Mr. Morgan have to stay alive and not get caught," I say. "When will the rest of us rescue Ying?"

"You won't," Val says. "Scott and his parents will go. You two will stay safe with me and Mr. Morgan."

"Here in Toledo?" I ask.

"It's not that bad a place."

"If we're going to be stuck here, you have to let me vike."

"No vikes," she says. "I haven't changed my mind."

I look at Scott, and it takes him a minute to meet my eye.

"I agree with Val," he says. "You don't know what can happen to you in a vike."

What does that mean? Does he think I'll become evil by observing Lillia?

"My soul line ancestor wasn't the one who killed her peers," I say.

"Are you sure?" Scott asks.

I want to say yes, but he raises a good point. I don't know what happened to Lillia. I've observed her on the ship losing most of her left pinky and again as she reached Psychen Euporos in Caesarea. Other than what's in our archives, I have no idea what else happened when she was an overseer.

"No, I'm not sure," I say. "That's why I need to vike. You guys need to trust me."

"I'm sorry, Zelly," Val says. "The vike portals are back in Sterling, but even if we could get to them, I'd still say no. If anything happens to you, it's catastrophic to our organization."

I stare at her. "You want to keep me and Simon stuck in this house, doing nothing?"

"That's the plan," she says. "Until we know more and until we can find a better way to protect all of us, we have to remain off the grid."

"At least give us those prepaid phones, so we can reach civilization."

Scott shakes his head. "Let's wait until we get Ying and bring Soul Identity back under control."

Val says, "In the meantime, read a book. Watch television. Wear your sunglasses and take walks. Act like you're just two normal kids on vacation, so our neighbors don't get suspicious."

I have nothing to say.

Their plan sucks.

Thirty-three

That night I lie in what must have been one of the Miller twins' beds. The walls are papered with posters of swimsuit models and rock bands from the early nineties.

I stare at the ceiling and think how impossible my life is without an internet connection.

My life is also impossible if I continue to let risk-adverse adults make decisions for me. I'm supposed to be figuring out how to survive. Cowering in Toledo without any way to research is stupid.

I need a vike portal.

I can assemble one from the parts I ordered online before we flew to Sterling. But those parts will arrive in Seattle. I'd fly there or even take a train, but then I'd have to use my credit card and show my driver's license. That would put me right back on the grid, and then the bad guys would know about Toledo.

But I know exactly what I need to do. I'm going to drive to Seattle.

This evening, when I was poking around, I discovered that Mike and Monica own a second car, an older model Toyota Camry, parked in the standalone garage that's facing the alley behind their house. I also found its keys hanging in the kitchen.

I know I need to drive west, but on which highways? How did people drive to new places before the internet, anyway? Did they just read the maps at the rest areas? That can't be how. There must have been a way they planned out their road trips.

Books. Real ones. What my grandparents used in the olden days. Mike and Monica have a bookshelf in their living room. I pull on a pair of jeans and a sweatshirt, and I walk downstairs. I turn on the light and search through the bookcase. There's a whole row taken by a set of encyclopedias from 1976, at least thirty Reader's Digest Condensed Books, and a spiral-bound Rand McNally Road Atlas from 2002.

I sit on the floor and open the atlas to an interstate map of the entire United States. I find Toledo and follow I-90 to Chicago, through a bunch of Midwest and Western states, and into Washington. At the bottom of the map are tables of distances and driving times. Seattle is around 2,300 miles away, and if I don't stop at all, I can be home in thirty-six hours.

The good news is that from Toledo, I can drive I-90 the whole way to Seattle. If I stay traveling west, I can't get lost.

I climb the stairs, grab my new clothes and toiletries, and shove them into two empty Target shopping bags. I carry them downstairs and take the keys from the kitchen. I open the back door, but I stop before walking out.

Money. I won't get far on the forty bucks that I have tucked in my wallet. Scott's mom mentioned stacks of cash in the van's glove compartment, so I find the van's keys. But the glove compartment is empty.

Back inside, I search for the Visa cards Val bought. But she must have brought them up to her and Scott's room.

Simon might have money. I carry my bags back upstairs and slip into his bedroom. He's lying on his back, sound asleep. I don't want him to scream, so I cover his mouth with one hand and shake his shoulder with the other.

His eyes jerk open and he lets out a muffled yell.

"Sy, it's Zelly. Hush and I'll uncover your mouth."

He nods, and I remove my hand. He sits up.

"Do you have any money I can borrow?"

"What for?"

"I'm getting out of here."

He shakes his head.

"You must have some money. I'll pay you back."

"Take me with you," he says.

"You don't even know where I'm going."

"Doesn't matter. It's better than staying here." Simon swings his legs out of bed. "I have money, but if you try to leave without me, I'll wake everybody up."

I sigh. "Are you sure? It's a long drive back to Seattle."

"You're going home? Is it safe?"

"It doesn't matter. I need to vike."

He says, "I have three hundred bucks. Will that be enough?"

I do the math in my head. If the car averages twenty miles per gallon, we'll need to buy one hundred and fifteen gallons. And we'll need more for tolls.

"It's probably enough."

I help him pack his stuff into another Target bag, and we creep down the stairs and into the kitchen. Simon grabs the bag of snacks he bought earlier, and we're out the back door.

Then he stops.

"What did you forget?" I ask.

"Sunglasses. To hide our eyes."

We grab our sunglasses, put them on, and stumble out back. I wince as the alley-facing garage door screeches open.

Simon waits while I back out the car. He pulls the garage door shut and hops in the passenger seat. I drive out the south end of the alley and loop back onto Cherry Street. I turn left, away from downtown, and we drive in front of the Millers' house.

"Still dark inside," Simon says.

"Maybe they didn't hear us leave."

"Should we have left them a note?"

I glance at him. "You want to go back and write one for them?"

He shakes his head.

I turn onto Central Avenue, follow the signs for I-75 South, and after five more minutes, take the exit for I-90 West and pick up our toll ticket.

I invest some time figuring out the car's cruise control, because I don't dare get a speeding ticket and have my name recorded in the police system. I'm not scared about Scott and Val figuring out where we are, but I am worried what the bad guys will do if they catch us.

Will the cops pull me over if they see me wearing sunglasses at night? I think they might.

"Let's stop at the next rest area and sleep until dawn," I say.

An hour later we reach the Indian Meadow Plaza, recline our seats all the way back, and try to suppress our worrying long enough to sleep.

"I still think we should have told them why we left," Simon says sometime during the restless night.

I feel a teeny bit bad about just picking up and leaving. But not bad enough to admit that to Simon. I keep my eyes closed and pretend to sleep until I do.

Thirty-four

I open my eyes and check the dashboard clock. It's already after eight, and we've wasted at least two hours of daylight. Simon is sound asleep, and I have plenty of fuel, so I decide to get on the road.

I reflect on my plan to drive us all the way to Seattle. It was impulsive, like most of my decisions, and now that I'm thinking it through in the harsh and realistic light of day, I can identify three issues with it.

First, we may not have enough money. I've already blown most of my own cash on tolls. The car seems to suck a lot of fuel, and the price of gas on the highway is more expensive than I had estimated. Guess that's what happens when you usually drive electric cars.

Second, we may be identified on the road. It would take just one slip-up to get pulled over. Or just one camera image without our sunglasses for Scott's software to betray us.

Third, even if we make it home anonymously and assemble a new vike portal, I still can't vike, because I won't have the source code. My laptop's sitting at Soul Identity headquarters.

These three issues will require creativity. Solving them will keep us busy during our long drive.

I stop at a travel plaza at the western edge of Indiana, and I shake Simon awake. We use the facilities, change our underwear, do a few jumping jacks, and fill up the gas tank.

I grab the snacks from out of the trunk, and we get back on the road.

I share the snacks with Simon as well as the three issues with my plan.

"Why didn't you do this analysis before we stole the car?" he asks.

"I was too upset to think it all the way through."

We ride in silence for the next three hours, which is good, as it requires my full attention to follow the jam of roads, find the express lanes, and navigate the correct highway splits through the mess of traffic that surrounds Chicago.

As we pull out of a travel plaza about twenty miles into Wisconsin, Simon points at my odometer. "Your first issue isn't a real issue. We have enough cash to get home."

"We do?"

"You just drove one hundred sixty miles on less than eight gallons. And the gas is cheaper here than it was in either Indiana or Illinois. We'll be fine."

"That's good news."

"I have even more," he says. "Your second issue about not getting caught is manageable. Just keep using the cruise control. And I'll remind you to wear sunglasses. But I've been watching you so far, and you've been doing great. The cops haven't looked twice at us."

"Thanks. Did you happen to solve the source code issue?"

"That one's all yours. You're the geek."

A geek dealing with internet withdrawal symptoms.

We pull back onto the highway. It's now two in the afternoon, and we'll be reaching Madison soon.

The third issue is bugging me. Driving all the way to Seattle when I don't have source code makes no sense. If I can't get to the code, we'd be better off trying to steal an existing vike portal. But those portals sit in Sterling, not in Seattle. The opposite direction.

Given our limited funds, we should decide soon if we should turn around and head to Sterling instead.

If I were Jeremy and I had sold my company to Soul Identity, would I keep a copy of my code, just in case?

I probably would.

"Don't all public libraries provide free internet?" I ask.

"I think so. Why?"

"Solving the third issue. I'm going to stop in Madison."

I exit the highway and follow signs for downtown. We pass some fast-food restaurants, and Simon points to a brick two-story building on the left.

"A library," he says.

I make a U-turn and park. We walk inside and up to the information desk, where a man sits in front of a computer. He's in his fifties, with a crewcut and tiny red reading glasses perched on the end of his nose. He's wearing a short-sleeved pink dress shirt, untucked, over his baggy jeans.

"Can we please use your computers to get online?" I ask.

He smiles at me. "Did you make a reservation?"

I shake my head.

"We only have one that doesn't require a reservation. Let me check to see when it's free." He types on his keyboard. "It's ready for you now."

"Great," I say. "Where is it?"

He stands and hitches up his jeans. "I'll take you to it."

We follow him to a room close to the stacks. It's got one desktop with a monitor, and four tablets, all bolted down along a counter. He points me to the desktop.

When he leaves, I open a private browser window and run searches for Jeremy on Vashon Island, wheelchairs, and vikes. Nothing useful comes up, but after a few attempts, I find a vikob.com with its location set to Vashon Island. It's Jeremy's house.

From there it's pretty simple to pull up the house's tax records and find Jeremy's last name. Once I have that, it's child's play to get his email and phone number.

I create a new Gmail account under the name Lillia Cagliari. I send Jeremy a message, saying that I wished I could visit the cannibals again, and to please write me back soon.

We hop back in the car and drive out of Wisconsin and into Minnesota. We fill up in Rochester, and Simon and I walk inside the gas station to pay.

While I'm scanning the road atlases and trying to choose a rest area where we can spend the night, Simon comes and stands next to me. He's got a frown on his face.

"What's wrong, Sy?"

"The clerks are whispering about us."

I pick up an atlas and flip through its pages, glancing at the guy and the girl at the registers. "What are they saying?"

"To keep an eye out, because we're going to steal something."

"Oh." I put the road atlas back on the shelf. "It must be our sunglasses."

"Other people in here are wearing sunglasses," he says. "Maybe they don't like teenagers. Or they hate out-of-towners."

"Or they suspect a frizzy-haired, brown-skinned girl is teaching a blond, white boy how to steal." I nudge him. "We did take the Millers' car a couple days ago."

He frowns. "Whatever it is, they're biased."

"Everybody's biased. We're not going to be able to fix them today."

"You're excusing their behavior?"

"I'm excusing nothing. I'm saying that who we are and what we've done is our past, and sometimes that's just the burden we need to accept."

"That's not fair."

"Yeah, I know. The world's unfair." I give him a hug. "Let's just leave. We can't afford extra attention."

We drive back onto the highway, and when dusk settles in, we stop at a rest area close to the border in South Dakota. Bad news, it's got a three-hour limit on stops. We risk driving another hour in sunglasses in the dark, and we end up at a well-lit travel center.

After hitting the bathrooms and filling up with fuel again, Simon hands me a bag of chips.

"We should eat a real breakfast tomorrow," he says. "We can afford it, and that way we won't stink up the car so much."

I lie awake for a while, trying to block out the sounds and the smell of Simon's peidos. He wasn't kidding about needing real food.

It was a good first day. We know we can make it all the way home. We kept our eyes hidden. And we may have found a way to talk to Jeremy.

I hope he emails me back.

Thirty-five

A family restaurant sits alongside this South Dakota travel center, and we hunker down at a table just as the sun is rising.

Simon orders the "Nana Nut French Toast" with eggs and bacon and orange juice, and I choose the misspelled "Vegtable Omelette" with hash browns, pancakes, and coffee. It's way too much food for a single meal, and we box what we can't eat and drive onto the highway before seven in the morning.

We need a library to check if Jeremy emailed me back. But the surroundings are flat fields holding nothing but a few cattle and even fewer windmills. A road sign shows Rapid City is 275 miles away, which I realize will put us halfway home. It's also our last chance to turn back, because we'll have spent half of our money.

Many cows and radio stations later, the plains give way to hills on our sides and mountains looming ahead of us. When we arrive in Rapid City, we follow a sign to the Visitor Information Center. A helpful lady directs us to the library, which isn't far away.

This librarian is young and pretty. She's dressed in a short skirt and a lacy blouse. And she's not helpful at all.

"You must first take off those sunglasses before I can assist you, young lady," she says.

"Sorry, but we have medical issues with our eyes," I say.

She frowns. "We prize politeness in Rapid City. Hiding your eyes like that is not polite behavior."

I wonder how polite the good citizens of Rapid City would think Scott was if they knew he had tapped into their video cameras.

I flash a slight smile. "Thank you for your help. Have a nice day."

And we leave the library.

"Please come again," she calls.

Back in the car, Simon asks, "Why didn't you fight back?"

"Because she could have called a cop. And we can't risk taking off our sunglasses, especially inside a library full of video cameras."

He sighs. "How will we check your email?"

"Find another library somewhere else, I guess."

But as I'm about to turn onto the highway, I see a Best Buy coming up on our right-hand side. "Hold on . . . these guys' display computers are online."

He laughs. "Smarty pants."

But his praise comes too soon, because we get spooked by two cops hanging around the laptops, and even though we wait for a half hour, they're stuck laughing and flirting with the sales associate.

I walk over to the prepaid phones, and I point at the cheapest Android device. "Can we afford twenty-five bucks?"

We count our money—one hundred and seventy dollars.

"Barely," Simon says. "It will mean no more breakfasts."

With tax, the phone costs a bit over twenty-six dollars. We walk back to the appliance section because it's empty. I connect to Best Buy's free Wi-Fi.

My email has a reply from Jeremy. He wants to talk.

I activate the phone, set up a new WhatsApp account, and

message Jeremy. A few seconds later, he tries to start a video call with me.

I don't trust him yet, so there's no way I'm going to show him where I am. I answer with audio, and his face pops up on the screen. He's in his wheelchair, pulled up to a worktable. Behind him lies the Puget Sound.

"Zelly, are you all right?" he asks. "And why are you calling yourself Lillia?"

I turn down the volume so just Simon and I can hear. "I'm being careful."

"Scott called me yesterday," Jeremy says. "He asked me to pass along a message if I heard from you. I am to inform you that it's difficult to stay hidden these days."

"Why would he say that?"

He shrugs. "No idea. He also said that if I help you build another vike portal, I'd forfeit my acquisition money. I checked my contract, and that ain't no idle threat."

"I don't need help building one. But I do need a copy of the code. Can you send it to me? I won't tell anybody."

"Why do you need it?" he asks.

"So, I can vike again. It's important. It may save my life."

He sighs and looks down for a minute. "I'm sorry, Zelly. I can't. I have too much to lose."

"Jeremy, please."

He shakes his head.

I try to think of something that I can threaten him with. But I've got nothing. Would he help me if I started to cry?

I'm busy working up some crocodile tears when he rubs his chin and says, "Zelly, I know a way you can vike that doesn't risk me losing all my money."

"Tell me."

"Giovanni Judd," he says. "He's crazy and paranoid, but he trusts me. We can visit him together. At his compound in Idaho."

"Why would I want to see Giovanni Judd?"

"Because he knows all about xanazo. Vikes. But ask me what's the real reason."

"What's the real reason?"

He grins. "Giovanni Judd can teach you to vike without a vike portal."

Thirty-six

Jeremy says the closest town to Giovanni Judd's compound is Wallace, Idaho. I tell him that Simon and I can meet him there in twenty-four hours.

"Something else," I say. "Can I borrow some money? I need a thousand bucks, in cash."

"No problem," he says,

That almost feels too easy. "Seriously?"

"Of course. I owe you anyway for solving that safety issue."

"I'll pay you back. Where should we meet?"

"The Center of the Universe."

"Where?"

He laughs. "Just search for it. I'll meet you there tomorrow at noon."

After I disconnect, I look at Simon. "Good news and bad news."

"It all sounded good to me."

"But Scott anticipated us. That means we're too predictable."

"Maybe, maybe not. He might have left you messages all over the place."

"Even so, let's get a different SIM card," I say. "Just in case the bad guys are now tracking this one."

I search for the Center of the Universe. Who knew it's at the intersection of Bank and 6th streets in Wallace, Idaho? It's been there since 2004, when the mayor of Wallace proclaimed it must be, since it couldn't be proven otherwise. This was in protest of the government declaring, without evidence, that the town's water must have been polluted by the neighboring silver mines.

People declare things without proof all the time.

We spend another twenty bucks to get a new prepaid SIM card. As we walk out of the store, I break the old card in half and throw it away. We stop at a gas station before heading out on the highway.

It's a beautiful afternoon, and the few extra trees and rolling hills we see out the windshield are much more pleasant than the previous flat lands. The miles roll on by. Simon chases radio stations. I daydream about viking back into Lillia as we pass through the rest of South Dakota, across a tiny northeast corner of Wyoming, and burrow our way into Montana as the sun sets in front of us. Good thing we wear our trusty sunglasses.

By nine o'clock we reach Bozeman, and we need a place to sleep. I turn into the rest area. A big sign on the door says that overnight parking is forbidden, but somebody has scrawled *Park at Walmart* across the bottom.

The rest area has free internet access, so when we get back to the car, I use the phone to connect to the Wi-Fi and find the nearest Walmart. It's two miles from us. We fill up with gas along the way, and when we arrive, we see at least thirty RVs already parked. We choose a spot near the edge of the biggest cluster, put back our seats, and try to relax.

"So many people," Simon says.

"They're all traveling. Just like us."

"But they're on vacation, and we're on the run."

I connect to Walmart's Wi-Fi, and I check the map. Wallace is four and a half hours away, so if we want to get there early, we'll have to leave by six. I set the alarm for five-thirty.

"My butt is so sore," Simon says. "I can't wait for this trip to end."

"Me, too. I'm even beginning to miss Sue's cooking."

We are silent for a moment, each lost in our thoughts.

"I've been thinking about Ying," Simon says. "Do you think Scott was able to rescue her?"

I shrug. "We don't have a way to find out."

That gets me wondering how I can communicate with Scott without the bad guys intercepting what I write. He found a way through Jeremy to tell us how difficult it was to stay hidden. Perhaps he was inviting us to reach out.

He knows what car we stole, so he knows our license plate number.

He must have used his eye surveillance system to spot our license plate.

I sit up and point at the Walmart entrance. "Time to go shopping."

I lead us to the greeting cards and gift bags, where I select a posterboard and a large black marker. On the way to the cash register, I pick up apples, bananas, and oranges. "Can we afford all of this?" I ask.

"We overspent on that SIM card, so let me check." Simon pulls a twenty and two fives out of his pocket. "This is what we've got left. But our tank is full, so we can get to Wallace."

"Jeremy better not let us down," I say.

Back at the car, I write my new email address on the posterboard using big, fat letters, and I prop it into the back windshield. I move our car under a parking lot light.

"You're sending a message to Scott?" Simon asks.

I nod.

He hands me an apple.

We listen to ourselves chewing.

"Do you still pretend your family is alive?" he asks.

"Sometimes. How about you?"

"Every night. I tell them what I did during the day, and I listen to them grumble about work and about me not doing my chores. Sometimes we laugh. Sometimes we cry."

"That sounds nice, Sy."

He nods. "And every night, before I fall asleep, I pretend that my mom kisses me goodnight. I can actually feel it on my forehead."

"My father used to lie on the floor next to my bed at night," I say. "He would tell me about this little girl named Olivia Gisellia who did so many brave things. My mom would join him, and we'd giggle at the way he made me the hero." I smile. "Sometimes at night I pretend he's still doing this."

A tear creeps out from under Simon's sunglasses and rolls down his cheek. I reach out and take his hand, and he squeezes back, hard.

"Ever since my vike," he says, "I can no longer imagine my parents. I try so hard, but they're not there. They've stopped coming to see me at night. I'm so scared, Zelly. I think they're gone forever."

I wrap my arms around him. He sobs into my shoulder, and I pat his back until his trembling stops.

He leans away from me. "I'm afraid about you viking again, Zelly. I keep wondering what part of you will get lost."

I pull him back into a hug. "I don't know, Sy. But if we don't figure out how to survive, our families' deaths will have been useless. I need to vike. Even if it means I lose part of myself."

One last pat, and he settles back and reclines his seat.

A long time later, he says, "Good night, Zelly."

"Good night, Sy."

I remember what he said about his mother, and I lean over and kiss his forehead.

When I recline my seat, he grabs my hand, and I lie still, listening to him snore, all night long, hoping that we can keep it together for just one more day.

Thirty-seven

The alarm goes off at five-thirty. I must have managed to fall asleep, at least for a little while. We both groan as we stretch.

I remember the sign I left in the rear windshield, and I check my phone. I have a single email from somebody claiming to be Yuno Hu.

I read it aloud. "Z, Glad you got my message. We found her. My folks are helping with rescue plan. Should be tomorrow. The others still at house. Hope you two are safe. Let me know if you need anything. PS don't do it."

"What doesn't he want you to do?" Simon asks.

"Make a vike portal, I guess."

I write back, "We are fine. Is home safe?"

I start the car and drive the two miles back to the rest area. In the bathroom, I pull my brush through my curls and frown in the mirror. Despite trying to clean myself in the sink, changing at least my underclothes every day, and using deodorant, I'm beginning to stink. When Jeremy sees us at noon, he's going to think we're uncivilized slobs.

When we're done with this trip, I'm going to stand under a showerhead until my skin looks more wrinkled than a chuchu.

We're back on the road before six. Simon peels the bananas and the oranges, and we gobble them up.

"Best breakfast ever," I tell him.

"That's the spirit," he says.

The last part of Montana climbs higher and higher on a steep and curvy road. The mountains make the car work hard, and our fuel gauge starts to flash. We coast downhill in Idaho, scrounge all the loose change in the car, and put five bucks in the tank.

We take the first exit for Wallace. The entire town is a few blocks long. We drive right through the Center of the Universe and keep going as I search for a place to park. I circle around to the right and spot a small motel, so I turn into its parking lot.

We both stretch, but before we get out of the car, I say, "We should leave everything here. Phone, keys, and clothes."

Simon raises his eyebrows. "I thought you trusted Jeremy."

I shrug. "Just in case."

We tuck the phone into the center console and put the keys over the visor. We move the remaining snacks and our bags of clean and dirty clothes to the trunk. We get out, leaving just the rear passenger door unlocked, and walk to the meeting place.

I spot a sign on the northwest corner that points to the Center of the Universe's plaque, which sits on top of a manhole in the middle of the intersection.

"We still have an hour to walk around," I say.

Wallace hosts three museums, two churches, a tattoo parlor, and quite a few bars and bistros. It takes us just thirty minutes to see most of the tiny downtown, so we waste time inside a Gems and Collectibles store right on the corner of our meeting place. I read the T-shirts while Simon examines and rearranges the rocks and minerals.

At two minutes before noon, we walk up to the store's plate glass windows and peek outside. Tourists wander into the intersection and take their pictures next to the manhole cover at the Center of the Universe.

When my phone tells me that it's noon, I look across the street, and I see Jeremy rolling his wheelchair into the middle of the intersection. I grab Simon's hand, and together we step outside.

Jeremy wheels over to us. "Welcome to the Center of the Universe."

"I always wondered where it was," I say.

He laughs. "Y'all ready to meet Giovanni Judd?"

"We are," I say. "How far away is his place?"

"Less than half a mile. Just follow my van."

"We can ride with you," I say. "If that's okay."

"Of course. Do you have any bags?"

I shake my head. "We're only here for the day. We need to be back by four this afternoon."

"What if . . ." He shrugs. "Never mind. Let's go."

We follow Jeremy to his conversion van. He uses his key fob to open the side door and lower the ramp. I sit in the passenger's seat, and Simon perches on the bed in the back.

"Imagine traveling in one of these vans," Simon says.

"Bigger than what you came in, I imagine," Jeremy says.

Simon doesn't say anything.

Jeremy glances over at me. "You guys are running away, aren't you?"

I'm still not sure I trust him. But we need him. Instead of answering, I ask, "How can you tell?"

"Scott's message. Threatening me about helping you build a vike portal."

"Then why are you helping us?"

He says, "You got Ying out of that vike and saved the sale of my company. I figure I owe you. Big time."

"Believe me, I was also happy everything worked out."

Jeremy reaches into a pack attached to his wheelchair and pulls out an envelope. "A thousand bucks, all in twenties. If you are indeed on the run, no sense having to deal with places that won't break big bills."

I fold the envelope in half and stick it in my pocket. "Thanks, Jeremy. I'll pay you back when we reach Seattle."

"No rush." He pushes the ignition button and uses a hand throttle just to the right of the steering wheel to pull the van into the street.

"Is it hard to learn to drive with your hands?" I ask.

"I've been doing it so long that I don't even notice." He shows me how it works. He pushes right and left for the throttle, and forward to brake.

Jeremy drives right over the Center of the Universe plaque and past the collectibles store. We round a corner, make a couple of quick turns, and stop in front of a gate that blocks access to a paved roadway. A video camera and speaker are mounted on a metal post outside Jeremy's window, and he reaches out and pushes the talk button.

A man's voice asks over the speaker, "Are they with you?"

Jeremy leans back in his seat. "See for yourself."

The gate swings inward. Jeremy follows the roadway around a tight corner, where it dead-ends in a turnaround in front of a narrow single-story house that's squeezed against a steep hill behind it. An old green farm truck is parked to the right.

The tiny house is white clapboard with blue trim. It has a red door and a large picture window on its front. Inside is a small living room with a couch and a television, a kitchen area to the right. A chimney above its steep roof has a trace of smoke rising from it.

"This itty-bitty house is Giovanni's secret compound?" I ask.

"Size doesn't matter," Jeremy says. "What matters is Giovanni Judd."

The front door opens, and an older man wearing a flannel shirt, jeans, and fancy Italian loafers steps outside. He's bald on top, his gray fringe of hair pulled back in a ponytail. He's wearing large glasses and carries an old shotgun in his hand.

"And that right there is Giovanni Judd, God bless him," Jeremy says.

Giovanni waves and goes back inside the house. He closes the front door. And just as I'm about to ask Jeremy what's going on, the front of the tiny house lifts, up like a garage door, exposing the rooms and furniture inside. The floor folds upward toward the walls like the bottom of a cardboard box, leaving behind a bright room that tunnels into the mountain.

"Whoa," Simon says. "That's awesome."

Jeremy pulls the van forward, and we enter Giovanni Judd's compound.

Thirty-eight

The tunnel curves to the right and opens into a garage area where a shiny motorcycle, a plain white utility van, and a silver Tesla are parked. Giovanni has put away the shotgun and taken off the flannel shirt, exposing a black turtleneck. He waves at us, a grin on his face. He stands by a closed steel door that has an electronic keypad hanging on the wall next to it.

Jeremy parks. Simon and I wait for him to unlock his chair and wheel out before we follow him. He heads for Giovanni, who welcomes him with a fist bump.

"Giovanni, I'd like to introduce you to Zelly and Simon," Jeremy says. "They both—"

"Their reputation precedes them." He bows his head. "Giovanni Judd at your service, Miss Oliveira and Master Green. Welcome to my humble abode."

I throw a glance to Simon. We've always flown under the radar. Does he know that we're overseers or is he just being polite?

"We're pleased to meet you," I say.

"The pleasure is all mine." Giovanni puts his thumb up to the keypad, and when it beeps, he enters a code, covering it with his hand. He pulls the door open and points inside with a flourish.

Jeremy leads the way, and Simon and I follow him into a foyer with a high ceiling, a slate floor, and yellow walls. Three couches form a U, and in the open area, a red velvet curtain hangs over a wide opening in the wall. A small table stands three feet in front of the curtain, and on it lies an assortment of drinks and sandwich ingredients.

It reminds me of the sitting area in the Psychen Euporos headquarters where Lillia and Junius waited during my last vike. Though these couches are for sitting and not reclining.

"Please take rest," Giovanni says. "And let me apologize for the bourgeois furnishings."

I sit next to Simon on the center couch. Jeremy maneuvers his wheelchair between ours and the one on the right, and Giovanni sits on the couch to our left.

But as soon as Giovanni sits, he pops back up and walks to the table. "May I serve you refreshments?" he asks. "I have coffee, tea, soda, water, and an assortment of sandwich fixings."

Jeremy wheels himself over to the table. "Don't mind if I do."

"Please, tell me your preferred sandwich, Master Green."

I say to Simon, "Let's just make our own."

We walk over to the table, and it's got Simon's and my favorite fillings. I make a cheese and guava Romeu e Julieta, and Simon prepares a cucumber and brie which he cuts into triangles.

"How did you know what food we like?" I ask once we return to the couch.

He taps his forehead. "I've spent a good portion of my life learning everything there is to know about the Soul Identity overseers, Miss Oliveira."

I sense Simon tensing up next to me.

"Overseers?" I ask.

"Don't worry, Miss Oliveira." He winks. "Your secret is safe with me."

I glance at Simon, who's biting his lip.

Giovanni's still talking. "The real question, though, is how I was able to get my hands on the guava and brie way out here in the middle of Idaho."

"How did you manage that, Giovanni?" Jeremy asks.

"I placed an order nine days ago, in anticipation of your visit. After you called me for help with Ms. Ouyang."

"I've been here four times, Giovanni, and you still can't remember what sandwich I like," Jeremy says. "Just a simple PB&J, and you never have it."

Giovanni frowns.

After a moment of uncomfortable silence, Simon says, "I didn't like them when I first came to America, but I've grown to love peanut butter and jelly sandwiches."

Giovanni says, "Then you shall have one. Excuse me." He disappears behind the curtain.

Simon leans over and whispers, "Is he a bad guy?"

"Let's hope not," I whisper back. "Else we're screwed."

Giovanni comes back with jars of peanut butter and jelly and sets them on the table. "Master Green, may I make you a sandwich?"

"I'll do it." Simon walks back to the table and makes two sandwiches. He brings them both to Jeremy, returns to the couch, and eats his cucumber and brie.

"You are the man," Jeremy says.

I say to Giovanni, "Thanks for your hospitality. Jeremy told us that you can teach us how to vike."

"Vike?" Giovanni asks.

"I'd better translate," Jeremy says. "Giovanni, she wants to learn how the ancients practiced xanazo."

Giovanni frowns. "You perverted the sacred name of xanazo?"

"Vicarious observation. Vike for short," Jeremy says. "I needed something marketable."

"Xanazo means I live again, and that conveys a multitude more meanings than mere observation can," Giovanni says. "It was practiced by the ancient overseers of Psychen Euporos in Miletus, Babylon, and Alexandria."

"Only those places?" Simon asks. "What about our other headquarters?"

"I have found no references after that. Either Origen fled before he learned how to do it, or all records have been lost."

Despite the creepiness about him knowing we're overseers, Giovanni could have information about Origen that will help me convince Val about the threat that Ying poses.

"You said that Origen fled Alexandria?" I ask.

"I did." Giovanni pushes his glasses up his nose. "Origen was the Iron Man of his time. He outfoxed and outran those who would murder him, and he single-handedly saved Psychen Euporos from destruction."

"Wait, Origen saved the organization?" I ask. "That sounds like propaganda."

He cocks his head at me. "Have you heard a different version? Maybe one from your own archives?"

This could easily become a distraction. I already know the best way to survive whatever Ying is planning. I need to vike—or xanazo if that's what Giovanni insists on calling it—back into Lillia of Cagliari and observe her outwitting Origen.

"Perhaps I'm uninformed," I say. "I'd like to learn more, but can we do it after you teach us how to xanazo?"

"Of course!" Giovanni says. "We can discuss the history later. Would you like to rest first?"

"They don't have time," Jeremy says. "They're leaving at four."

Giovanni whirls around to face Jeremy. "Impossible! Nobody can learn to xanazo that quickly."

"How long does it take?" I ask.

He stares at me, hand on his chin. "Have you already visited the Gallery of Past Lives?"

I ask Jeremy, "Is he talking about the vike space?"

Jeremy nods.

"I've been there," I tell Giovanni. "Twice."

He furrows his forehead, strokes his chin, and says, "Two days and not a moment less than that. And don't worry about tonight. We have two beautiful guestrooms."

Simon and I may have spent the last three nights sleeping on bumpy car seats, but I'm not ready to stay in this underground compound. We'll have no phone access, no private way to contact Scott, and we'll be dealing with an unknown level of surveillance.

Especially since he knows we're overseers.

"Learning for two days is fine," I say. "But we'll stay elsewhere. We don't want to bother you."

"It would be an honor," Giovanni says.

"Thanks, but we already have plans."

He frowns. "As you wish."

"I can sleep here," Jeremy says.

"You can go home, Jeremy," Giovanni says. "No need for you to stay."

Jeremy glances at me, then back at Giovanni. "No, I think it's better that I stick around."

Giovanni lets out a sigh. But he musters up another smile as he faces me and Simon. "Perhaps we should start with a tour. Once you see my accommodations, you just might change your minds."

Thirty-nine

Giovanni leads us into the hallway behind the velvet curtain.

"To the left is the rest of the living space," he says. "We can keep this part of the tour short."

We walk through a large and modern kitchen and a small dining room. Giovanni points out a bathroom, and we peek into two guest bedrooms.

"May I remind you that you are most welcome to spend the night," Giovanni says.

"I'm claiming one of these bedrooms," Jeremy says. "You two can share the other."

Giovanni looks at me and raises his eyebrows.

I shake my head.

"As you wish," he says. "My own suite is also on this side, but that is not part of the tour."

He brings us back to the curtain and leads us to the right of the foyer. A hallway opens into a large, high-ceilinged room that's roughly the size of our dining hall back in West Seattle.

The right side of the room is cluttered with tables covered with scale models of groups of buildings. Straight ahead of me is a sizable collection of sculptures and artwork, illuminated with museum lighting. On the left side of the room, large portraits of Mr. Morgan and Ying hang high on the wall.

"Ms. Ouyang has been gracing my wall only since yesterday," Giovanni says. "It's nice to have more than one overseer again."

"Where did you get the portrait?" I ask.

"I commissioned it myself, based on a photo I found on the internet."

Creepy.

He brings us to the right side of the room. "Each of these tables contains a scale model of the headquarters as they existed at the end of their reign."

Simon and I walk around the tables. The models are labeled Miletus, Babylon, Alexandria, Caesarea, Istanbul, Bratislava, and Sterling. I examine the Sterling model, and it includes the offices, the parking lot, and the guest house.

"I'll bet you've hung out in each of these places," Jeremy says.

Giovanni raises his hand like he's taking an oath. "Other than Sterling, I am sure that I've spent more time at each site than any other living member. These models are accurate in all dimensions, except Miletus. I had to guess based on Thales' descriptions."

I move to the Caesarea model, and indeed the building I entered during my second vike is accurate. It's got the stairway leading up from the wharves, the walled garden around it. It even shows the logo over the doorway, just like I saw.

But it's not quite accurate. There's an extra building next door that I don't remember seeing when I viked to Caesarea.

"Are you sure this is correct?" I ask. "This building here isn't familiar."

He smiles. "That building was in fact built by your own soul line ancestor, Lillia of Cagliari. It was the very first guest house, and it was necessary, as she had pulled away from the protection and sponsorship of the church."

The more I learn about Lillia, the more I realize she's exactly the kind of overseer I need to learn from. She not only survived—she thrived.

"Have you used xanazo to visit Lillia of Cagliari?" Giovanni asks.

"Yes, but earlier in her time in Caesarea," I say. "Just as she arrived."

"Then you must see this beautiful specimen!" He leads me to the back of the room, and points to a framed mosaic of the Psychen Euporos logo. "Do you recognize it?"

The mosaic is faded, but it's clear to me where it's from. After all, I just saw it a week and a half—and eighteen hundred years—ago when it was fresh.

"This was above the entrance to the main Psychen Euporos building," I say.

"It is my greatest Caesarea find." He shows us various artifacts that he's dug up from the different headquarters. He has a bust of Alexander the Great from the Alexandria Library, a glass vase emblazoned with our logo from the Bratislava headquarters, and what he claims is the top of a Byzantine column that once was part of our headquarters structure in Istanbul.

There are many more artifacts, and Giovanni insists on showing all of them to us. At some point I just can't absorb any more. Giovanni Judd is a total freak for all things Soul Identity, too excited by these ancient pieces of rubble.

I'd love to know why he's so obsessed with us, but we're here to learn how to vike. I stay patient for as long as I can, and then I ask, "When can you start teaching us your xanazo method?"

"It's not my method. It's not even Soul Identity's method. Our founder, Thales, learned it when he kidnapped the Egyptian priests and stole their collections."

"But he didn't kidnap them," Simon says. "Thales saved those priests' lives from persecution."

"Of course that is what you learned," Giovanni says. "History is written by the victors. I, on the other hand, have searched high and low across Egypt. I could find no evidence of persecution."

Simon looks like he wants to say more, but I hold up my hand.

"We'll have plenty of time later to debate what took place 2,600 years ago," I say. "But right now, we need to learn how to vike."

"Xanazo," Giovanni says. "It's not the same."

He leads us to the left corner of the room, in between the artifacts and the portraits. It's a glassed-in area with its own door, a small conference table, and three chairs.

"We end the tour here in my documents room," he says.

Finally.

"I have an extensive collection of what I call my Gallery of Rogues. It contains information about the people and groups, along with their tools and techniques, who have tried to destroy our beloved organization."

"Is The Alert Foundation in it?" I ask.

"Your kidnappers? Of course they are," he says. "They are my most recent entry. You can peruse the collection at your leisure; you may find it instructive."

Giovanni points to the back of the room. "This side contains everything I was able to recover about the art of xanazo. If you take a seat at the table, we can get started."

Forty

Giovanni grabs an oversized black portfolio and sits down with us, placing the folio under his elbows as he leans forward.

"First a little background," he says. "When I worked at DARPA, my team hunted for potential new weapons. This led me into researching the mystical worlds of astrologers, fortune tellers, and witches."

Simon leans to me and whispers, "Told you he researched witchcraft."

"In those days, the agency was going through a post-Cold-War identity crisis," Giovanni says. "They were unable to recognize the value of my work. They might have mocked me right out the door, but I'm the one with the last laugh."

I see a lonely man sitting in a lonely room in his lonely underground compound. This is his last laugh?

"First, I wallowed in an early mid-life crisis," he says. "But one lucky day I was introduced to Soul Identity, and that changed my life forever. I inherited a small fortune through my soul line collection."

"Sweet," Jeremy says.

"It most definitely was sweet." Giovanni unzips and unfolds the folio. It opens to what looks like a religious icon, painted on silk. A man with curly brown hair, a gold halo around his head, the top of a green robe covering his shoulders, on a bright red background.

"This is Alexios Palaiologos, my only documented soul line ancestor. He lived in Constantinople in the fifteenth century, and he was part of the extended imperial family. He was also the head of the depositary for Psychen Euporos."

That explains the green robe.

Giovanni flips to the next sheet in the folio, and it's a parchment document. "His letter to me is written in Byzantine-era Greek, which I didn't know at the time. I had to get it translated. Besides the money, Alexios left me with a secret—the ancient overseers survived the political turbulence by using xanazo to rapidly grow their wisdom and experience."

My instincts to gather knowledge and survive are no different than those of the ancient overseers.

Giovanni says, "Alexios wanted his overseers to use xanazo, because the Ottomans were about to overthrow Constantinople."

"He wanted to give their experience a boost," I say.

"He did, but those overseers didn't see the value. They chose instead to flee, and they shifted the headquarters to Bratislava. My soul line ancestor felt that was a huge mistake."

Giovanni turns to the next page in the folio, a large and faded map. I can make out coastlines, islands, and mountains. "For the two years preceding the fall of Constantinople, Alexios protected the xanazo knowledge he had gathered by secreting it in caches at each depositary. He left me, his soul line descendant, this map, and he sent me on a quest to re-introduce xanazo to our organization."

I stand up and lean over the desk so I can inspect the map. "Where is this?" I ask.

"The big body of water in the middle is the Mediterranean Sea." He pulls a clear sheet of plastic from behind the map and places it on top. "If I overlay today's countries, it should make more sense."

Giovanni points out our early headquarters cities: Miletus and Istanbul in Turkey, Babylon in Iraq, Alexandria in Egypt, and Caesarea in Israel. Each of these cities has a small picture of a building next to it.

"These sketches show what the depositaries looked like. Alexios hid a cache for me in each of the ruins."

"Your soul line ancestor sent you on a grand treasure hunt," I say.

"The grandest of them all," he says. "Alexios pointed me in the right direction, but he left me with quite the puzzle to solve. It required me to go back to school and get a PhD in archaeology, and to sponsor digs on each of these sites. It took me twenty years to gather all the knowledge."

Giovanni flips to the next sheet, a painting of two naked men, sitting so close that one man's chest is pressed up against the other man's back, his chin resting on the other man's shoulder. Their arms and legs are both entwined, and the palms of their hands and the soles of their feet are pressed against the other's. Hieroglyphs are written above the painting, and at the bottom, the original Soul Identity logo.

"This is my oldest record of xanazo, as it was practiced in ancient Egypt," Giovanni says. "It's the spell from the Book of Rebirth that Thales stole from the priests. Somehow Alexios obtained it, and I recovered this painting from where he stashed it in Miletus."

He turns to the next sheet in the folio, and it's a photograph of a bronze sculpture. A woman sits behind a man in the same position as the previous painting. She's pressed up against his back, their palms and soles pressed together. The Soul Identity logo is engraved onto the woman's back.

"I found this sculpture in Babylon," Giovanni says. "But the authorities confiscated it from me. It ended up in a Baghdad museum that has since been bombed to pieces."

He flips through the next few sheets and shows us more examples of people in the same xanazo position, along with the same logo, depicted on a tapestry, a line sketch, and a photograph of a mosaic. None of them are wearing clothes.

"These are all from Alexandria," he says. "Getting the headquarters back to Egypt must have made xanazo popular. Or perhaps it was the influence of their Roman rulers. We Italians are a lusty people, always seeking adventure."

I'm interested in how different this xanazo is from Jeremy's approach to viking. It looks like a shared experience, which sounds way more fun than viking alone. "Does the xanazo spell require two people?" I ask.

"It does," Giovanni says. "And this could be the reason why I found no evidence of xanazo in Caesarea. Origen went there alone, and he served as the sole overseer for years until Lillia of Cagliari was found. Maybe he was never shown how to xanazo. But more likely, because he was a Christian priest, he stupidly refused to engage in xanazo with a woman."

I feel cheated by Origen for not teaching my soul line ancestor how to vike. How selfish he had to be to deny her! And how selfish Ying is for wanting to run Soul Identity without me.

"So how does xanazo work?" Simon asks. "You just sit in that position and the vike starts up?"

Giovanna laughs. "No, that wouldn't be much of a spell." He flips back to the original painting from the Egyptian Book of

Rebirth. "This provides the basic idea of what must be done, but it's written with lots of metaphors that required years of research to understand. I had to use everything I learned from Alexios, plus plenty of old-fashioned guesswork, to figure it all out."

"You can teach us, right?" I ask.

"I will teach you," he says. "Soon. But you need to know a few more things."

Giovanni's teaching methods are too slow for people in danger. You can slap Jeremy's vike portal on your head, calibrate it, and think about our logo to get into vike space. No need to sit through all of Giovanni's lessons.

I hide my impatience. "Bring it on."

He points at me. "You may be surprised to hear that you already practice a simple form of xanazo. You just don't realize it."

I raise my eyebrows.

"When you dream about things you've never experienced, xanazo is reliving a moment from a past life. When you get that incredible sense of déjà vu, xanazo is pointing out that your soul line ancestor has been in the same situation before. Even when you think you see a ghost, that's xanazo overriding your vision senses with somebody you saw in a previous life."

We sit in silence for a minute, and I ponder what Giovanni just said. Can dreams, déjà vu, and ghosts all be examples of our brain's interactions with our previous lives? Can we access it all the time?

"Are you saying that nobody needs spells or vike portals?" I ask.

"Not if all you want is a cheap, undirected version of xanazo," he says. "If you sufficiently let your mind wander around, eventually you'll relive something from your past. People slip into this state when they meditate or while they're performing routine work. They think they're having visions, watching people's auras, or seeing UFOs."

"I don't want the cheap version," I say. "I want to choose the experience. Can we get back to the spell?"

"Yes, of course." Giovanni points to Jeremy. "I helped this young man come up with a new electronic version of the spell for modern times. He tells me you've seen the code. Do you recall how it worked?"

I try to remember each step of what we did. "First, we blocked out all our senses," I say. "We had to imagine that we were drawing the original Soul Identity logo. After that, the vike portal sent an activation command and a go-back-to-sleep time to our PCC."

"That is right, Miss Oliveira," Giovanni says. "In essence, Jeremy's device performs the work of the second person. We built technology to allow people to practice xanazo alone."

Giovanni closes the portfolio and stares at us through his big glasses. "It's just about four o'clock, so that's enough for today. Your homework is to come up with ways the ancients could use partners to xanazo. When tomorrow comes, I'll show you if you're right."

Forty-one

We agree to meet at nine in the morning. We refuse the ride that Jeremy offers us, and Simon and I walk out of the compound, through the parking garage, down the tunnel, and out the front door of the fake house. We follow the long driveway, put on our sunglasses, press a button to open the gate, and walk back onto the street and into the little town of Wallace, Idaho.

"It's like we're back from another planet," Simon says.

I glance at the old houses around us. "Or back from the future," I say. Then I think about Giovanni's museum. "And from the past too, I suppose."

On our way to the Camry, we detour into the town's grocery store. They have a deli, and we spend some of Jeremy's money to pick up orange chicken and lo mein. We stay away from the snacks, but we do buy bottled water and fruit.

"Would you like to stay in a hotel tonight?" I ask. "We can afford it."

"I'm sure we'd need identification," Simon says.

When we reach the car, I connect to the hotel's Wi-Fi and search for how we could stay at a hotel anonymously. Simon's right. It's not possible to check in without ID unless it's a seedy hotel.

"We can just sleep in the car," he says. "Again."

That would suck, as I want to experiment with xanazo.

And then I get an idea. I ask, "You wanna go camping?"

"Like in a tent?"

I nod. "With sleeping bags. What do you think?"

"That's got to be better than another night in the Camry."

I search for camping in the Wallace area, and I find an RV park that's a few blocks away from where we are. They have both campsites and dry cabins, but they don't have any booking info online.

They do have a phone number, so I call, and they tell me that a dry cabin is available for just one night. We'll need to bring our own bedding. The total price is under fifty bucks. I give them the name of Lillia Cagliari and my new email address, and I ask them to hold it for me for the next ten minutes.

We walk over to the RV park and find the owner. I pay him cash, and he shows us the cabin. It's next to the highway, which is noisy, and it's even smaller than Giovanni's fake house. But it's clean and cheery with a tiny porch, two sets of bare bunk beds, and an overhead light.

It's perfect.

I locate a Walmart fifteen miles away, and we purchase sleeping bags, pillows, and bath towels. We're back at the RV park before six. The place is empty. It's a great time to finally take a shower. I stand under the water, thinking of all the events from the past two weeks that have led us here, in the middle of almost nowhere, thrilled that we're going to sleep in uncomfortable beds and eat cold food.

And if we can figure it out from the sparse clues Giovanni shared, we're going to vike.

I return to our cabin. Simon has already moved the beds together and laid out our sleeping bags on the top bunks.

"Do you like it?" he asks.

"I love it." I give him a hug. "And I love that we're camping here together."

"Best adventure ever," he says.

We eat the cold Chinese food and wash it down with water, each of us lost in our own thoughts. We throw away the trash and brush our teeth in the restrooms.

Back in the room, we huddle around the phone and check my new email account. I have a receipt and directions from the RV park, a message from Jeremy, and an email from Yuno Hu, aka Scott Waverly.

Jeremy's message asks if we want to do anything in the evening. I check with Simon, and he shakes his head, so I decline and offer to meet for breakfast in Wallace at eight.

I open the email from Yuno Hu. Scott writes, "Z: Hit snag during rescue. We need to talk ASAP. PS, Why'd you stop?"

I reply to Scott, asking him for his new phone number so I can reach him on WhatsApp. He's online and replies within a minute, and I start a video call with him.

Scott's face fills the phone's screen. "Zelly, it's nice to see you," he says. "And you too, Simon. How goes your journey home?"

I pan the phone around the room so he can see our cabin. "We's going to sleep in real beds, which is so much better than another night on the car seats," I say.

"Living the high life," he says. "Hey, you asked if home is safe. The answer is no, it's not. More of these same, gray-uniformed guards have it staked out. They even detained George and Sue for a day, but they were able to sneak away."

"Did you identify the guards?" I ask.

He frowns. "We've now ruled out The Alert Foundation. Their skeleton crew is all in New York City, talking to nobody."

"So who do you think they are?" Simon asks.

"We'll figure it out," Scott says. "They're not making it easy. I tried to use my eye surveillance, but none of them are Soul Identity members."

"And you still think Ying is innocent?" I ask.

Scott shrugs. "We're now fifty-fifty on whether she's being held or whether she's allied with these people."

I'm not fifty-fifty. I'm one hundred percent sure she's allied with the bad guys. But until Scott and Val find out for themselves, nothing I say will matter.

"Zelly, what's in Wallace?" Scott asks.

"Don't you know?"

"I have a guess. Did you find Giovanni Judd?"

"We did. He's like Soul Identity's biggest fan."

"Just be careful," he says. "For all we know, he's a bad guy."

"He knew we were overseers," I say.

"He knows about you and Simon?"

I nod. "He claims our secret is safe. He seems to be on his own quest to become important."

He tilts his head. "Why are you risking yourselves?"

I don't want to get Jeremy in trouble. And I think Scott would kill me if he knew I was trying to vike again.

I glance at Simon as I answer. "We were passing through Idaho, and I thought it might be good to understand his relationship with Jeremy's company. So, we dropped on by."

Scott raises his eyebrows. I doubt he bought my story.

Simon leans forward. "Speaking of bad guys, Giovanni showed us a collection he's built of all the attacks on Soul Identity. He called it his Gallery of Rogues."

"We can find something useful in there," I say.

Scott sucks in his breath through his teeth. "Keeping that kind of collection sounds like the man's obsessed. Be careful."

Scott promises to let us know the moment he has more information about Ying or the bad guys. We tell him that we'll let him know when we're back on the road to Seattle, and we hang up.

I ask Simon, "You ready to figure out how to vike?"

He smiles. "Didn't you listen to Giovanni? It's called xanazo. Get it right."

Forty-two

"What did Giovanni teach us about the xanazo spell?" I ask Simon.

We're sitting on top of one of the bunkbeds, leaning against the wall. Simon is making a list on the back of the Walmart posterboard, which he holds in his lap.

He writes, "It takes two people."

"He mentioned meditation," I say. "And that one person acts like the vike portal."

He adds these. "The examples he showed us all displayed the old Soul Identity logo." Simon writes that down.

"They sit one in front of the other," I say. "Touching soles and palms. Naked."

Those get added, but he says, "The naked bit worries me."

"It's cringy," I say. "But it's what we saw."

We both stare at the list. I point to *One person acts like the vike portal*. "I bet that if we solve for that, the rest will come easy."

I grab his marker, slide the posterboard over to me, and list out what the vike portal person needs to do. Block the senses, activate the PCC, and tell the PCC when to sleep.

"How does a person do these things?" Simon asks.

"This has to be where meditation is used," I say. "Let's read about that."

We search on the phone for ways to meditate, and we spend a long time reading about various techniques. They all come down to a few things. Eliminate distractions, set a timer, and focus on something rhythmic, like breathing or a mantra. If your mind wanders, bring it back.

We research how the ancients practiced meditation. We zero in on Hindu meditation, since it's the only method we can find that was documented before Soul Identity existed.

Ancient Hindus believed they could shape themselves into perfection by meditating on the deliberations and desires of their current and past lives. They used yoga poses, special breathing, and mantra chanting. They focused their thoughts on themselves until they felt separated from everything else.

We read about yoga nidra. This is a way to enter and stay in a hypnagogic state, somewhere between consciousness and sleep. Yoga nidra requires a guide to help you get relaxed, shut down your outer senses, and talk you into a conscious deep sleep.

I tell Simon, "If we put meditation and yoga nidra together, we should be able to block our senses. We can visualize the logo to activate the PCC. One of us can be the guide, and the other the viker."

"But how will the guide put my PCC back to sleep?" he asks. "I don't want to get stuck like Ying."

We waste two hours watching yoga nidra videos and searching for hypnagogic wake-up sequences.

"We're going to have to experiment," I say. "Figure it out as we go."

"Or we can wait for tomorrow," he says. "When Giovanni can help us."

"What are you worried about?"

"Getting stuck in a vike with nobody to pull us out."

"How about this," I say. "You can vike, and I can be the guide. If I can't get you out, I'll load you into the car and drive you to Giovanni's."

He crosses his arms. "It sounds too dangerous."

"You want to be the guide instead?"

"No, because if we have a problem, I can't drive."

"Sy, let's just try it," I say. "The bad guys, whoever they are, have been in Sterling since Sunday. It's already Thursday. The sooner we figure this out, the sooner we can rescue Ying and save Soul Identity." I take his hand. "You know, our magic garden."

He stares at me. "You promise to get me out if there's any problem?"

"I promise. Just like I saved Ying."

"You're the one who got Ying stuck!"

He's right. I can't argue that. "But I did get her out," I say.

After a minute, he says, "Okay, Zelly. I want to save Ying. She's worth the risk. Let's do it."

I hug him. "We should move to the lower bunk," I say. "In case we fall out."

We climb down, and I bring the posterboard.

"Umm . . . should we get naked?" Simon asks, staring at the floor.

"You want to try it in our underwear?"

He glances at me, his cheeks red. "I was hoping you'd say that."

I check to make sure the cabin door is locked, and I pull down the window blinds. I take off my shirt, jeans, shoes, and socks. I fold my clothes and leave them on the top bunk.

Simon has undressed down to his underwear. He puts his clothes next to mine.

I sit down in the middle of one of the lower bunks. "Remember the pose?" I ask.

He swallows.

I spread my legs wide enough for him to fit between them. I pat the empty space.

He climbs onto the bed and sits between my legs, barely touching me.

"Come closer," I say. "Every picture we saw had the people skin to skin."

He scoots back even more. My chest is against his back, and my thighs squeeze around his legs.

"Lean back a bit," I say. "I have to get my chin onto your shoulder."

He leans back, and I blow into his ear.

Simon jumps. "Zelly, this is serious!"

"Sorry, I was quebrando o gelo."

He swivels his head toward me.

"Breaking the ice," I say. "Turn around. I'll be good."

He faces forward, and I wrap my arms around his chest and extend my legs alongside his.

"I need to put my palms and soles against yours," I say.

Simon crosses his legs, and I press the bottoms of my feet onto his. He crosses his arms and lets his hands rest, face up, on his knees. I lean forward and place my palms on top of his.

"Anything else?" I ask into his ear.

He shakes his head.

We sit still for a minute. "This isn't so bad," I say. I snuggle myself a little tighter into his back, and I squeeze his hands. "Try a mantra to get relaxed."

He lets out a soft oooommmm, waits a few seconds, and does it again. I join him on the third om, in harmony.

We sound good together, and I'm feeling more relaxed.

I remember the yoga nidra videos. It's time for me to guide him. I talk into Simon's ear while he chants his mantra. I tell him to focus on his breathing, to focus on himself, to let the sensations of the world disappear. I walk him down the right side of his body, and his left, from his fingertips to his toes, telling him to release his sense of touch. I do the same with his sight, his smell, and his taste.

When every sense except for his hearing is blocked, I tell Simon that he's about to enter the vike space, and I ask him to imagine using a lightsaber to draw the old Soul Identity logo. I walk him through drawing the two sides of the pyramid and both Eyes of Horus.

And, amazingly, I find myself in a vike space, standing alone and naked on a hovering disc. But this space is different. I have no ribbons of light on my left. No breeze, no chanting, and no whiff of cinnamon, either.

What do I do here? I lean on my disc to move up and down, left and right, forward and backward, and even around in a circle, but I see nothing. I hope Simon isn't stuck like me, as he'd be pretty scared. I need to help him. I force my disc up and let it rise for a long time, but I never reach the top.

I promised Simon I'd rescue him, but I'm stuck in this space with nowhere to go, and I can't help him.

I screwed up.

Tomorrow morning the RV park owner will find us wrapped around each other. He'll call an ambulance or the police. They'll read our eyes while they're poking at us, and the bad guys will find us and catch us and kill us.

All because I had to vike, had to do this xanazo, and couldn't wait.

But then I realize there's one thing I haven't tried. Hopefully, it won't kill me. Since I find no other options, I hold my breath and step off the disc.

I'm awake, and Simon is, too. I let out a groan. "I'm so sorry, Sy. I screwed up big time, but everything's all right now. We made it back."

He leans forward, uncrosses his arms and legs, and turns around, staring at me. His eyes drop down to my bra and his mouth falls open.

I cross my arms over my chest.

His gaze rises back to my eyes. "It worked, Zelly! I flew the airplane again, and I landed it this time!"

"You viked?"

"I viked, and it was incredible. You're incredible!" He holds up his hand for a high-five, and when I just stare at him, he laughs and pulls me into a hug.

"It must have been short," I say. "Do you want to go again?"

"It lasted a few hours, but I'd love to do it again. Can you leave me in longer? For at least an hour of real time? That would give me a few months."

I guide him through his next xanazo. I can't last a whole hour in my empty vike space, but I stay for as long as I can, and Simon comes back thrilled.

"My turn," I say.

I explain to him how I ended the vike by jumping off the disc. We switch positions. I scooch in close to Simon, cross my arms and legs, and get the palms and the soles of his feet pressed against mine. I start the mantras, Simon helps me draw the logo, and he guides me into the vike.

I reach my vike space, this time complete with the cinnamon, the chanting, the breeze, and the ribbons of light. I direct my hovering disc up to Lillia of Cagliari's ribbon, and I jump in, feet first, a couple years past the point where she first met Origen.

Forty-three

"*The carpentum is waiting, ma'am,*" *the young lady says.* Her hair is pulled into a bun, tied with a silver ribbon. She wears a white robe bordered with an olive-green strip. "Are you ready to leave?"

"I am." You let out a big sigh. "Three days alone with him in that stinky carriage. I can't fake it for that long."

"You can," she says. "You must. It's how we survive."

You sigh as you roll up the sleeve covering your left arm. "Do you have any more salve? I'm scratching myself again."

She examines the red streaks and scabs that rise from your elbow up to your shoulder. Her hands are warm on your forearm. She crosses the room and returns with a small clay pot. She removes its fabric covering, and a sweet smell fills your nose. She dips her fingers into the pot and applies the salve to your skin.

She puts a dot of the salve onto the stump of your little finger, where it's missing the top two joints. "For luck."

"I need all I can get."

"Take the rest of the salve with you." She slips on the fabric cover.

"Thank you, Tabitha. See you back in Caesarea."

You put the pot in your robe's pocket, and you walk out the door and through the gate. Four horses stand in front of a covered wooden carriage. The driver and groom step down from its bench in the front. They help you climb in through the carriage's side door.

The man inside is lounging low in the seat. His body is slim. Gray hair streaked with white flows in loose, curly locks down to his shoulders. He wears a dark green robe and leather sandals, and he's staring at you, smiling at you.

You sit across from him, and the carriage lurches to a start. A few sharp turns, and it picks up its pace, rocking back and forth. You watch a large stone building pass by the window on the door.

A while later, he lets out a laugh.

"Everything okay?" you ask.

"The council ended better than I dared to dream."

You raise your eyebrows. "You didn't think you'd fail, did you?"

He shrugs. "Beryllus can be stubborn. He didn't budge at all last year. And this time, bringing a pagan woman—"

"Hey!"

"Bringing an *alluring* pagan woman with me made it all the harder for him to focus on what I was teaching him." He holds up his hands, fingers splayed wide. "But then, the moment he recanted, when he told everybody that he, the Bishop of Bostra, would follow only the teachings of Origen—that moment was one of the most satisfying of my life."

"You're so proud of yourself," you say. "But aren't Christian priests supposed to be humble?"

"In public, absolutely. But here in this bouncing carpentum, days from Caesarea, with our privacy assured?" He leans forward and grabs your hands and pulls you toward him and kisses you full on the lips. His tongue darts out and probes at your mouth. "I need no humility. I just need you."

You pull your head back and push on his shoulders with your hands until he falls back to his seat. You smooth the wrinkles in your light green robe with your hands. You lie back and smile at him.

"Oh, Origen, if your critics ever found out about us."

He laughs. "My critics still spread the lie that I castrated myself as a teenager. They have no such suspicions."

You are silent, staring out the window flap at the passing scenery. Rocky hills, a dusty road, and the occasional olive grove dot the landscape.

"What did you think of Bostra?" Origen asks.

"It's landlocked," you say. "No bustling port. Dust and sand everywhere. A huge amphitheater with nothing interesting going on. I feel sorry for the poor soldiers stationed here."

"The church, though," he says, "is the biggest in Arabia. It reeks with power, even though the dummies in Antiochia gave it to Beryllus, and he almost messed everything up."

"But you thwarted him. Psychen Euporos is back in charge. We overseers are back in charge. The bishops have been beaten."

"For now. If Heracleides prevailed and Beryllus kept preaching that the soul died with the body, all my efforts for us to rely on the church would have failed." He purses his lips. "But thanks to my brilliance, they abandoned the path of mortalism and hopped on the track of something compatible with us."

"Not just on the track," you say. "You convinced Beryllus to join Psychen Euporos. That is huge."

"Most people eventually join, Lillia."

"Not many Christian priests. As you said, they can be stubborn."

"They'll convert once we get their theology straightened out, and then we'll be glad for that stubbornness," he says. "We're a big step closer after this Second Council of Arabia. We have bishops and priests from all over the world spreading the good news about the immortality of the soul. Once that message goes out, their congregations will flock to Psychen Euporos."

"Which gives us more gold."

He smiles. "And more gold gives us more influence. And more influence gives us more power."

"That's why this council was so important."

"Exactly," he says. "We're the overseers, Lillia. The two of us are transforming Psychen Euporos to become the decision-makers of the world. Not just a resource for tiny despots and rebels, but for the kings and emperors who we will let shape the future."

A flush comes over your body. "The two of us?"

"The two of us."

You lean forward and drop your hands into his lap. "Did I tell you how amazing you were yesterday?"

He closes his eyes and arches his back. You inch the hem of his green robe up, over his knees, and halfway up his thighs.

"I'm pretty amazing, too," you say.

"You, Lillia of Cagliari, are the most amazing woman I have met." He grabs his robe and pulls it up to his waistline.

You examine his exposed body. "Definitely not castrated."

He stares at you, breathing hard. "Lillia . . ."

You glance out the open window. You raise the hem of your robe, stand up, push his legs together and straddle them. You lower yourself onto him, feeling every tiny advance radiate through your body.

When he starts to thrust, you shake your head. "No need to rush."

And the carriage rocks, slowly, leisurely, until you do need to rush, raising your body up, up, and almost out, and down, down, all the way down, again and again, until his rough hand across your mouth stifles your screams.

You lie forward on his chest, your hands behind his head grasping his long locks.

"You are perfect, Lillia of Cagliari," he murmurs.

You watch his eyes as they close. When he starts to snore through his nose, you pull his robe back down over his knees.

You sit down across from him, slip your hand under your sleeve, close your eyes, and scratch at your arm, re-opening the scabs, drawing sharp pain and wet, hot blood.

Forty-four

I grab at my left arm, but the scabs aren't there, and neither is the robe. I feel Origen's arms and legs wrapped around me, and I try to tear myself free, twisting my body and kicking him off.

"Zelly, stop!"

I freeze. A blond boy stares at me with concern. He's not Origen, he's Simon. I'm back from my vike, and I'm Zelly, not Lillia.

"Are you all right?" he asks.

I let out a sigh. "It was rough this time."

"What happened?"

I remain silent for a moment, thinking it through.

"Origen was power hungry," I say. "He spoke like Ying did in her speech. How we needed to shape the events of the world. He even manipulated the Christian religion to make reincarnation part of their theology."

I grab the sleeping bag and pull it over us. "And now I know how Lillia survived."

"That's great news."

"It's not great news," I say. "Lillia was afraid of him. She seduced Origen, and even slept with him, telling him how awesome he was. Meanwhile, she was going crazy."

I wonder if Ying viked into the same encounter between Origen and Lillia. If she did, she would have had a whole different perspective. She would think that Lillia was head over heels in love with Origen and that he was using her.

This explains why Ying won't discuss her vikes with me.

Ying wouldn't realize that Lillia performed an act of survival. That the sex she offered wasn't love. That the sex was merely part of a transaction.

Maybe in ancient times romantic love was bestowed on the few. And maybe that hasn't changed much over the years.

"You'll need new tactics," Simon says. "I can't imagine Ying being seduced by you."

"I'm sure I can find ways to show Ying that she's awesome."

But we need to do more than proclaim Ying's awesomeness. We have to figure out her plan to get rid of us. I was hoping that Lillia would ask Origen how he killed the Alexandria overseers, but I think Lillia was too scared of him to broach the subject. I need to backtrack on Lillia's ribbon of light, to her initial trip from Delphi to Caesarea, before she became an overseer. When Junius might have told her something useful.

"I'd like to vike again," I say. "Are you up for another one?"

He grimaces. "I can't last long in that vike space. It freaks me out."

"I don't mind if the vikes are short."

"Can we eat something first?" he asks. "I'm starving."

We get dressed and put on our sunglasses. We walk fifty yards to reach the next-door pub, and the waitress leads us to a booth. We each order brownie sundaes, and she brings them out right away.

"A brownie with ice cream on top isn't a sundae," Simon says. "It's not what I expected."

"And we're not the customers they expected." I take a big mouthful of brownie. "Two kids wearing sunglasses at night, ordering dessert, paying in cash. They must think we're runaways."

"We sure don't look like we were going to be two of the three most powerful people in the world."

"What do you mean *were*? We're still going to be," I say.

He sighs. "I hope so."

I stare at him until he meets my eyes. "I'm not giving up," I say.

Simon nods.

"Anyway, it's good nobody knows about us. Otherwise, the normal crooks would be trying to kidnap us."

"Speaking of crooks," he says. "Do you trust Giovanni?"

"He's definitely eccentric and probably a conspiracy theorist," I say. "But we don't need to trust him."

"We don't? He's probably one of the bad guys. Or at least working for them." He scans the room and hunches forward onto his elbows, dropping his voice. "He acts like he's a fan of ours and treats us super well, but somehow he knows we're overseers. And did you see the way he talked to Jeremy? That wasn't normal."

"It was pretty rude."

His eyes open wide. "He wanted us to sleep there, Zelly. We don't know him, and that's just weird. He told us it would take two days to learn how to practice xanazo but look how we've already figured it out. He knew our favorite foods and just happened to have them in stock. He's either crazy, or he's working with the bad guys."

"You're right."

"We shouldn't go back tomorrow," he says. "Unless you want to get caught."

But Giovanni has information that we could learn from. "What about his Gallery of Rogues?"

"It's not worth the risk. We shouldn't go back. We know how xanazo works, so we can vike anytime we want. Besides . . ." He swallows.

"Besides what?"

"If he's bad, then Jeremy is too, and the rudeness Giovanni shows him is just an act. It would be those two men against us. Trapped inside that cave."

When the waitress checks on us, Simon orders the mac and cheese bites appetizer. I ponder what he said while he scarfs that down and I finish my brownie sundae.

Have I been so focused on Ying that I missed seeing Giovanni for what he is? Did he contact Ying and flatter her and promise her the world?

I doubt it. Jeremy told us the dude was too paranoid to make a video call. He lives in a cave under a hill. It's a nice cave, but it's weird. Anybody so scared of the world can't be interested in running it.

"We drove all this way, figured out how to vike, so we'd know what Ying learned from Origen about getting rid of us," I say. "And we still don't know."

"True."

"How about this," I say. "You guide me through a few more xanazo sessions, and if I can figure out Origen's tricks, we won't go back to Giovanni's."

Simon signals the waitress for the bill. "You can vike all night long if you need to. I just need to do it in short bursts."

"Deal." I pay the waitress and leave her a big tip.

It's chilly, so after Simon wraps his arms and legs around me, I pull one of the sleeping bags over us.

We sit quietly for a moment. I've been trying to act nonchalant in front of Simon, but in truth, our conversation about Giovanni and Jeremy being bad guys has unnerved me. I want to run away as fast as I can.

But where would we go? We have a little bit more than nine hundred bucks, and that won't get us very far. Plus, with Scott's hijacked readers everywhere, there's nowhere left to hide. I don't want to spend the rest of my life behind sunglasses.

The best path forward is to learn as much as we can. I need to put away my fear. I need to focus so I can find out how Origen eliminated his fellow overseers. I start chanting my oms, and Simon guides me into blocking my senses and drawing the logo. When I get to the vike space and I hover my way up to Lillia's ribbon of light, I use the back of my hand to search for a time when Junius and Lillia sailed on the ship from Delphi, before they reached Caesarea. When I find a good spot, I jump in.

Forty-five

"**Y**ou must listen to what I am telling you!"

The man's eyes narrow. The acne on his face is red and angry. His white tunic gleams in the harsh sunlight.

"I am listening. I'm just . . . it's hard for me to concentrate when bad memories flood my head."

The sails snap as the breeze changes direction and the ship shudders. You grab the rail and breathe through your nose and flood your lungs with salty air.

He glances down at your hands. "Did you lose that pinky out at sea?"

"I don't want to talk about it, Junius."

He holds up his hands. "Fine. But please concentrate. We will soon arrive, and you still have so much left to learn."

"We can continue. I'm sorry."

A seagull lands on the railing and squawks. Junius waves his arms, and the gull flies away.

"The Pythia's influence has plummeted," he says, "Instead of Delphi, the rich and famous sail to Caesarea to bow at the feet of Origen."

"So?"

"The man doesn't even believe in the gods. He says we're demons!"

"Who cares what Origen says?" you say.

He stares at you. "Lillia, why did you seek out the Oracle of Delphi?"

You gaze out over the water. After a minute, you say, "Disease ravaged my ship, took my partner, and left me unable to continue the venture alone. I needed to consult with the Oracle about my future path to ensure I made no mistakes."

"Exactly," he says. "People like you have been coming for centuries to read the omens and hear the oracles. In those days, no wars were fought, no colonies established, no serious businesses started without the Pythia first sanctioning them."

"But not anymore," you say.

"That's right. Psychen Euporos has hijacked our business. With their financing, they steal influence. And with their ties to the Christians, they've convinced the world that our prophecies are evil."

"Then change," you say. "Become relevant to this modern world. Lend money and finance wars. Speak a clearer message to the common people."

"All good ideas, but the Pythia has ordered what we must do," he says. "You, Lillia, are destined to bring unity between Delphi and Psychen Euporos. You will lead the people back to us."

"Your Pythia has too much faith in the abilities of a former ship's servant," you say. "Why would she think I can do this?"

"She doesn't think it, Lillia. The gods think it, and she knows it. The gods won't let you fail."

You snort and turn away, tapping your fingers on the railing as you stare at the waves. You see land in the distance, a solitary cloud hanging above the coastline.

"In all my years on the water," you say, "I have learned to trust what the gods have to say. Even though they tend to speak in riddles, they have saved my life many times."

He faces you, saying nothing.

"If the Pythia says the gods have chosen me, I will do what is asked of me."

He raises his hands to his heart. "Thank you, Lillia."

"But I need help."

"We will be with you every step of the way."

You raise your eyebrows. "How can that be?"

He beckons to a young lady who is standing nearby and looking out to sea. "I want you to meet somebody."

The lady is dressed in a white robe, a silver ribbon braided into her dark hair. "Hello, Lillia. I'm Tabitha," she says.

"Tabitha has been a priestess in Delphi," Junius says. "She is assigned to support you. When you get to Caesarea, we will arrange for her to be hired into Psychen Euporos and established as your personal scribe."

"How will that help?" you ask.

"Tabitha knows what needs to be done."

"And I can be your friend," Tabitha says. "From what we've heard, working with Origen isn't easy. He's smart. Dedicated. Focused. You'll need an ally."

"Am I your first attempt to stop Origen? Or did the Oracle send others before me?"

Junius glances at Tabitha. "We tried before," he says. "Twelve years ago, when Origen was still in Alexandria. We scoured the world and found two overseers. Two men."

"But it didn't work," Tabitha said. "Within a year of arriving, Origen and Demetrius had them brainwashed. They grew soft in the luxury of wealth. They forgot their mission. They betrayed us and confessed our plot to Origen."

"We had no choice but to eliminate them," Junius said. "And we found another overseer. But because he refused to work with us, we got rid of him, too. We do not let traitors to our cause survive."

"Lillia won't betray us." Tabitha rests her hand on your arm. "This time we'll succeed. The Pythia says so."

"If the gods will it," you say.

Junius stares at you. "Unfortunately, Origen knows what we tried to do. He and Demetrius escaped unharmed. And now that he's fled to Caesarea and strengthened his ties to the church, our task is made all the harder."

"We believe the gods blessed us by sending a woman overseer," Tabitha says. "We can use the strength of a woman's faith and the allure of a woman's touch to succeed where men have failed."

"But he's castrated," you say. "He isn't tempted by women. This is known."

"The castration story was a lie put out by Demetrius before he died," Junius says. "They pretended to argue, just to give the Caesareans a reason to show their loyalty to Origen. Trust me, Origen is as lustful as any powerful man. And Tabitha can teach you ways to transform that lust into whatever you want. Whatever *we* want."

"I am committed," you say.

Tabitha grabs your hands. "You, Lillia of Cagliari, will be the one to restore the true religion to the people and bring them back to Delphi. You will help us to defeat Origen and remove Psychen Euporos from the clutches of the Christian church. Your name will be known the world over. Lillia of Cagliari will be the hero of legends told and songs sung. You, Lillia, will—"

Forty-six

The sleeping bag cocoons my legs. Simon's hands and chest and thighs press against me. The events of the past few days weigh down my mind.

What I observed in this vike overwhelms me.

What just happened, anyway? How did we shift to Lillia bad and Origen good? I keep my eyes closed and my breathing as steady as I can, hoping Simon doesn't notice I'm awake until I can get my thoughts together.

But I'm not that lucky.

He squeezes my hands. "Zelly?"

I sigh.

"Did you discover Origen's tricks?"

How am I supposed to answer that? Do I tell him that although Origen may be power hungry, he's not the bad guy we thought he was? That he didn't kill the Alexandria overseers? That Lillia was probably the one doing the seducing as she schemed to murder him?

I've been convinced that Ying is trying to get rid of me and Simon. But these were crazy, muddy thoughts like I've been viajando na maionese, swimming in mayonnaise. Because come to find out, Ying's got plenty of valid reasons for being scared of me.

From her own vikes, Ying must have learned that the Delphians killed the Alexandrian overseers, and that Lillia was sent by the Oracle of Delphi. Ying knew that sooner or later I'd vike into Lillia's ribbon and observe this myself.

Ying wasn't learning new ways to kill me. No, she's been wondering when I was going to try to kill her.

How dense can I be?

I'm happy I'm facing away so I don't have to catch Simon's eye. I'm embarrassed I was wrong. And I'm scared that I'll start acting like Lillia.

I've already begun to act like her.

"Did you learn anything new?" Simon asks.

I disentangle myself from his arms and legs and pull my shirt and pants on.

"I need a break," I say. "Viking twice in one day has left my mind all jumbled. I need to sort things out in my head. Can we talk about it in the morning?"

Simon looks confused, even a little hurt, as we climb up to the top bunks, bundle ourselves in the sleeping bags, and say goodnight to each other.

But I don't sleep. And after several hours of tossing things back and forth in my head, I wonder if I missed something in my research on Origen. I reach for the phone to dig in deeper on how he died.

In the year 250, a plague broke out in Rome, killing five thousand people every day. Emperor Decius ordered almost everybody in the empire—not the Jews, though, because of the special status Julius Caesar gave them—to make a sacrifice to the gods. When the Christians refused, he had them persecuted. Origen was arrested and tortured for two years until Decius died in battle. When Origen was released, he was broken, and he died less than a year later.

I'm sure that Lillia took advantage of the plague. She might have whispered in the Emperor's ear to write that decree. She probably turned over Origen to the authorities. She may have even killed him in the end.

With Origen out of the way, Lillia became the executive overseer.

My soul line ancestor was conniving and evil. Will she rub off on me like Origen has rubbed off on Ying?

I don't want to vike back into Lillia's ribbon of light ever again.

If Ying isn't trying to kill me and Simon, maybe the bad guys aren't bad after all. It would be reasonable for Ying to feel she needed the protection of a security force to stay safe from me, given what I now know about Lillia.

And if Ying shared her concerns with Scott and Val, it explains their why they worked very hard to block me from viking.

If Simon wasn't sleeping, I'd scream and pound the walls.

It took just this one vike to twist up everything I believed into a big knot. I'm struggling to wrap my head around the idea that my paranoia is false, that my soul line ancestor could have infected my mind.

Did the vike make me paranoid, or have I always been this way?

Am I already a danger to Ying?

I need to talk to Scott about this. When it's six in the morning in Sterling, I ping him, and he replies right away.

I ask Simon, "You awake?"

"All night long. Just like you."

"I'm ready to talk about what happened in my vike."

"Yay." He sits up and stifles a yawn.

"But Scott needs to hear. And Val, too."

I organize a group call while Simon flips on the light. He comes back to sit next to me and puts his arm around my shoulder. I snuggle into his side.

"Rough night?" he asks.

"The worst. Thanks for giving me time to think things through."

He rubs my shoulder. "Did you get it all sorted out?"

"I'm not even close. But we're at the point when everybody needs to share what they know and start working together."

"Good."

"I'm going to tell them," I say. "Our fears. That we can vike. What I learned last night. Everybody needs to know everything."

Forty-seven

I start the video conference. Scott and Val are already online, waiting in their own windows on the screen of my phone.

"Isn't it four in the morning in Idaho?" Scott asks.

"Neither of us could sleep," Simon says.

Val leans forward. "Is everything okay? Do you need help?"

"We're fine," I say. "But we're out of sync with you. I want to put together everything we know so we're actually working together."

Val raises her eyebrows. "Everything?"

I nod.

"I can do that," she says.

"We'll go first," I say. "Before we left Seattle, I ordered the parts needed to build my own vike portal. Simon and I stole the car from Toledo so we could go home and get it working."

Val frowns.

"What do you expect?" Simon asks. "Ying's trying to kill us."

"You still believe that?" Scott asks.

"We did, but not anymore," I say.

Simon stares at me, and I hold up my finger.

"But let's back up," I say. "We contacted Jeremy, and he said that Giovanni Judd could teach us how to vike without using any tech."

"Vikes don't need vike portals?" Val asks.

"They don't," I say. "Remember Simon found out that Giovanni ran diggings in all the old Soul Identity cities? His soul line ancestor left him buried details on how the ancient overseers practiced xanazo. He plans on teaching us later today."

"But we don't need him," Simon says. "Zelly and I figured it out last night. It takes two people, and it's not fun if you're the guide."

"The guide?" Scott asks.

"One person guides the other person's vike," I say. "Jeremy's tech makes it so you can vike alone. The vike portal is the guide."

Val's biting her lip. "And did you vike, Zelly?"

I sigh. "You don't want me to, do you?"

"You saw what it did to Ying," she says. "She's got this idea that Soul Identity should be a power-based organization, and I'm sure that's coming from Origen."

"We saw," Simon says. "And we noticed changes in ourselves."

"What kinds of changes?" Scott asks.

"I got scared of boats," I say. "And I've gotten way more comfortable with telling lies."

"I'm losing memories of my parents," Simon says. "On the other hand, I've learned to fly all kinds of aircraft."

We said we'd share everything.

"More importantly, I know that my soul line ancestor did bad things," I say.

Simon looks at me, his eyes wide.

I grab his free hand. "Origen wasn't the evil one. Lillia was. And she may have already influenced me."

There, I said it.

"You learned Lillia's history," Val says.

I nod, biting my lip.

"Ying is terrified of you, Zelly," Val says. "After her first vike, she told me and Scott that Lillia had been recruited to kill Origen."

I close my eyes. As if that could block it out.

Val keeps going. "Ying said she saw Lillia was missing most of her little finger. That matched what you said at Jeremy's, and she figured you were only a vike or two away from learning how Lillia betrayed Origen."

"Is that why Ying lied about her vike?"

"Yes, and it's why she wanted to vike again. It's why she begged us to stop you from viking."

Simon asks me, "Did you watch Lillia kill Origen last night?"

I shake my head. "I saw how she was recruited." I tell them about the Oracle of Delphi and what Junius told Lillia.

I say, "I'm the one you all should be scared of."

"We're not scared of you, Zelly," Scott says. "We're scared of Lillia taking over. For instance, you've started using an email account in Lillia's name."

Now the tears run down my cheeks. Simon tightens his arm around my shoulder.

When my voice won't betray me, I say, "Okay, we're done sharing."

"I'll share ours," Val says. "I'm still in Toledo with Mr. Morgan. I've been able to communicate with a handful of employees I trust. We're beginning to figure out what's happening in Sterling."

"What's your theory?" I ask.

"That a mercenary organization—we don't know who yet—grabbed Ying and took control," she says. "It's more than a theory. They've informed our employees that Soul Identity is illegal, our operations are being shut down, and everybody will receive layoff notices on Monday morning."

"But none of what they said is true," Scott says. "My parents and I now have eyes and ears inside their electronic communications and throughout the buildings. They haven't shut anything down. They're using their own people to run the operations, and they're busy redirecting funds in the depositary to a bunch of new investments. Ying's name is used to authorize everything."

"Are they stealing the money?" I ask.

"Not really." Scott holds up a sheet of paper. "Money is being moved out of tech and real estate, and it's shifting into the hands of smaller non-business groups, some dedicated to keeping their people in power, and some dedicated to overthrowing their local government. A few crime syndicates and weapons suppliers, too."

"The good news is we have a built-in safeguard," Val says. "Without unanimous consent from both overseers, they can only move ten million dollars each day. They need my approval to do more."

"We assume this increases their urgency to either capture or kill Archie and Val," Scott says.

"We can't let that happen," Simon says.

None of us speak for a minute.

"Anyway," Scott says. "We see their actions and we know their motive, but we're still missing the big picture of who they are."

"How do we find that out?" Simon asks.

"You guys mentioned yesterday that Giovanni has a Gallery of Rogues," Scott says. "You could find out what he knows about this group."

"We can't go back to Giovanni's," Simon says. "He's one of them."

"Simon and I don't agree on this," I say. "I believe Giovanni is in love with Soul Identity. He's not trying to overthrow us."

"What if he thought that Soul Identity was being mismanaged?" Val asks. "Would he want to correct it?"

I think how Giovanni used his wealth to bring xanazo back to life. And how he has chosen to live in a hole in the side of a hill, afraid of people eavesdropping on his calls and tracking him.

"Yeah, Giovanni would take extreme measures to correct the parts of Soul Identity that he thought were wrong," I say.

"Then I agree with Simon," Val says. "It's not safe for you two to go back there."

"You don't even know who the bad guys are," I say. "We need to see what information Giovanni has."

"Even a name would be great," Scott says. "Something to kickstart our research."

"We should just get out of Idaho as fast as we can," Simon says.

"But that information," I say. "We're stuck without it."

We're all quiet for a minute or two.

Simon sighs. "Zelly's right. We need to try and get it."

We spend the next hour discussing logistics. I share the location of Giovanni's compound. Val and Mr. Morgan will get a trusted crew to fly them out on the corporate jet to pick us up this evening at Coeur d'Alene Airport, and the four of us can fly to Sterling. Scott will refine his plan for Ying's rescue and share it with us.

"Stay as safe as possible," Val says. "And run at the first sign of trouble."

Forty-eight

Simon and I each take showers and pack our belongings. At a quarter to eight, we put on our sunglasses, load up the car, and drive it back to the motel parking lot so we can walk unobserved to meet Jeremy.

He's waiting for us in his wheelchair on the northwest corner of the Center of the Universe.

"Hope you're down for an old-fashioned breakfast," he says.

Jeremy leads the way up the street, almost to where we parked our car. He wheels into a converted red and green garage that advertises itself both as a restaurant and as an antique store.

Inside, old license plates cover the ceiling behind the exposed ductwork. The wooden floor is offset with red and green trim, with hanging lights over each table. Antique signs and photographs take up almost every inch of the walls.

This whole town is trapped in its past.

The waiter seats us and hands us the menus. Jeremy and I order coffee, and Simon asks for an orange juice. Everybody gets the pancakes.

When the waitress leaves, Jeremy says, "You made a good choice not staying underground."

"Was it claustrophobic?" I ask.

He shakes his head. "Giovanni couldn't stop talking about what an honor it was to have two future overseers in his home. I thought he'd never shut up."

"What's the deal with you two?" I ask.

"What do you mean?"

"He insults you every chance he gets."

He sighs. "We had a big fight over selling the company. But Val was both generous and persuasive with her offer, and it would have been stupid for me to refuse the sale." He holds up his fist to Simon. "Little man, getting me those PB&Js was righteous."

Simon bumps his fist. "Any time, mate."

"Do you trust Giovanni?" I ask Jeremy.

He frowns, and I study his face. My eyes wander to his muscled arms and chest bulging under his t-shirt. Yesterday—and for the past two weeks—I found Jeremy super cute. But today Simon is more my kind of guy.

"Giovanni is overly smart," Jeremy says. "He's difficult to work with because his assumption is that he's always right. But I've never caught him in a lie. If you want to know something, just ask him. I've found that he tells the truth when he's confronted."

The waiter brings the pancakes, and we eat in silence. When we're done, Simon asks Jeremy, "What are you going to do with all the money you made?"

"First off, I've ordered a bigger, better, badass-er van," he says. "When they deliver it, I'm hitting the road with my lady friend, if I can convince her to take a year off from work. After that, I'm starting another company to research lightweight exoskeletons. I want to walk again."

"Take us with you," Simon says.

Jeremy laughs. "And let you miss running the world? I think not. Giovanni would kill me for sure."

I wonder if Jeremy can help reduce the risks we're about to take.

"About today," I say. "The reason we're here is to learn to xanazo. And Giovanni acts somewhat . . ." I hold up my hand palm side up, fingers splayed.

"Random?" he asks.

I make a face. "That he is, but I was thinking of something else. In Brazil we'd say santo do pau oco. A saint of the hollow wood. He's behaving in a way that he's not."

"Ah. You're saying he's a poser. Or that he's got a hidden agenda?"

I nod.

"Tell you what," he says. "I'll keep him on track and focused. And I'll keep my eyes out for any bad behavior."

"Thanks. I hope it's not necessary."

Jeremy pays the waiter. We get into Jeremy's van, and he drives the short distance to Giovanni's driveway. The gate opens, the house folds up, and we enter through the tunnel and park in the garage.

Giovanni gives us a deep bow. He thumbs and keys open the door, and we follow him into the foyer. This time he leads us directly through the curtain and to the fishbowl-like document room.

"I apologize for the lack of breakfast," he says. "Jeremy assured me that he would take good care of you. Did you have enough to eat or should I prepare something more?"

"We're fine," I say. "Thanks."

When we're seated, he rubs his hands together. "Last night I assigned you homework. Did you complete it?"

I glance over at Simon, then back to Giovanni. "You wanted us to think about how humans could replace the tech in Jeremy's vike portal."

"Exactly. What ideas did you have?"

"We listed what the vike portal needed to do," Simon says. "It has to block senses, activate the PCC, and put the PCC back to sleep."

"Correct," Giovanni says, steepling his hands. "What else?"

"We think you need two people in a xanazo because one gets to vike while the other serves as the guide," I say. "We assume that you can use meditation to block your senses, and the guide can assist with envisioning the logo and waking the viker up."

Giovanni claps his hands. "Bravo! That's exactly what must happen."

I glance at Simon and hope that que ele não dê com a língua nos dentes, he doesn't spill the beans.

"Can you show us how to be guides?" Simon asks.

He's so smart.

"Absolutely," Giovanni says.

"Great," I say. "I can guide, and Simon can vike."

"No, that won't work," Giovanni says. "I must first show you how I guide you, and after that, you may try guiding Simon."

"Um, Giovanni," I say. "All the pictures you showed us yesterday had the xanazo people naked."

"Yes," he says. "That's required. Both participants must have nothing touching their skin."

"Can we try doing it with clothes?" Simon asks. "Or at least in our underwear?"

Giovanni shakes his head. "It wouldn't be authentic, and it wouldn't work. Believe me, I've tried."

"Yikes," I say. "I think I'm better off waiting for a vike portal."

He says, "I realize this is uncomfortable, Miss Oliveira, but I want to assure you that there is nothing sexual about this. I take no pleasure. It is merely a necessity."

I point at Jeremy. "How about you demonstrate xanazo on him? I can learn to guide by watching."

"Me?" Jeremy says. "No way am I gonna take off my clothes with Giovanni."

But when he throws me a glance, I stare back at him, willing him to say something.

Jeremy needs to step up, like he said he would.

And he does. He says to Giovanni, "Dude, even if it's less efficient, can't you show them first with your clothes on and let them do it with each other?"

Giovanni frowns at me. "Do you want to learn to xanazo or not?"

"Can I stay in my underwear?"

He shakes his head.

Simon was right. This guy isn't just a socially inept fan of ours. He's creepy. I cross my arms. "I'm not comfortable enough to do this without clothes."

Giovanni throws up his hands and looks up at the ceiling.

"Then, Miss Oliveira," he says, "I am sorry to inform you that you will not be learning the art of xanazo."

Jeremy told me at breakfast that Giovanni wouldn't lie if you asked him a direct question. It's time to test that out.

I stare in Giovanni Judd's eyes, unblinking.

"Are you absolutely positive there is no way you can teach me to xanazo without me taking off all my clothes?"

He stares right back at me, and he lies right to my face.

"Yes, Miss Oliveira. I am positive. Xanazo cannot be taught by rote. I am sorry."

If Simon and I hadn't viked while wearing underwear and wrapping ourselves in a sleeping bag, I wouldn't know that this pervert is taking advantage of his power over me.

We need to get out of this cave. It's not like we can hop out of a window. I'll have to be thoughtful as I plan our exit.

But we can't leave until we explore his Gallery of Rogues.

After a minute, I say, "I definitely want to vike again. But I don't want it enough to do it naked with you."

Jeremy frowns. "Zelly—"

"How about this," Simon says. "Zelly and I can take a time-out. We both want to vike, but I think she needs to warm up to the idea."

"That's an excellent suggestion, Master Green," Giovanni says. "Take whatever time you need to get Miss Oliveira comfortable. I'm happy to wait."

"Can you give us a few minutes alone?" Then Simon adds, like he just thought of it, "How about we take a peek at your Gallery of Rogues as we clear our heads?"

"As you wish, Master Green." Giovanni points to the filing cabinets. "Like I said yesterday, my collection is at your disposal."

Jeremy reaches up and grabs Giovanni's arm. "While we wait, the two of us need to have our own conversation."

They both leave, and when Simon opens his mouth, I shake my head with the tiniest of movements.

"Let's see the collection," I say, for the benefit of the microphones and cameras that must be monitoring us. "After that we can figure out how to get comfortable."

Forty-nine

Simon and I open the cabinets housing Giovanni's Gallery of Rogues. They contain thick, black portfolios, one for each century.

I'm curious to see what he knows about Origen and Lillia, so I pull out the portfolio for the third century AD. I open to the tab labeled Delphians and find a bunch of plastic-covered documents, none of them written in a language I can read. I flip to the end, where I find an English summary.

It says that over the course of twenty years, the Delphians attempted two takeovers. One in Alexandria, which was thwarted by Origen after two overseers died. And another in Caesarea, which was blocked by Lillia of Cagliari after Origen died.

The summary goes on to explain the techniques the Delphians used. In Alexandria, they infiltrated the servants, and they placed plague-infested linens in the overseers' sleeping quarters. All four overseers got deathly sick, but both Origen and Demetrius survived.

It says that in Caesarea, Origen was killed by a Delphian assassin posing as an assistant, but Lillia happened to walk in, saw what happened, and strangled the assistant to death.

But I know better. When Lillia became executive overseer, she rewrote the history, removing all mentions of her working with the Delphians.

My soul line ancestor got away with murder.

I close the portfolio and put it back. If Giovanni got this history wrong, what are the chances that we'll get any useful information from his other files?

Even if it's useful, how can we trust it?

Simon clears his throat, and I face him. He inclines his head toward the portfolio opened in front of him. It's the most recent one, the twenty-first century. I come and stand behind him so I can look over his shoulder.

Simon flips to the beginning. There's a thick section from twelve years ago about a fake overseer starting WorldWideSouls, ending with a showdown in Venice. The next section from ten years ago talks about neo-Nazis attacking Soul Identity personnel in a cave in Slovakia. A final section from five years ago explains what happened when The Alert Foundation took us hostage. The rest of the sections are empty.

I reach over his shoulder to close the portfolio, but Simon grabs my hand.

I raise my eyebrows.

"Keep reading," he says.

I flip the portfolio's tabs. After four empty sections, I find a plastic-covered single sheet of paper, titled "BiggerGuns."

The paper says BiggerGuns is a private military organization that has been planning a takeover of Soul Identity for almost a decade. Six years ago, they induced a heart attack in one of our previous overseers, and they located and attempted to place two new overseers around the time we were kidnapped. But these potential overseers were intercepted and killed, leaving BiggerGuns without a way to implement their takeover plan.

There is further analysis hypothesizing that BiggerGuns wants to control, not destroy, Soul Identity. They are waiting for Ying, me, and Simon to grow up so they can grab us and take charge through us. They don't care about the organization. They just want to direct where the money goes.

At the bottom of the page, it claims that BiggerGuns has infiltrated several departments of Soul Identity, with details in an attached appendix.

I flip through the rest of the tabs in the portfolio, but I don't find the referenced appendix.

Simon closes the portfolio and returns it to the filing cabinet.

"Wow, just reading about what happened to us brought back a ton of bad memories," he says.

He's speaking for the benefit of the microphones.

I shake my head. I want to say more, or at least smile, but I don't dare.

Inside, though, I'm dancing. Thanks to Giovanni's mistake, we know who the bad guys are.

"Is your mind clear, Zelly?" Simon asks. "Can we talk about learning to xanazo? I really want to vike again."

Simon's smart enough to keep pretending. I close my eyes and take a deep breath.

I say, "I won't get naked with Giovanni. I'm seventeen, and it's not appropriate."

I may be answering Simon's question, but I'm speaking loud enough so Giovanni and Jeremy can follow along.

If Giovanni knew we viked in our underwear last night, he'd know I'm blustering. But his request remains inappropriate—not because I'm seventeen, but because Giovanni is taking advantage of his power over me.

"And if he insists?" Simon asks. "Do we just leave?"

"We'll have to give in, eventually." I glance around the room. "I'm struggling so hard because we're sitting in this fishbowl of an office. I need to vike in a place where I can relax."

"And like Jeremy said, you should practice first with your clothes on."

"Yes, I will insist on that."

"Cool," Simon says. "Does this mean you're ready?"

"Let me think about it," I say.

We sit without saying anything. Since we already do know how to xanazo, I'm thinking through a possible escape plan. It's crazy, but it could work.

Because we must escape. Giovanni thought he had hidden everything, but we found that page about BiggerGuns. They're the group behind the gray-uniformed guards we saw in Sterling. And Giovanni must be working with them, trying to detain us. He's wasting our time, slow-walking us instead of teaching us to xanazo.

We must get out of this compound before we're trapped.

"We need to leave," I whisper, trying not to move my lips.

Simon raises his eyebrows.

"We make him teach us in Jeremy's van," I whisper. "But I need a little more time to get organized. Can you stall?"

Simon nods. He says in a loud voice, "I'm getting hungry. Can we get something to eat before we do the xanazo?"

"I'm sure we can," I say. "Let's go find these guys."

Back in the foyer, Giovanni sits on a couch next to Jeremy's wheelchair. They stare at a tablet that Giovanni holds.

"Did you come up with a solution?" Jeremy asks.

As if he doesn't know. I'm sure they watched us from the tablet.

"We did. I'm sorry for my earlier reluctance. I'm ready to proceed."

Jeremy smiles.

"But I have three requests."

"How can I help?" Giovanni asks.

"Your document room is too exposed, and I won't be comfortable there. I want to vike in the same place I did it last time. In Jeremy's van."

"That's fine with me," Jeremy says. "The bed is clean."

"It's unorthodox," Giovanni says, "but we can make that work."

Make that work? What is so screwed up in his head that he can act with such a cara de pau?

"My second request," I say. "We take Jeremy's suggestion and do a dry run with our clothes on."

Giovanni throws a glance at Jeremy, who gives a subtle nod.

"I am happy to accommodate," Giovanni says.

"Thank you," I say. "And one more request."

This is the important one.

"You both wear blindfolds when we xanazo for real. If you insist that I must undress, I insist that you do not watch."

"Absolutely not," Giovanni says. "That's not how xanazo works."

"As far as I understand, you don't use your eyes to xanazo," I say. "Why would you need to see my body? Why would Jeremy?"

He crosses his arms and stares at the floor. But after a minute of frowning and muttering to himself, he says, "Blindfolds it is."

I show him as big a smile as I can fake.

"And I have a request, too," Simon says. "I need a snack before we start."

"Of course, Master Green!" Giovanni says. "Allow me to bring out sandwiches." He heads toward the curtain.

"Can I help you get them?" I ask.

"Please, stay here and relax, Miss Oliveira. I shall serve you."

"I insist." I follow him to the kitchen, where he retrieves two platters of finger sandwiches from the large refrigerator. They're already prepared.

"I made these for lunch, but we can eat them now." He hands me the platters. "Take these, and I'll bring beverages."

Why would he pre-make our sandwiches?

As I carry the platters to the foyer, I have this crazy worry that he's done something to the food. I decide I won't eat anything, just to be safe.

Simon has no such worries. He eats five of the eight quarters of the brie and cucumber finger sandwiches.

When Simon's full, the four of us step into the underground garage.

I grab Simon's arm and whisper, "Be ready to run. Follow my lead."

Fifty

Inside his van, Jeremy maneuvers into the space for the driver, back-first so that he's facing us. "Giovanni, sit on the bed," he says. "Simon, come up to the passenger seat. And Zelly, just stand by the door for now."

Once we're all in, Giovanni asks, "Shall we begin?"

"I'm ready," I say. "For the practice run."

"Excellent!" He scooches his body back until he leans against the driver's side of the van. He spreads his legs wide and pats the mattress. "Come and sit here, Miss Oliveira."

I throw a glance at Jeremy as I climb onto the bed.

"Do you remember the position from the pictures I showed you?" Giovanni asks.

"I do." I cross my legs, cross my arms, and rest my hands on my knees. "Is this right?"

"I shall verify. First your legs and feet." He leans forward against my back and runs his hands down each of my legs.

"What do you think you're doing?" I grab his wrists and hold them in place.

"I'm getting your legs into the correct position."

"You need to rub them to do that?"

"Giovanni," Jeremy says, "remember what I said."

"Let me do this properly!" Giovanni snaps at him.

I let go of his wrists, and he continues, this time directing me how to move my legs instead of touching them.

"What makes this a correct position?" I ask. "I want to learn."

"Each foot must be tucked under the opposite knee. And the sole of each foot must be at a right angle to your body."

"Got it."

"Now your arms and hands." Giovanni grasps my bicep and slides his hands down to my forearm, brushing his arms alongside my ribs. "Again, I apologize. I just want you to get this right."

I almost forgive his hands on my arms, but he gets sneaky and presses up against my breasts.

I don't say anything, even though I know that's stupid. We're about to escape, and I don't want to make a big deal.

I ask him, "What's the proper position here?"

"Your hands must be on top of your knees, palms up, so I can reach around and place my palms, fingers, and thumbs on top of yours."

"Okay."

Giovanni scooches himself forward until his chest and crotch are pressed up against my back and my butt.

I'm so glad I insisted that we stay dressed for this.

He pulls his legs together until the soles of his shoes touch mine. He places his palms on my palms, his fingers and thumbs on mine. He rests his chin on my left shoulder. "We are now in the proper position."

"What comes next?"

"The next step is for you to relax and enter a state of meditation. We're going to chant a mantra together."

I'm not sure how I could ever relax with this creep pushing his body against me, taking advantage of me. But I'm not going to tell him that. "Which mantra?"

"Hamsah. It's Sanskrit for 'I am that.' It's done like this." He demonstrates, whispering a long drawn-in HAAAAHM on his inhale, holding it, and a faster SAAAH on his exhale.

We practice saying hamsah a few times.

"Once you're relaxed," he says, "my job will be to guide you into blocking out your sight, touch, smell, and taste. I'll help you imagine drawing the logo. That will allow us both to enter xanazo. You will find yourself in the Gallery of Past Lives, and after a minute or so, I will bring you out."

"Awesome," I say. "How will you do that?"

"All in good time, Miss Oliveira. After you complete your first xanazo, I will teach you."

This loser is stuck on his power trip. He's creepy and touchy-feely, and he's withholding information. I pull myself out of his embrace and get off the bed.

"Thanks for doing this dry run," I say. "I understand what I need to do."

He bows his head. "I am at your service, Miss Oliveira. Are you ready to perform your first real xanazo?"

I'm about to say yes, but when I think how he grazed my body with his hands, claiming it wasn't sexual, something snaps in me.

"On second thought, I'm not going to do it. This won't work for me."

"I'll do it." Simon's voice is slurred, and his eyes are droopy.

"No, Simon. He may say he means nothing by it, but this dude ran his hands down my legs like he owned them. He rubbed my arms and brushed up against my breasts for no reason except that he could."

Giovanni sits on the bed, his mouth hanging open.

"Zelly," Jeremy says. "I'm sure he didn't mean any harm. Did you, Giovanni?"

I stare at him. "What the heck, Jeremy?"

"I meant no harm whatsoever!" Giovanni says. "And I apologize profusely for making you uncomfortable."

I stand, arms crossed, staring at Giovanni.

I want to smash his smug face. But if I don't get him blindfolded, we won't be able to escape.

I take a deep, calming breath. "Sorry about that," I say. "I can be pretty sensitive, as you can see. Let's continue. But I won't need any help with positioning. Are we clear on that?"

"Of course, Miss Oliveira," Giovanni purrs. "Jeremy, what do you have that we can use as blindfolds?"

I glare at Jeremy, and he shakes his head. "Nothing comes to mind."

"I have neckties in my closet. Allow me to retrieve them." Giovanni climbs off the bed, steps out of the van, thumbs and keys the panel, and enters the foyer. He leaves the door propped open.

I whirl around to face Jeremy. "People who act this way when they have all the power make me sick."

"I'm sorry, Zelly. Do you want to stop? I can get you out of here."

I don't trust him, but I need him to help us escape without realizing he's doing so.

"You agree that what he's doing is wrong?"

He nods. "But you want to vike, so I think you'll need to deal with his crap."

"What would keep me calm is knowing that I can stop at any moment."

"You'll be in a vike. You can't just stop."

"I'm not worried about the time that I'm viking, as he said he'll be in xanazo, too," I say. "I'm thinking about the moments when we're getting ready. When he presses his naked body against me. I won't be able to relax if I don't feel in control."

He frowns. "That makes sense. I think I can help."

Jeremy maneuvers his wheelchair over to a kitchen drawer, pulls out a steak knife, and hands it to me. "Will this work?"

I bury the knife into the crack between the mattress and its frame. "I was hoping for a gun. Or a Taser. You must have something like that in here, Jeremy."

He scratches his goatee. "Okay, you want the good stuff. Simon, my man, can you grab me something from the glove compartment?"

But Simon doesn't answer because he's fast asleep. His head leans to one side, and he's snoring.

And now I'm all alone. I'm glad I didn't eat those sandwiches, but I wish Simon didn't, either.

I do my best to swallow my panic and pretend that I don't know Simon was drugged. "I guess he was tired," I say. "I'll do it." I move to the front of the van. "What am I looking for?"

"I have a stun baton in there. It's black, almost two feet long."

I pull it out of the glove compartment. The baton is shaped like a mini baseball bat, but it's heavier.

I hand the baton to Jeremy, and he shows me how to use it. "If he attacks you, and I sincerely doubt he will, just jam this into his chest and slide the button up."

He demonstrates, and the baton gives a menacing-sounding crackle.

"It's a hundred million volts," he says. "Hold it on him for three seconds, and he'll go down and stay down for a while."

I put the baton into the same mattress crack as the knife. "I hope I don't need it."

"Me, too," he says. "But I want you to feel safe."

I tell Jeremy that I'm going to the bathroom. On the way back through the foyer, I bring with me both platters of sandwiches, and I set them on the van's countertop.

I'm as ready as I can be. I just need to wait for Giovanni to return with the blindfolds.

Fifty-one

Giovanni comes through the foyer door. Instead of his slacks and shirt, he's now wearing a white bathrobe and slippers. He's holding three striped neckties colored red, blue, and black.

He steps into the van and holds up the neckties. "These should work well as blindfolds."

"Perfect," I manage to say without any sign of revulsion.

Giovanni hands a necktie to Jeremy. "Put it on, please."

Jeremy wraps the necktie over his eyes and around his head, tying it in the back.

Giovanni drapes a necktie over the back of the passenger seat. "I see Master Green decided to take a nap."

Does he really think I'm that stupid?

He licks his lips. "Are you ready, Miss Oliveira?"

While holding his gaze with my eyes, I kick off my shoes, unbutton my jeans, and slide them off. I place them on the edge of the mattress, jam my fingers into the gap to make sure Jeremy didn't remove the stun baton and knife, and use my jeans to cover the gap.

"My, my, Miss Oliveira." His voice is almost a whisper.

Giovanni wraps the necktie around his neck and unties his bathrobe, all the while staring at me. He lets the bathrobe drop to the floor.

I take off my shirt and stand facing him in my bra and panties. I place the shirt on top of my jeans.

"Put on your blindfold," I say.

"Are you sure you need me to wear it?"

I stare at him.

"Let me situate myself," he says.

He backs up to the edge of the mattress and hikes himself onto it, all the while holding my gaze. He leans against the side of the van and spreads his legs. He takes off his glasses, folds them, and reaches out to set them on the counter.

"Without my glasses, I'm quite blind," he says.

"Just put the blindfold on so we can do this."

He ties the necktie over his eyes and spins the knot to the back.

I walk closer and box the air in front of his face, but he doesn't flinch, so I assume his sight is blinded.

Then I look down, and I wish I didn't.

The creep has an erection.

I need to channel Lillia.

Maybe not Lillia, because when she was in a similar situation with Origen, she slept with him. No way am I going to do that.

I channel Zelly the fearless. I yank the stun baton out of its hiding place, and I jam it into Giovanni's disgusting crotch, and I slide its button all the way up.

Giovanni lets out a scream and arches his back, and if I wasn't so pissed off at how he made me feel powerless and dirty, I might feel sorry for him.

But I don't feel sorry at all. All I feel is rage, and I count to three as slow as I can before turning off the baton.

Giovanni is suffering huge shakes and twitches, but I can't watch him, because Jeremy has taken off his blindfold and is propelling his wheelchair at me.

I scramble up on the mattress and toward the back, out of his reach, pointing the baton at him.

"Stay away from me," I say. "I'll stun you, too."

He holds up both hands, and when I lower the stun baton, he darts his hand into the mattress crack and pulls out the steak knife.

"Jeez, Zelly, what did you do?"

"He had a hard-on! I told you I wasn't going to put up with his crap."

"You did ask him to teach you to vike."

"Why would you defend him?" I stare at him and lower my voice to a growl. "You need to back off. Now."

"Just relax, Zelly. And put down that baton."

I shake my head.

Jeremy rolls backward, away from me and toward the front of the van. He lunges toward his left and grabs Simon under his arms, pulling the top of his limp body onto his lap. He holds the steak knife to Simon's neck.

He narrows his eyes. "I said put down that baton."

"If Simon loses even one drop of blood, I will kill you."

"You can't stun me. Not without hurting Simon."

Darn it.

Since he's got Simon half on his lap, Jeremy is immobile. This gives me time to take the necktie off Giovanni's head, push him onto his side, wrestle his trembling arms behind his back, and tie his hands together. I also put on my jeans, top, and shoes.

"What's your plan, Zelly?" Jeremy asks.

"To get out of here," I say. "Are you working with them?"

"Them?"

I stare at him. "Let Simon go."

He shakes his head. "You must see that you can't win."

"What do you mean I can't win?" I hop off the bed, walk over to him, and jam the baton against his neck.

"You'll just hurt Simon. Don't you dare."

I dare. I slide the button up, and Jeremy screams. I count to three, and I catch Simon in my arms as he slips off Jeremy's lap.

Hopefully, the drugs that Simon ingested work like anesthesia, and he didn't feel anything.

I lever Simon back into the passenger seat, grab the extra necktie, and bind Jeremy's hands behind his back. I use Jeremy's necktie to bind Giovanni's feet. I move the steak knife from Jeremy's lap to the counter.

After that's done, I sit on the floor, wrap my arms around my legs, and allow myself to sob for five minutes.

Giovanni groans.

"What have you done?" he asks, squinting at me.

The guy had all the power, and he used it against me. I did what I had to do. And he deserved every volt.

But I don't need to tell him that.

His eyes flash, and he opens his mouth, but I hold up the stun baton.

"I've got plenty of charge left."

He rolls onto his back and sits up. I throw his bathrobe over his lap and put his glasses on his face.

"Who's BiggerGuns?" I ask.

"Bigger who?"

"Don't play dumb," I say. "You missed a page when you were cleaning up your Gallery of Rogues."

He grimaces.

"So, who are they?"

He looks up. "They are the ones who will bring Soul Identity back to its former glory."

It sounds like something Ying would say.

"What does that mean?"

He shakes his head, and even my threats to zap him again don't make him talk.

I point out the front windshield. "I want to drive out of here. How do I raise up that fake tiny house out front?"

"It requires my thumbprint. Just like the door to the foyer."

"Got it." I gesture at the sandwiches on the counter. "You laced the sandwiches with something to make us sleep, didn't you?"

He glares at me.

I walk over to the sandwich platters. There are Simon's three cucumber and brie, and all eight of my Romeu e Julieta quarters, left. I pick up a cucumber and brie quarter and hold it in front of his lips.

"You get an early lunch today," I say. "Eat it."

He squeezes his lips together.

I hold up the stun baton and make it crackle.

"Eat it. Now."

He opens his mouth, and I shove the sandwich inside, making sure he doesn't bite me. He chews and swallows. We do this for one more cucumber and brie quarter, and then for half of the Romeu e Julieta quarters.

"How long before you fall asleep?" I ask.

Giovanni says nothing.

I hop off the bed and crouch next to Jeremy, who's beginning to stir. He lets out a moan and sits straight up, fighting the necktie that binds his hands. He opens his eyes.

"Oh, my God," he says. "You're crazy."

"I was really hoping you were a good guy."

"I am."

"Good guys never hold knives to the throats of children."

He exchanges looks with Giovanni, but he doesn't say anything.

I bring the sandwich platter to him. Just like Giovanni, Jeremy needs the threat of the stun baton to open his mouth. I push the remaining sandwich quarters in one at a time, until he's chewed and swallowed them all.

"How long?" I ask Giovanni again.

He stares daggers at me.

I move to the front and check Simon, but he's still out cold. I slip the passenger seatbelt around him and recline his seat back halfway.

The men remain silent. Which is fine with me, as I take the time to think about what I must do before we can meet up with Val and Mr. Morgan at the airport.

After ten minutes of waiting, Giovanni's eyes start to droop. Two minutes later, his head has fallen forward, and his breathing is steady and deep.

I don't know if he's faking it, so I zap him on the neck with the stun baton, just for two seconds. He doesn't scream, so I'm assuming he's asleep.

I check Jeremy, but he's still awake, fighting sleep. He opens his mouth to say something to me, but then his eyes close and his head lolls to the side.

I zap him, too. Just to make sure.

I pull hard on Giovanni's legs, and he slides off the mattress. The back of his head bangs against the floor, but I don't see any blood. I drag him down the ramp of the van and leave him on the garage floor.

I roll Jeremy's wheelchair to the top of the ramp. I search his pockets and take his key fob. I give the wheelchair a mighty push, and it rolls down the ramp, colliding with Giovanni's limp, naked body at the base. The wheelchair flips forward, and Jeremy spills onto the floor, just beyond Giovanni.

I roll them onto their sides and make sure they can breathe. I use Jeremy's key fob to retract the ramp and close the side door.

Simon is still asleep, but we need to go. Since there is no driver's seat, I kneel behind the wheel, which is a bit awkward but doable. I push the ignition button.

I try to remember what Jeremy said about the hand throttle. Push to brake, right and left for gas. I push, then shift into reverse. I shove the throttle to the left, and the van jerks backward hard enough that I am thrown into the steering wheel.

I push the throttle forward to brake, and I try again. This time I inch the throttle to the left, and we creep backward, slow enough that I can cut the wheel and turn around. I shift and drive into the tunnel that leads to the fake house. I round the corner to find a wall in front of me.

I remember that I need Giovanni—or at least Giovanni's thumb—to move the house out of the way. Should I go back to get him? Or his thumb?

I could do what the kidnapped lady did to Lillia and just bite off Giovanni's thumb.

I ponder this for all of ten seconds, and I decide that it would be more expedient and a lot less gross if I act like I'm in the movies and just bust my way out.

I wish Simon was awake to see this. He'd be cheering me on.

I pull the throttle hard, and the van lurches forward and picks up speed. I grip the steering wheel and brace for the impact as we hurtle into the wall, but the van is big, and we bust through with ease, plowing into the tiny house's living room.

The furniture stops the van's progress. It must be bolted to the floor. I back up as far as I can, and I ram the van into the couches. They spring loose, the van rips into the front wall, and we're through.

I stop in the driveway, hop out of the van, and walk to the front. One of its headlights is smashed, and there are pieces of glass stuck in the grill, but other than these cosmetic issues, the van looks fine. Jeremy should be thanking me when he gets it back.

The house, though ... That's a total mess. Well, good riddance. Simon and I have a plane to catch.

Fifty-two

I drive us to the motel parking lot, and when nobody is looking, I somehow drag Simon's unconscious body out of the van and into the Camry. I leave the van unlocked and its key fob on the front seat. I grab our sunglasses, and I drive toward Coeur d'Alene Airport. It's an hour away, so we should be there by noon.

Or twelve-thirty because I end up taking the next exit and stopping at the town park and spending a minute just breathing.

Simon stirs, but he's still unconscious. My insistence to go back into the compound might have left me with bruising, but Simon, who pleaded with me to stay away, who went along with my plan even though he knew better, ended up both drugged and stunned.

I hope the information we gleaned about BiggerGuns is worth its cost.

Giovanni drugged the sandwiches. He must work for them. Jeremy may not. But even so, I can't trust him. When push came to shove, he held a knife to Simon's throat.

Simon moves again, and I reach over and stroke his cheek.

He opens his eyes. "Zelly."

I laugh and unbuckle my seatbelt and leap over the console and into his lap, giving him a bear hug even though it hurts my ribs to squeeze him.

"You're awake!"

"Why are we back in this car?"

"You remember nothing?"

"We got into the van, Giovanni tried to grope you, and I couldn't keep my eyes open."

"He drugged you." I fill him in on Giovanni coming back in his bathrobe, why I shocked him, what Jeremy did, how I fed them the laced sandwiches, and how I drove through the walls of the fake house.

"And I stunned you too, Simon. I'm sorry."

"At least I didn't feel it." He bursts out laughing. "I'll bet Giovanni felt it! I can't believe you zapped him in his bits and pieces."

That gets me laughing, and for the next few minutes, every time our giggles begin to subside, one of us snorts, and we start all over again.

When our nervous energy dissipates, I place my hand on his cheek. "I'm glad you're okay, Sy. Jeremy scared me to death when he held that knife to your throat. I can't lose you."

He buries me in a hug.

After a few more minutes of sitting, recovering, I let Simon go. "It's time for us to save Ying."

I drive the rest of the way to the airport's private jet centers, and it takes us a while to check the FBOs to discover where the Soul Identity jet parked.

"They landed at noon," the receptionist says. "But if you think you're leaving soon, I'm sorry. The pilots rented a car and left here twenty minutes ago."

"The rest of our group should already be on the jet," I say.

"Nobody else deplaned. Do you want to check who is on board?"

We do, but when we refuse to show our identification, she refuses to let us through.

"You can wait for the pilots," she says. "They said they're returning the rental at three." She gives me the Wi-Fi password and points us to the lounge.

I send a message to Val, and she vouches for us and escorts us back to the jet, where we see Mr. Morgan reclining, staring out the window.

Val hugs her arms. "Scott and his parents went dark fifteen minutes ago," she says. "He texted me they were letting themselves get captured by the gray uniforms but nothing since. We need to get to Sterling and figure this out."

"Where did you send the pilots?" I ask.

"I didn't send them anywhere," she says. "They're running an errand, retrieving a package that would take an hour or so. I've been calling them to come back, but they're not answering."

"We can't trust the pilots," I say. "In fact, we can't trust anybody at Soul Identity." I tell her about what we read and what we went through to get that information.

Val massages her forehead. "Just when it felt like we were getting ahead of the curve."

"Sorry," Simon says.

"Don't be sorry. Just be safe. Soul Identity needs you." She stands up. "I'll ask the receptionist to find us another pilot."

While Val is gone, I search from my phone for information on BiggerGuns.

They've been around since the turn of the century, and most of their work has come from the government for overseas fighting, logistics, and guard duty. Since they're privately held, there is little information about their corporate structure.

I find an article on private military organizations and how they are expanding overseas in search of new revenues from other countries.

If BiggerGuns is feeling the pinch, that would explain what Scott said about them shifting our investments into crime syndicates and weapons suppliers.

Good thing we have safeguards to limit the money from moving faster. BiggerGuns must be frustrated at the speed they can get to it. Frustrated enough to try to catch us all.

The BiggerGuns corporate website is generic. It's got a public relations email address and little else. They don't tweet. They don't have a Facebook page. Nobody on LinkedIn lists them as their employer, and nobody is complaining on Glassdoor. If they are real, they are real quiet.

I do find a cached copy of a defunct web magazine article from ten years ago that contains a tangential reference to BiggerGuns' role in one of the Middle East wars. It mentions the founder, Adam Monarch, and shows a photo of him in a desert-camouflage combat uniform, complete with rifle, helmet, and sunglasses. But other than saying he is a former special forces officer, the article provides few details on him or the organization.

Did Giovanni leave that report page in the portfolio as a false flag, so we'd blame somebody else and not him? No, that doesn't make much sense. If Giovanni was the head of the bad guys, he wouldn't have needed to drug us, and he wouldn't have wasted time being a handsy creep.

Giovanni is unfit to run a takeover operation, no matter how much he knows about Soul Identity.

I check my messages and find a new email from Yuno Hu. I tap it open, and read, "Z: Pilot evil. Find another way back. Tell V we are ok and that I love history. See you at midnight."

Val returns and informs us, "If you can believe it, no pilots in the whole region are free until tomorrow. No jets are available for charter, either."

I show her and Simon the message from Scott.

"Why would he get himself captured?" I ask.

She shrugs. "He's done that kind of thing before. Scott loves any plan with trickery. He'd build a wooden horse in the driveway if I let him."

"Giovanni's rogue research would show that this is Scott's thing," I say. "They will anticipate his tricks."

She balls her hands, and I see her knuckles go white. "We need to get to Sterling. Now."

"But not with our pilots," I say.

"I'll find a commercial flight." She pulls out her phone.

"That won't work," I say. "We can't use our identification."

She sighs. "We need a jet pilot."

"I'm a jet pilot," Simon says. "At least, my soul line ancestor was. I can fly this plane."

Fifty-three

"You're not a jet pilot, Sy," I say.

"I can fly this plane."

I hold my hand up to his forehead. "That stun gun left some damage after all."

He knocks my hand away. "I can."

"If this jet and the four of us go down," Val says, "Soul Identity is lost."

"This jet is a Bombardier Challenger 600 class," Simon says. "It won't go down. I've flown it many times."

"How is that possible?" I ask. "Your soul line ancestor was Asian. I remember the dragons."

"His name was Yun Fei, and he was an airline pilot in Beijing. He retired in the early nineties, moved to France, and flew for rich people. On an older version of this plane."

"The nineties wasn't that long ago," I say. "Why is he gone and you're here?"

He shrugs. "I haven't observed that far yet. At this point in my vikes he's based in France, flying around Europe. He's an excellent pilot."

I put my hand on his shoulder. "I viked to a ship as Lillia, but I can't sail one. Can you really fly this?"

"I know I can."

"Let's go to the cockpit, Simon," Val says. "Show us what you know."

Simon takes us up front and sits in one of the two pilot's seats. He points out the various flight controls like the throttle, flaps, and rudder. He tells us about the displays, and the wheel brakes, thrust reversers, and autopilot. He shows us how to program a flight plan into the guidance system, and how to use the weather radar. He pulls the flight checklist out of pocket to the left of the seat and walks us through it, and then how to check for the center of gravity, how to verify the temperatures of the oil and fuel, and a whole lot more that I can't remember.

Simon knows this jet. And he's more excited than I've ever seen him.

Do I trust him enough to ride with him?

I hold up my hand, which causes him to stop showing us how he'd adjust the air conditioning system.

"How long would it take you to get this plane ready to leave?" I ask.

"I'd have to run through the checklist. Probably a half hour."

"Can you get everything ready to go and we'll decide then?"

"Of course." Simon reaches behind the seat, pulls out a captain's hat, and puts it on his head. He grabs the flight checklist and heads out of the cockpit. "Follow me."

He leads us through the visual inspection, telling us what he's doing at each step. He pokes, prods, pulls, and pushes the wings, wheels, and various connectors, checking off items on his list. He kicks the chucks out from under the wheels.

We go back to the cockpit. I sit in the co-pilot's seat, and Simon talks through each lever and gauge that he plays with. He programs in Worcester Regional Airport as our destination and shows us the full flight plan.

We climb out of the seats, and the three of us stand in the main cabin.

"I've done everything except inform air traffic control," Simon says. "We're ready to fly."

I put my hand on his shoulder and stare him in the eye. "One to ten, Sy, how sure are you that you can get us to Worcester?"

He stares back at me without blinking. "Nine."

I sigh.

"But I can make that a ten."

"How?" Val asks.

"Help me vike for just ten minutes. I can get a few more flights in. If I'm lucky, they'll be on the same model as this jet."

"This is crazy," Val says. "It's like we're putting our lives in the hands of a pilot who has only flown Flight Simulator. We should find another way—a safer way."

"What's our alternative?" I ask. "Drive all the way to Massachusetts?"

"There's really no safe option," she says.

"There never really is with Soul Identity," I say. "But when we have good reason to, we need to take the risk."

Val wears a solemn expression. "My good reason is to help Scott before he gets himself killed," she says. "But you and Mr. Morgan should stay, so Soul Identity can survive if we crash."

I'm about to argue, but Simon grabs my arm and says, "I won't fly without Zelly. She is my co-pilot."

Val turns to me. "What's your good reason to take this risk?"

I stand still for a moment, thinking.

"Ying needs our help," I say. "And Soul Identity needs saving. I'm not going to let these jerks screw up my chance to be an overseer."

Val raises her eyebrows at Simon. "And you?"

"I just want to fly," he says. "And yeah, help save Soul Identity."

"You will fly us to Worcester without crashing?" Val asks him.

"I promise."

Simon stands straight and tall, not at all like a fourteen-year-old. The stance of an older man, the confidence of an adult. The swagger of a pilot.

"I trust you," I tell him.

Val takes a deep breath and lets it out. "Let's get his confidence all the way to a ten. Vike him up, Zelly."

Fifty-four

I need to find a spot with enough room for me and Simon to vike. The plane has single seats on each side, so I choose one that's facing backward, diagonal to Mr. Morgan, who's still staring out the window. I raise the seat's footrest all the way up and recline its back a little. The armrests will be in the way, so I take the bottom cushion off the seat next to Mr. Morgan and use it as a booster.

"This is how you vike without a portal?" Val asks.

"This is how you xanazo. Don't freak out." I kick off my shoes, take off my shirt, jeans, and socks, and climb onto the seat.

With a shy smile to Val, Simon strips down to his underwear and sits between my legs.

Mr. Morgan watches us. We must be more interesting than whatever is outside.

"I can see why you had to zap Giovanni," Val says.

"He wanted to do it completely naked," I say. "There's no need for that. He's a pervert."

I pull Simon back, wrap my arms and legs around him, and make sure the palms of my hands and the soles of my feet touch his. I rest my chin on his shoulder.

"No more than ten minutes," Simon says. "That'll give me around ten days. I'll find Yun Fei's latest, busiest flying time."

He starts his oms. I join in and when he's relaxed enough, I guide him into blocking out his senses and drawing the Soul Identity logo.

And then I'm in my empty vike space, standing on my hovering disc. And as I stand there in the silent darkness, with neither cinnamon scent nor breeze to focus on, and no way to sit or lie down, I realize that the ancients had a built-in failsafe that is missing in Jeremy's vike portal. Nobody will over-vike, because there's no way a guide could last for more than an hour of torture in this senseless place.

Speaking of torture, Simon went through his share of it this morning. I hope that he'll be able to stay awake all the way to Worcester. Giovanni might have drugged him with the sandwiches, but I'm the one who zapped Jeremy while he was holding Simon.

If the plane goes down because Simon is just too worn out, it'll be my fault. The four of us will die, and so will Scott and his parents. Ying, too, depending on whose side she's on.

I wonder why Scott would let himself and his parents get captured by the BiggerGuns people.

Val says he likes tricking the bad guys, and she mentioned a wooden horse. Scott's email said that he loves history.

I read *The Odyssey* a couple years back. Odysseus was the book's great trickster. After ten years of besieging the city of Troy, the Greeks decided to give up, but Odysseus had them leave behind a big wooden horse full of Greek soldiers. The Trojans rolled the horse into the city, the soldiers popped out and opened the city gates, and the Greek army sacked Troy.

It sounds like Scott and his parents will unlock a gate and wait for us to rush in. I think about what this would look like.

And then I realize that I have lost track of the time. I jump off the disc and exit vike space.

I open my eyes and see Val leaning over me.

"It's been fifteen minutes," she says. "We have to take off soon."

I peek at Simon. He's whimpering, and he pulls his arms around his chest and shakes his whole body.

"You okay, Sy?"

He groans.

"Sy? We're back from the vike. We're in the jet. It's time for you to fly."

"You left me in there too long, and I reached the end of the ribbon." He opens is eyes. "I died, Zelly. It was horrible. I was stuck in an empty space forever."

As if I haven't caused him enough pain today. I squeeze him in my arms. "I'm so sorry, Sy. I lost track of time."

He shivers like he's a dog shaking off water. "I'll be fine," he says. "Let's get in the air." He stands up on shaky legs, pulls on his pants and shirt, and slips into his shoes.

"Are you sure you can do this?" Val asks.

"I'm positive. Zelly, come and be my co-pilot."

We head to the cockpit, settle into the pilot seats, and strap on our seatbelts.

"Did you get more practice?" I ask.

"Too much." He glances over his shoulder and drops his voice. "Yun Fei died in an airplane crash on takeoff. He was the pilot."

I open my mouth, but I don't know what to say.

"It's okay." He pats my knee. "I saw what he did wrong. I won't make that same mistake."

My worry is wasted. Simon talks to the air traffic controllers, taxies to the runway, and takes off, with no problems at all. He climbs to a cruising altitude and engages the autopilot.

"Easy peasy," he says. "We'll land in four hours. Around nine-thirty at night, local time."

"I can't believe you picked this up from your vikes," I say.

Can I gain any useful skills from my own vikes?

Just as I'm getting comfortable, Simon unbuckles his seatbelt. "I need the lavatory," he says.

"You're leaving me up here? Alone?"

He smiles. "It's on autopilot. Call me if there's a problem. I'll be back soon."

But he isn't back soon. Or even a half hour later. The longer he takes, the more worried I get.

When I can't wait any more, I call out to Val, and she comes up front.

"Where did Simon go?" I ask.

"He said he needed a nap and that you had this under control."

My guts twist themselves into a knot. "I can't fly the plane!"

"Me either." She sighs. "The poor kid looked exhausted, and the plane seems to be steady. Can we let him sleep for a while?"

We don't really have a choice. I close my eyes and I try as hard as I can to not panic and to ignore the fact that we're in the air, with our pilot, trained solely through a series of vikes, passed out in the back. And that he's unconscious because he's been drugged, zapped, and left at the end of the vike space ribbon for far too long.

My heart is pounding, and I can't seem to catch my breath.

What would Lillia do?

She'd be brave. She'd figure it out. And she'd survive at all costs.

She's exactly like me.

Fifty-five

Val heads back to the passenger cabin, and I'm alone in the cockpit, wondering what happens if Simon can't wake up in time to land this plane.

I find the manual in Simon's seat pocket and read about the autopilot system, hoping that it's smart enough to get us on the ground. The manual uses lots of confusing abbreviations, but after a while I find a feature called autoland, designed for passengers to use if the pilot becomes incapacitated. The manual says to activate it once we're close to the airport, shows me where the button is, and suggests that I verify the airport is rated for handling autolandings.

I search for the instrument landing specs for Worcester Regional Airport, and I find that two of their runways are rated for autoland. That's one less worry.

The flight system shows we have two hours left. I figure I can stare at the manual and worry myself sick for those two hours or I can stop worrying and trust in the autopilot. Because even if something did break, I wouldn't know how to do fix it.

That makes my choice easy. I walk out of the cockpit and back to the passenger cabin, thinking that Val and I can do some planning for our rescue mission.

But Val is next to Simon, fast asleep. I don't have the heart to wake her up.

I do try to wake up Simon, but after shaking him, pinching him, and even holding his nose until he gasps, he doesn't open his eyes.

Only Mr. Morgan is awake. He's on the other side of the aisle, staring out the window. I take the seat facing him and ask, "What do you see out there?"

He glances at me, but he says nothing. Not that I expect him to talk. He hasn't spoken since the tumor-removing brain surgery he got the day we met him five years ago.

Even a one-way conversation would be nice. I ask him, "Would you like me to explain what's going on?"

He turns back to the window, which I interpret as a yes.

I tell him, "Until last night I was convinced that Ying would follow in Origen's footsteps and try to kill me. But instead of confronting her about it, I tried to outsmart her. That made things worse.

"I was seeing everything she did as a personal attack against me." I lean forward. "But now I've realized that Ying wasn't attacking me. She—no, not just her. *Everybody* is afraid of me and my past. And they should be afraid. My soul line ancestor was evil, and even now I can feel her influencing me."

That hurts, but it needs to be said.

"Meanwhile, Ying got herself mixed up with bad people from BiggerGuns. We're flying back to Sterling to help Scott rescue her. And then we'll kick BiggerGuns out of Soul Identity before they ruin everything."

I reach out and take his hand. "Did that make sense, Mr. Morgan?"

He faces me. I peer into his eyes, but I don't see even a glimmer of understanding.

"And just so you know, our plane doesn't have a pilot right now," I tell him. "Simon got it in the air, but he's passed out, right over there."

I point, and Mr. Morgan stares at Simon.

"He's had a rough day," I say. "Drugged, stunned, and then I screwed up and kept him in his vike too long. I guess he needs a good nap to recover."

Mr. Morgan swings his head back to me, and I think it's best that he can't understand what I'm saying.

"The good news is that this plane is flying itself," I say. "Nobody's controlling it. Nobody's watching it. It's scary, but it's also okay. When we get closer, I'll try to wake up Simon. If he can't wake up, I'll press the autoland button. You don't have to worry about anything."

It helps to put words to my own anxiety.

His gaze has dropped into my lap, and I touch his chin to guide his head up so I can look into his blue eyes.

"You're kind of like this Soul Identity plane, Mr. Morgan. You've been flying on autopilot for the past five years. But don't worry about that either. We'll get the organization through this rough patch. We'll help Scott with his plan, and together we'll rescue Ying. We'll save your magic garden from the bad guys. And meanwhile, you'll keep living, breathing, flying along, staying alive until we can handle things ourselves."

Just talking it through gives me a sense of peace.

Mr. Morgan smiles at me, and he twists his body to stare out the window again.

We sit still for a while, holding hands, saying nothing. When I feel calm enough, I let go of his hand and kiss his cheek.

"Thanks for listening to me," I say.

"Be strong, Flora," he whispers.

My heart feels like it'll leap out of my chest. "Mr. Morgan, you can speak!"

But he's quiet, leaving me wondering if I imagined his response.

Did he mistake me for a young Madame Flora?

His lips move, but I can't hear anything. I bring my head down lower, my ear as close to his mouth as I can get.

"Xanazo," he breathes. "Help me."

I pull back. "You want to vike?"

He blinks at me with his watery eyes.

Was that a yes?

The monitor shows we have ninety minutes of flight time left. Both Val and Simon are sound asleep. And despite the reassurances I just gave Mr. Morgan, I have no idea if this plane will land.

This could be the last ninety minutes of our lives.

If Simon can learn how to fly a jet, if Ying can become obsessed with power, and if I can feel Lillia shaping my thoughts, then a soul line ancestor from Mr. Morgan's past might bring him something in this waning time he has left.

"Let's do it," I tell him.

I help him undress. His paperwhite skin is covered with freckles and moles, hanging loose over the bones beneath. He starts to shiver, and I find a blanket to pull over our legs. I wrap myself tight against his body once I get his creaky legs and arms into place.

Sole to sole, palm to palm, skin to skin. My chin on his bony shoulder.

"When you get to the Gallery of Past Lives, fly around a bit," I say. "It's easy. Touch the longer ribbons of light to find one you like. Then jump into it, feet first."

I have no idea what he heard or what he understood. I ask him to chant with me, but he stays silent, and I chant the oms alone. I talk him through relaxing, and I guide him through drawing our organization's old logo.

And wonder of wonders, I'm in vike space, which means the xanazo worked.

While I wait in the darkness, I think about what Mr. Morgan might be doing, who he might be observing. He's only the third in his overseer line, but he may have a bunch of unrecovered soul line ancestors to choose from.

Val told us that Mr. Morgan's brain surgery erased all his memories, but he called me Flora. Maybe they're not erased after all, just hard for him to access.

Will the vike help him recover his own thoughts? Or load up somebody else's?

I wait in the empty vike space for as long as I can. When I feel anxious, I start a slow spin on my hovering disc, and I count the rotations. I reach three thousand, and I jump off the disc to end the vike.

I open my eyes and find myself back in the main cabin. Val and Simon are still asleep. The flight monitor shows we have twenty minutes left. From my ears and the tilt of the plane, I can tell that the autopilot has started our descent. If I can't wake up Simon, I'll have to activate the autoland.

Unfortunately, now Mr. Morgan is also unconscious. I shake his shoulder, but he doesn't wake up, even though I push and pull his arms and legs to get his clothes back on. He's not heavy, and I'm able to carry him back to his seat and strap the seatbelt across his lap.

Fifteen minutes to go. I try again to wake up Simon, but he's not budging. I slap his face, pinch his legs, blow in his ear, shout at him, but he's sound asleep.

I wake up Val and tell her to keep trying with Simon. Then I go to the cockpit to figure out how to get this plane landed. Before we crash.

Fifty-six

Seven minutes left. We're close enough to the ground that I can make out streetlights and car headlights piercing the darkness below.

I've moved to the left pilot's seat. If I'm reading the altimeter right, we're at two thousand feet. There are several panel lights blinking and at least two different kinds of urgent alarms whooping at me, but nothing makes any sense.

I press the autoland button on the flight control system. The instrument panels go dark, and the alarms stop.

The silence is better than all that clamor. Or is it?

"Val!" I call. "Is Simon awake?"

"I'm still trying," she calls.

"You'd better come up here with me."

A minute later she enters the cockpit. "Why's everything dark? Where's the instrument lights?"

"They all went out."

"That can't be good."

She sits in the co-pilot's seat and straps herself in. "What did you do?"

I point to the autoland button. "I pressed that."

She pulls out her phone and uses its light to shine on the button. "It says to press twice to confirm."

"I only pressed once," I say.

She presses, and the main display lights up with the word AUTOLAND filling the screen in big, black letters.

A female computer voice says, "Emergency autoland activated. The airplane is being controlled by the emergency autoland system and will land at the closest airport. Please do not touch any of the flight controls. Your destination is . . ."

Ten agonizing seconds crawl by.

". . . Worcester Regional Airport."

I slump back in my seat. "It worked."

"You did it, Zelly."

"Let's hold the congratulations until we're on the ground."

The side display suggests that we contact ATC, which I assume means the air traffic controllers. I pick up the radio and press the microphone button.

"Is anybody out there?"

"Worcester Regional Airport ATC," a lady's voice says. "We see you are attempting an autoland. What is your emergency?"

"Our pilot is unconscious and won't wake up," I say.

"Are you the co-pilot?"

I say to Val, "I have to tell him something."

She shrugs.

I key the radio microphone. "The co-pilot is also unconscious. I looked in the flight manual and found the autoland button. Please, don't let us die."

"You'll be fine, ma'am," the ATC lady says. "Your landing gear is down. You're going the proper speed. You're on an appropriate flight path, and we have no cross winds tonight. Just don't touch anything, and you'll be on the ground in a jiffy."

The computer voice tells us to put on our seatbelts and stow any loose luggage. Val leaves to buckle up Simon. When she returns, the screen says we're landing in two minutes.

"I tried to wake up Mr. Morgan, but he's also fast asleep," she says.

"He talked to me, Val. He called me Flora."

She shakes her head. "He hasn't spoken in five years."

"I didn't imagine it," I say. "It was just a whisper. He asked me to xanazo."

"He what?"

"He wanted to xanazo. I got him into vike space, and I left him there for at least a half hour. But he didn't wake up when I ended it."

After a moment of her looking at me with unblinking bug eyes, she laughs. "I don't know what to say, Zelly. Other than good for him. Maybe when he wakes up, he'll tell us what happened."

The monitor says ten seconds. I reach out and grab her hand, and the plane hits the runway with a jarring impact. But we're still alive. The reverse thrusters engage, and we roll to a stop.

Val takes off her seatbelt and gives me a hug. "Thank you, Zelly. You got us here in one piece."

"Simon got us in the air," I say. "And the autoland got us down."

"Don't sell yourself short."

I don't know if it's short. In my mind, all I've done in the past two weeks is make things worse for everyone. Getting Ying stuck, stealing a car, zapping Simon, and sending him off the end of a vike ribbon.

Because of me, both Simon and Mr. Morgan lie unconscious in the passenger cabin.

The autoland has left us parked at the far end of the runway. An ambulance, lights flashing in the dark, heads our way.

"We have to get out of here before they come," I say.

Val gestures with her thumb over her shoulder. "We won't be able to carry them."

"Let's leave them," I say. "We can rescue them tomorrow."

She hesitates for a second, but then she nods. "If we strap them in up here, it'll add to the general confusion."

We scramble to the back and carry Simon and Mr. Morgan into the cockpit, buckling them into the pilot seats. Just as we finish, the ambulance arrives.

I hand Val a pair of sunglasses. "We still need these."

She puts them on, then pulls on the door's lever to open it. She lowers the staircase and calls to the two paramedics below, "The pilot and co-pilot are both unconscious. Come quickly!"

The paramedics run up the stairs and into the cockpit. Val and I hustle down the stairs, make a U-turn under the plane, cross the runway, and strike out through the grass. I give her a boost over a fence, and I scramble up and over it myself. We jog down a slight hill and into the woods.

I check my phone and point to the left. "There's a road about a mile that way."

Twenty minutes later we reach Mulberry Street, surrounded by nothing but pine trees. Val uses her phone to request an Uber.

"Hey, who was our driver last time?" she asks.

"Boubacar. He was afraid Mr. Morgan was going to die."

She grins. "He must be the only XL driver in the area. Three minutes."

Fifty-seven

When Boubacar's car appears, we step into the road and flag him down.

We climb in the backseat, and Boubacar taps his phone. "We're heading to Soul Identity?"

"Yes," Val says. "No . . . Hang on. I'm searching for a restaurant close to the campus that's open."

"Good luck with that," he says. "Sterling rolled up its sidewalks an hour ago."

"Found one. I'll put it in the app."

Boubacar checks his phone. "You sure you two ladies want to go to a tavern?"

"It's our only choice," Val says.

Hold on, why am I letting Val make these decisions? If we follow her risk-adverse instincts, we'll never rescue Ying and we won't be able to stop BiggerGuns.

I need to take charge.

I put my hand on Val's leg. "You can't go to Soul Identity."

She presses her lips together.

"If they capture either you or Mr. Morgan, they'll have unanimous consent. That's game over."

She sighs.

I point up the hill at the flashing red lights. "Boubacar, please follow that ambulance."

Boubacar looks at Val, and when she nods, he shifts into gear and executes a U-turn. He drives toward the airport, but as we get close, the ambulance speeds out of the entrance with its lights flashing.

Boubacar accelerates to keep up, and soon the ambulance turns into the emergency room entrance of St. Vincent's Hospital.

We watch the paramedics pull two rolling stretchers out of the back and wheel them inside.

Simon and Mr. Morgan are unconscious because of what I did. But that has become Val's problem, because only I can rescue Ying.

I ask her, "You'll get them somewhere safe?"

She nods.

"I'll find Scott and we'll bring Ying out of there. Trust me."

She stares at me. "Can I really trust you, Zelly?"

"Why would you ask me that?"

She sighs. "Let's see. You lied about trapping Ying in her vike. You stole a car and ran away. You and Simon viked, several times, after I asked you not to. And it seems Lillia is influencing you in ways I don't understand."

I cross my arms. "I was right about Ying. She tried to capture us. Running away led us to BiggerGuns. And all those vikes just flew your plane to Sterling."

We both look at each other, and I see she still has doubt in her eyes.

I reach out and squeeze her hands. "I'd do anything to save Soul Identity. You must know that."

She nods. "I do. Now go. Find Scott. Rescue Ying. We'll figure the rest out." She taps on her phone. "I changed your destination back to the guest house. I was going to scope things out first, but if you're alone, you might as well just head there. Go to the first maintenance shed on your way to the main building. There's a reader inside. It opens a door that takes you to our bunker."

"Bunker?"

"It's for situations like this."

"If you have a bunker, why didn't we go there last week?"

"We didn't know if Ying had access."

"But now you know?"

"Scott verified that nobody's been there. It's safe." She turns to Boubacar. "Keep the fare rolling. Come back for me once you drop her off."

"Yes, ma'am," he says.

We both get out. I give her a hug. She heads into the hospital, and I move to the front seat.

Boubacar shifts into drive and glances at me. "You were part of that big group I picked up last Sunday. With the old man I thought was gonna die."

"I was."

"Did he live?"

"So far."

"Good," he says. "Oh, and I deposited your phones in the mailbox. Did you receive them?"

"Not yet. But we've been busy."

We drive in silence.

Then he asks, "If I may ask, why did you return to Sterling?"

I look at him. "To take back what's ours."

"Bad people took it from you?"

"The worst."

"I have some experience with bad people," he says. "Mostly back in my home country. And now bad people are showing up here."

"Here in Sterling?"

"Right here. They arrived this week. I just brought four of them to the same tavern you were going to. They are full of swagger, and they have military haircuts, tattoos, and concealed weapons."

I didn't think of it earlier, but there must be plenty of BiggerGuns people all around Sterling these days.

"Were they coming from Soul Identity?" I ask.

He nods. "From the guest house. They were rude, talked to me like I was an idiot, and left me no tip."

"Jerks."

He faces me, his eyes wide. "I am happy you're not going to that tavern by yourself."

As we reach the Soul Identity campus entrance, Boubacar asks, "If you succeed, what will you do to the bad people?"

"I want to kill them."

He looks at me. "But you won't, will you?"

I shake my head. "I suppose we'll just chase them away."

Boubacar sighs. "They will become bad somewhere else."

I frown. "What would you do?"

"That's easy. My people are the Jola, so I'd show them the Jola Way."

"Jola?"

"It means payback. We Jola are renowned for it, whether for good or evil deeds. We always pay back. It is our way."

"What if these bad people stole your money?"

"I would steal theirs."

"And if they tried to destroy your company?"

"I would destroy theirs."

"And if they helped you?"

"I would help them," he says. "The Jola Way means I must always pay them back."

I toss that idea around for a minute. "An eye for an eye."

"As long as it's kept to just one eye." He wags his finger in a circle. "If you take my eye and I take both of yours, then you will pay me back even more. The cycle never ends."

"But if you don't escalate, it's over?"

"It is." He smiles. "The magic of the Jola Way. No holding of grudges. No remembering of ancient history."

Soul Identity is built on the promise of being able to remember your history and carry over your grudges. Could the Jola Way work for our members?

Probably not. But we overseers could apply the Jola Way to how we deal with each other.

We arrive at the guest house, and I ask Boubacar to continue past the driveway and stop next to a large maple tree sheltering us from the windows.

I put on my sunglasses and get out. "Thanks for the lesson, Boubacar."

"The Jola Way. Give it a try." He drives off.

I walk down the dark street, toward the main Soul Identity building. After a couple hundred yards, I spot a tiny maintenance shack in the middle of a well-lit lawn on my right.

I dart across the grass, open the door, and step inside.

The shack isn't much bigger than one of those old telephone booths, and it has no windows. When I close the door, it's pitch-black.

I take off my sunglasses and pull out my phone's flashlight. The room has a row of rakes and shovels hanging on hooks, a garden hose on a reel, an extension cord, and stacked boxes of light bulbs. On the wall closest to me, I find a shelf with gardening gloves and two pollen masks. An overwhelming smell of fresh-cut grass gives me the urge to sneeze.

I shift the pollen masks to one side and see a small black reader with a tiny blue light shining in between two plastic lenses. I maneuver the garden hose reel and climb on top of it. I stand on my tiptoes, and I'm just able to get my eyes up to the lenses.

It beeps.

A faint thump and the middle of the floor slides open, leaving a two-foot-wide opening. Ladder rungs descend into the darkness on the far side.

I step into the hole and onto the top ladder rung. When I drop below floor level, I see a red-lit button on the ceiling. I press it, the ceiling slides shut, and the button's light blinks out.

Twenty rungs down and I touch bottom. My phone's light helps me spot a wall switch. I stand in a concrete hallway, pipes and electrical conduit running overhead, puddles of water on the edges of the floor. A closed door is at the end of the hallway fifty yards ahead.

That must be the bunker. I walk down the hallway and put my eyes up to the reader mounted on the wall.

The door swings open. Inside is a large room with a high ceiling, four desks with their own computers and screens, and a row of clocks on the wall. Large flatscreens hang from the ceiling, cycling through various surveillance videos.

Two people sit at the desks, their backs to me. They turn. It's George and Sue.

George is wearing my modded eyeglasses. "Look who decided to show up," he says. "Come on in, Giselle Oliveira. We could use the help."

Fifty-eight

"What are you guys doing here?" I ask Sue.

"Scott sent us to meet you."

"Last week you were retired, cooking us meals."

She smiles. "Before I learned to cook, I ran operational security for Soul Identity. Scott asked us to help him out, so here we are."

I nod. "What's his plan?"

"He's opening a gate forty minutes from now so we can extract Ying."

Good news: Val was right. Scott's building his Trojan Horse.

Bad news: If he's that predictable, it means that Giovanni will figure this out and warn BiggerGuns.

"We got here two hours ago," George says. "We've been building out our situational awareness. Didn't even have time to eat."

I look around the room. "What is this place, anyway?"

"It used to be the boiler room," George says. "Until we got rid of the steam heating back in the eighties and sealed it off. Twelve years ago, after the mess with WorldWideSouls, I had it built out as a command center in case we ever needed it. We call it the bunker."

"Just like the White House," Sue says. "Except not quite as far underground."

"And no nuclear football," George says. "But other than that, we can monitor what happens in Sterling and in our offices around the world. We have phones, full internet, and Wi-Fi. Beds and a kitchen. Even a bathroom with a shower. But that's not the best part."

I raise my eyebrows. "There's a best part?"

"Nobody else knows about this place. Just the overseers and Val. And Scott. And Sue and me. Now you. We're safe here, hidden in the belly of the beast."

It doesn't sound like we're all that hidden. And we don't need to be safe. We need to find Scott and rescue Ying.

"Have you seen Scott on the surveillance?" I ask.

"We have." Sue types on the keyboard in front of her and points to the monitor over her head. On the screen, Scott and his parents sit in chairs around a small table. "They're in the dungeon, in Val's old office, not doing much of anything."

"Why would they be put down there?"

"No idea," George says.

"Do you have a recording?"

"We run a professional operation. Of course we have a recording. Sue, can you show it on the overhead?"

Sue brings up a video stream on the other monitor. "What are you looking for?"

"I'd like to know what they're doing," I say.

Sue plays it back at high speed, and it shows Scott and his parents sitting pretty much like they are now.

How can they open a gate just by sitting there?

I ask Sue, "Does the dungeon give Scott access to things he can't reach from outside?"

"The alarm, automation, and video surveillance systems are all housed down there. They're firewalled from the internet."

"So those are the gates," I say.

She nods. "He must have needed three sets of hands to pull it off."

We cycle through the live video surveillance from around the campus, but other than an occasional guard, the buildings are empty.

"Has Scott contacted you since you got here?" I ask.

They both shake their heads. "We sent him an email, but he hasn't answered," George says.

I pull out my phone and send a message to Scott, saying that I'm in the bunker with George and Sue.

When my phone buzzes, it's Jeremy, not Scott. He wants a video call.

I walk to the far side of the room, so he won't be able to see where I am, and I stab at the answer button. Jeremy appears on the screen, and he gives me a smile.

"I was hoping to never see you again," I say.

His smile fades away. "Look, all I can say is that I'm sorry."

"When I needed an ally, you betrayed me. You were supposed to be the good guy."

His eyebrows go way up. "What are you talking about? I armed you with a stun baton. And a knife."

"Which you then held to Simon's throat."

"I had to keep Giovanni thinking I was on his side. He was watching us."

"Why would you be on his side?"

He drops his voice to just above a whisper. "So he doesn't ask his BiggerGuns pals to kill me." He leans forward. "I knew you were going to zap me, Zelly. I would never hurt you. Or Simon."

I want to believe his lies.

"Why did you call, Jeremy?"

"Believe it or not, I'm just a dude who wants to help."

I stare at him. "Where are you?"

"Still in the Idaho compound. Giovanni's going crazy. Says we're missing all the action. But we woke up from his stupid sandwiches too late to find a jet."

"I'm disconnecting, Jeremy. Is there anything else?"

"They intercepted a message from Scott to Val. They know about the bunker, and they're about to destroy it."

I try to keep my face expressionless. "What bunker?"

He closes his eyes for a second. "The one you're sitting in. I don't want to see you hurt, Zelly. Get out of there. Quickly."

Jeremy looks at something off the screen. His head jerks back, his mouth falls open, and he disconnects.

I put away my phone and turn to George and Sue. "They know about the bunker."

They both go rigid in their seats.

"They know about the bunker," George says. "Evacuate immediately!"

"What about Scott and his parents?" I ask.

"They still need to open the gate," Sue says. "We'll find another way to reach them."

"We've got to leave right now," George says. He heads to an exit on the opposite side of where I entered. We follow him into a hallway. George uses his eyes on a reader hanging next to a door on the right, and when it clicks open, he goes inside.

A few seconds later he bursts out, carrying a wooden box that's the size of a desk's center drawer. He hands me the box and hurries down the hallway. At almost the end, he points to a ladder on the left.

"Climb up," he says.

I hesitate for a second. Does George know where he's going?

Up is farther from immediate danger, and it's likely closer to the gates Scott will open. I tuck the box under one arm and climb. At the top along the ceiling is a red button. I juggle the box, press the button, and the ceiling slides open. I climb through, which isn't that easy to do without handholds.

I use my phone to light up the space. It's another maintenance shed but bigger. Instead of gardening tools, it contains drums of oil and boxes of automobile parts. Instead of fresh-cut grass, it smells like gasoline.

I help Sue into the room, and the two of us hoist George up by his armpits when he climbs to the top of the ladder.

I open the door a crack and get a view of Soul Identity's parking lot. It's almost empty.

George hands me a set of car keys. "See the plain white van out there? That's ours."

We burst out of the shed and run to the van. I unlock the door as I get close. We hop in, with me in the driver's seat. I set the box down and drive toward the parking lot exit.

"We have to figure out what gates Scott will open," I say. "Do you have a place we can go?"

George points. "The guest house. We can reconnoiter from my old gadget room."

Fifty-nine

Three guards stand outside the guest house, and that means we can't stop. I drive past them and turn around at the next intersection.

"Your gadget room is as poorly kept a secret as the bunker," Sue tells George.

"How do they always know where we're going?" he asks.

I return to the parking lot. We're down to six minutes before Scott opens whatever his gates are. I ask, "Do you guys have any weapons?"

George points to the box he had me carry out of the bunker. "Open that up."

I lift the lid and pull out a short crowbar and a flashlight from a Styrofoam inset.

I hold them up, one in each hand. "These are your weapons?"

"That's all I have," George says. "Back in the day, we'd have been well-armed. The drones would be up, and we'd be watching infrared and heartbeat monitors from the bunker. We'd have won already."

I take a deep breath and try to unwind the knot in my stomach. Scott is counting on us to burst through the gates he's opening, but we have no base, no weapons, no way to coordinate with him. Meanwhile, Sue is distracted by George, who is stuck reliving the glories of his past.

I've got four minutes to get this rescue back on track.

"I'm going to the dungeon," I say to Sue. "You want to come with me?"

She sighs. "George can't go in there, and I can't leave him out here by himself."

I nod, trying to keep my sense of relief from showing.

"You've got this, Zelly," she says. "You can do this alone."

But I'm not alone. I've got Lillia to call on. If she has indeed infected parts of my thinking, she can help me survive.

"What's the best way to reach the dungeon?" I ask George.

"You can go in the main lobby and take the elevator down, but that way is exposed. You're better off using the fire exit next to the loading docks."

He hands me the crowbar. "The door is locked from the outside, but this should get you in."

I check my phone. It's three minutes until midnight. I walk across the parking lot and around the building toward the loading docks.

But two guards stand on the docks, and they carry machine guns in their arms. My crowbar is the knife at a gunfight. My plan has been thwarted. Again.

I want to scream. Over the last five days I stole a car, drove two thousand miles, sweet-talked Jeremy and Giovanni, learned to xanazo, escaped a sexual assault, almost killed Simon and Mr. Morgan, and landed a jet. There must be a way to overcome these two guards.

But if there is a way, I don't know it, and neither, apparently, does Lillia. There's nobody left who can help create a diversion. And as much as I'd like to be the action hero, I'm not going to sprint, unarmed, toward blazing machine guns.

I retreat before the guards can spot me, hating every step I take back to the parking lot. But as I round the corner of the building and see the main entrance, I realize how stupid I am. Why am I wasting time trying to open the gates myself? That's Scott's job, and he's doing it at midnight.

Midnight is right now. And the gates, which can only refer to the main entrance, are right in front of me. If Scott and his parents did their job, I can walk right in.

Of course, if Scott didn't succeed, I'm dead.

Lillia wouldn't walk in. In fact, I feel a chunk of my brain, probably occupied by her, screaming at me, telling me that Ying isn't worth saving. That it's better to stay alive, to live to fight another day.

But the rest of me disagrees. I drop the crowbar, take a deep breath, and walk up to the main entrance.

The front doors open as I reach them, and I step into the two-story lobby. Mr. Morgan's and Ying's portraits stare at me from above the empty reception desk. Nobody sits on the lobby furniture.

I veer to the right, over to the employees-only entrance. The door gives a click as I come close, and I don't need a badge or my eyes to pull it open and walk down the hallway.

I round the corner. The elevator door is closed. I press the down arrow, and the door slides open. I push the button for the basement, and the elevator hums as it descends.

In the basement, a wall placard tells me the datacenter is toward the right, so I go left. Again, the door clicks just before I reach it, and I pull it open.

I walk down the center of the hallway and peek in the first window on the right. Scott and his parents are facing me, sitting in front of three separate monitors. I rush past the window and through the door.

Scott leaps to his feet and gives me a big hug. He pulls back, and his face breaks out into a wide grin. "You made it!"

"She almost didn't," Scott's mom says. "I thought for sure she was going to rush those guards by the loading dock. With just that crowbar."

"Yet here she is," Scott's dad says. "Right on schedule."

"Here I am," I say. "You opened the gates. Let's rescue Ying."

Scott shakes his head. "You must go by yourself."

Sixty

"It takes all three sets of our hands to keep you safe," Scott says.

"Seriously?" I ask.

"It's why we let them capture us."

"Check this out." Scott's mom gestures to her monitor. "I keep the good guys off the videos." She shows how she is making me and the monitors disappear from the video of this room, and how George's van can't be seen from any of the parking lot cameras.

"My job is to clear the alarms and open the doors," Scott's dad shows me how the automation controls can be overridden. "When those doors clicked as you approached? That was me."

"And I reroute the BiggerGuns guards," Scott says. "I have most of them busy breaking into the bunker. I sent the rest of them to protect the gadget room and the loading docks."

"You meant for your message to get intercepted," I say.

"I told you all that I was clearing the gates," he says. "I don't know why everybody wanted to run their own operation."

I shake my head. "And here I thought BiggerGuns was being brilliant. You sent them to us."

"I was keeping the gates open so you can get to Ying," he says. "Which is what you need to do. Before everybody comes back."

"Where is she?"

"The overseer floor."

"What's she doing here so late at night?"

"She lives in her suite. It's a golden prison cage, and she doesn't even know it."

"Where's Val?" Scott's dad asks. "We thought she'd be with you."

"I told her not to come," I say.

"And she listened?" Scott asks.

"She agreed that we'll lose if BiggerGuns has both her and Ying."

"Good thinking, Zelly," Scott says.

Funny that I don't feel a buzz when Scott compliments me. I guess a lot has changed since last week.

It's still nice to know that he likes my decision.

I tell him, "We had to leave Mr. Morgan and Simon on the plane once we landed, so she followed them to the hospital."

"Why the hospital?"

"They were both unconscious."

I don't tell him that it was my fault.

"Who'd you get to fly the plane?"

"Simon figured it out. He learned from his vikes."

He opens his mouth, pauses, and waves his hand in dismissal. "You'll have to explain everything later. Get Ying first. She's in the office suite across from Val's."

"Does she want to be rescued?" I ask.

"She'd better want rescuing," Scott's mom says. "After all we've done."

"Convince her if you have to," Scott says. "Just so you know, there are no cameras in the suites. You'll be on your own."

"Can you get us out of the building?"

He nods. "We'll create a small diversion in ten minutes. I'll text you."

"What if she won't come?"

"Just make her come," he says.

"Mamão com açúcar," I say. Papayas with sugar.

Scott raises his eyebrows.

"Piece of cake."

"Let's hope it is." He reaches out and grips both of my shoulders. "Be smart, Zelly. And see you soon."

Why would he tell me to be smart? Can he sense how weak and unprepared I feel? How I regret not having a better plan?

I used to think my impulsiveness was my superpower. Now it's going to get me killed.

With all three members of the Waverly family keeping me electronically invisible, I feel like a ghost as I walk down the hall, through the door, to the elevator, up to the third floor, into the marble foyer.

Not a ghost but a doomed prisoner heading to her execution. I walk away from the depositary toward the overseer offices.

Scott's dad does his job too well. All the doors click open without giving me enough time to prepare. Before I'm ready, I stand in the hall outside of Ying's suite.

My phone buzzes, and it's a message from Scott. "Eight minutes before our diversion," it says.

I open the door and enter Ying's office.

She's not at her desk, which is raised to standing height. Her computer is awake and logged in. I walk over to see what's on the screen. Her email app shows boring business summaries, and her messaging app shows she's been chatting to somebody named GJudd.

Giovanni resurfaces.

I'm not surprised that Ying is talking to him, but his name on the screen puts a roar in my ears and a numbness in my body. An image of this morning's session flashes in my head. How he sat naked on Jeremy's bed, growing a boner, thinking he's so clever, using his power over me.

I also feel shame how I acted, how I puxei o saco dele, kissed his butt, until Simon and I could escape. Seeing his name makes me want to zap him again, right over the internet. Forget those eyeglasses I built. I need to invent a remote stun baton for dealing with creeps like Giovanni.

I lower the desk just enough for me to reach the trackpad and keyboard, and I scroll back to see what he's been telling Ying.

They first chatted on Tuesday afternoon. Giovanni brags that Simon and I are coming to his place. He wants to impress us, and he asks her what our favorite foods are. Ying tells him our sandwich preferences. Sneaky.

Giovanni is just as sugar-sweet to Ying as he was to Simon and me. He showers her with compliments about how smart and accomplished and insightful she is. He tells her that he's thrilled to work for her, and he asks what else he can do to make her life better.

And he lies to her. When Ying asks him on Wednesday night for an update on us, he tells her not to worry. That we're spending the night with him. On Thursday morning, he claims that he tracked down Val and Mr. Morgan all by himself and that he's directed the pilots to divert the jet to Idaho so they can capture us.

I scroll through his falsehoods, looking for how he explains Simon's and my escape after I zapped him when he tried to get me naked. All Giovanni tells Ying is that he sent us away when we displeased him and that she shouldn't worry about us anymore.

I can't blame him for trying to make himself look good.

Coming to the present time, a little less than an hour ago, Ying tells Giovanni that Val and I are headed to Sterling, but that she's been assured by Adam that the situation is well under control. BiggerGuns has intercepted Scott's email to Val that talks about a rendezvous with George and Sue at a bunker and at a gadget room. The email shows an attack plan of Val and me entering Soul Identity through the loading dock.

That was the end of the chat. The indicator shows that Giovanni is typing. I wait a few seconds, and his new message pops up.

Giovanni asks if Val and I have been caught yet.

I'm about to answer, but Ying's reply appears first. "Not yet. Should be soon."

Ying must be chatting from her phone. Where is she?

"Are you protected?" Giovanni writes.

"I'm in bed, safe and sound," she types back. "I'll let you know when it's over."

Ying is one room away.

Sixty-one

Ying is not a hostage.

And she has her phone in hand. I may not be able to rush into her room fast enough to prevent her from letting BiggerGuns know that I'm here.

My best chance is to keep her occupied, so I pull out my phone just as another message arrives from Scott. "Four minutes," it says.

I dismiss his message and send Ying a text. "Hey, it's Zelly. Can I call?"

She answers right away. "K."

I call her, and just as she answers, I kick open her door, rush to the bed, jump on top of her, rip the phone out of her hands, and throw it on the floor.

This will just make it harder for her to trust me, but I can't have her alerting BiggerGuns.

Ying lets out a scream, pulls my hair, and kicks at my legs, but I hang onto her.

"Girlie, it's me," I say. "Just stop for a minute."

She stiffens. "Zelly?"

"Who else would it be?"

She's remains still and silent. Then, "Let me up."

"You're not going to call anybody?"

"Of course not."

I let her go, and I retrieve her phone, shut it off, and put it in my pocket.

"Give me that," she says.

I shake my head. "We need to talk. And we need to escape. Can you get dressed?"

"Escape? I thought you had come to kill me." She crosses her arms. "Why would I leave?"

"Don't tell me you're letting BiggerGuns destroy Soul Identity on purpose."

"Is that what you think they're doing?"

"They're shifting our money. Firing our employees. What would you call it?"

She grabs my hand, and her fingers are warm on mine. "Zelly, this may be hard for you to accept, but BiggerGuns is saving us."

I pull away. "Saving us from what?"

She grabs my hand again, this time with both of hers. "From Mr. Morgan. From Val. From you and Simon. And everybody else who wants to keep Soul Identity powerless. BiggerGuns is helping me restart and refocus our beautiful organization, before the decline makes it too late."

Restart? Refocus?

"Do you mean something like what Origen did?"

She takes a deep breath. "You viked again?"

I nod.

"Then yes, exactly like that," she says. "If Origen hadn't pulled Psychen Euporos out of Alexandria, we would have collapsed when the city burned."

"He tried to hand us over to the church. Tell me how that was any better."

She lets go of my hand and switches on the lamp. She's in her pajamas, her hair in curlers. "He used the church to grow, so we'd become known throughout the world. Just like I'm using BiggerGuns."

Doesn't she know that the church betrayed Origen? And that Lillia had to kill him?

Maybe she hasn't viked all the way to the end of his life.

But maybe she has, and she's testing me. I had better come clean.

"When I overheard you telling Scott that you viked back to Egypt," I say, "I got scared that you were going to kill me, just like I assumed Origen killed the Alexandria overseers. But that was before I knew better."

She bites her lower lip.

I swallow the saliva that's gathering in the back of my mouth. "You told me and Simon that you viked into Philo, but we knew you were lying. I sabotaged your second vike because I didn't want you to wake up until I figured out how to protect myself. I'm so sorry I did that."

She takes my hand again and says, "When I woke up from that first vike, I already knew that the Delphians killed the Alexandrian overseers and that they had recruited Lillia of Cagliari. I saw her missing finger, and I realized she was your soul line ancestor."

I whisper, "I didn't learn about Lillia's recruitment by the Delphians until this week."

She squeezes my fingers. "You know, I begged Val to stop you from viking, so you wouldn't get any ideas from Lillia on how to kill me."

I was right about Ying's fear of me and my past.

As we sit there, it occurs to me that both Ying and I went into self-preservation mode and acted before we bothered to verify anything or talk to each other.

So much for Val's lesson on most respectful interpretations.

My phone buzzes, but I ignore it.

While still holding her hands, I ask, "How will we find a way forward without killing each other?"

She shakes her head. "Can we?"

"Not if we continue to act like we're Origen and Lillia." I sigh. "I hate what my soul line ancestor did to yours."

"But Lillia eventually redeemed herself, didn't she?"

I nod, but I catch myself. "Wait, what did you say?"

"Lillia redeemed herself." She cocks her head to the side. "You don't know?"

"No. Tell me."

"You'll just have to vike back and see for yourself."

"Did you vike until the end?"

She shakes her head. "I didn't get that far. And you and Val have all the vike portals."

I wonder if the promise of another vike can convince her to leave. "Our chance to exit comes in two minutes. If you want to vike again, let's go."

"You need to vike, not me," she says. "I don't have time for that anymore. I need to make sure Soul Identity gets stronger and more visible than it's ever been. That's my job now—to make us better."

I let go of her hands and walk over to the window. The fields are lit up and at least ten guards march from the direction of the guest house toward our building.

"Ying, come here."

She stands next to me, and I ask, "How is our campus overflowing with guards carrying machine guns better?"

"Those guards make us powerful. BiggerGuns funnels money to game-changing events all over the world. We're choosing who leads which countries, and who's overthrown. Everyone will know us, and we'll be back as the global power brokers."

"Why do we want to do that?"

"Because that's our job as overseers," she says. "Thales just wanted to make money, but Cyrus understood that we could help him rule the world. Origen got it, too. But since those days, we've been coasting down a long and slow slope of decline."

Ying thinks just like Origen.

Another buzz on my phone. Scott says we've only got a minute, and to get ready.

I say, "I need to get out of here before your BiggerGuns guys catch me. You should come, too."

She waves her arms like she's brushing me off. "Go, Zelly. Escape if you must. I'll handle the dirty work that's needed to restore Soul Identity to its former glory."

The power has corrupted her, and Ying's lost her head.

Maybe it's BiggerGuns' fault for giving her the means. Or it's Giovanni's fault for egging her on. Or Val's fault for not teaching us better and for not anticipating this.

Maybe it's nobody's fault but Ying's.

It's not going to be my fault for not stopping her. She's ruining everything.

I size her up. I can take her. I can grab her by those ridiculous hair curlers and pull her down the hallway, into the elevator, and out the front doors. Scott can help me from there, and we can clean up the leftover BiggerGuns guards and end this nightmare.

I play it out in my mind, and it's beautiful. If I start right now, I can do this.

But I won't. If I give up on Ying, I'll have to run Soul Identity without her, and I don't want that. Both Ying and I were meant to be overseers.

I glance at my phone, and I choose to ignore Scott's "Where are you???" message.

I tell Ying, "I'm staying until we figure this out. Together."

Sixty-two

"There's nothing to figure out," Ying says. "Everything is going fine. Soul Identity hasn't been this powerful for many years."

I should just drag her out of this building. But it's too late for that.

The first step is to get us in sync with each other. We're both making assumptions after learning only part of the story. We need to see how it ends.

"How about this," I say. "We choose one day in the lives of Origen and Lillia. Once we've both viked it, we'll know what to do."

"Does that mean you have a vike portal with you?"

I shake my head. "We don't need a vike portal. Simon and I figured out how the ancients practiced xanazo. I can show you."

"Why would I need to vike?"

"I'm betting that once we see how Origen and Lillia's story ends, we'll stop disagreeing on what we need to do."

"I've already learned enough of their story."

"That's what you think. Your first vike was right around when Lillia arrived in Caesarea. Is that right?"

She nods. "It started in Alexandria. Origen visits an old friend, and she warns him that the Delphians are sending Lillia to Caesarea. Origen reaches home just in time to welcome her."

"I viked into that arrival, too. The first time Lillia meets Origen."

She bites her lip. "Um, Zelly. There's something else you need to be aware of."

I wave my hands. "That they're sleeping together? Yeah, I observed them. Old history."

Her mouth twitches. "Kind of embarrassing, huh?"

"I thought it was pretty sexy."

"They are . . . um . . ." Her eyes meet mine and dart away. "They're good together. Not just in bed. They make good partners."

"They do," I say. "Did your second vike continue from there?"

"It did. For five or six years. Origen gets the whole church behind him. He even convinces them to believe in reincarnation. He signs up the leaders as members. He's incredible, and it works, Zelly. The right move. Just like teaming up with BiggerGuns."

"Perhaps," I say. "But I want us to vike into the last day of Origen's life."

"Have you viked it already?"

I shake my head. "I got as far as their trip home from that council in Bostra."

She raises her eyebrows. "You rode in the carriage?"

I nod, and Ying smiles at me and mimes fanning her face.

I put my hands together. "Can we do this? Are you ready to learn how to xanazo?"

"You really think it will help?"

"I know it will. Because we'll get a shared understanding. And we'll be able to stop the past from controlling what happens to us. This is our life, Ying. It doesn't belong to Origen and Lillia."

She frowns. "They have much to teach us. Wisdom to offer."

"And we can learn from them. But we need to see how their story ends before we make any more decisions."

She closes her eyes for a moment, and then she nods.

"And when we've both viked, we'll figure out what happens next? Together?"

She smiles. "I can't wait for you to see what I've seen. Once you do, it will be good to have you as a partner. We don't have to work against each other."

That last comment of hers gives me doubt as to how open her mind is. But I'm going with the most respectful interpretation.

I just hope she does the same for me after she watches Lillia kill Origen.

Ying isn't thrilled with the idea of viking in our underwear, but I shut off the lights first, and we both undress in the semi-darkness. We climb onto her bed, with me resting up against her headboard and her sitting in front of me.

I show her how to cross her legs and arms. I press our soles and palms together, and I put my chin on her shoulder.

"I'm your guide," I say. "You'll be viking, and after a minute, which is about a day in vike time, I'll end it. Then you can guide me."

I press my chest tighter against her back, and it's like I'm pushing myself up against a wall. "You're so tense, Ying. Relax."

We spend a few minutes sitting still, breathing in unison, before her shoulders and back soften.

"Better?" I ask.

"This is perfect."

I squeeze her as best I can with my arms and legs. "I'm liking it, too." I sway, just the teensiest bit, side to side.

But even though this is nice, time is short.

"Start letting go of your senses. Join me in this." I start a low chant of ooommm, letting it flow out of my exhale and ending in a drawn-out hum. Ying joins me, and I adjust my pitch so we're in a sweet harmony.

I guide Ying through the process of blocking out her senses, taking it slow, savoring it. When all she has left is her hearing, I help her imagine she's drawing our ancient logo—the triangles, the eyes with their beautiful brows and lines and swirls.

And I'm alone in my empty vike space, standing on my hovering disc, already missing Ying, hoping I get my timing right, so she doesn't end up in the same end-of-ribbon void that I left Simon in. After counting to sixty, I jump off my disc and become aware of the room and of Ying in my arms.

She gives a little jerk, and she lets out a long breath.

"Zelly?"

"I'm here," I say. "What did you see?"

She's quiet for a moment. "You'd better experience it for yourself."

Well, at least she's not attacking me for what Lillia did.

I'm a little scared that she's going to get her revenge and leave me in the vike space until I fall off the ribbon. But I put that fear firmly behind me and trust that our last five years growing up together count for more than our shared past lives.

I explain about the empty vike space and how to end the xanazo session. I remind her to keep it short. When she's ready, we switch places, and it feels just as good as it did with me behind her.

I lean back and snuggle into her arms. I start the oms, and she joins in. She guides me all the way into my vike space, complete with its ribbons of light, the breeze caressing my skin, the barest scent of cinnamon wafting in the air, the soft chanting in the background.

I raise my disc up to Lillia's ribbon, and I feel my way to Origen's death. I back up along the ribbon until early that morning, and I jump in feet first.

Sixty-three

You lie down next to the man and stretch your arms far enough around his back to embrace him, squeezing his body tight against you.

"Good morning," you murmur.

"Let me sleep," he says.

You kiss his cheek. "Come on. Seize the day. Only old men and boys waste their days in bed."

"Sixty-nine is definitely an old man's age."

"Sixty-nine is young enough for me."

You stand up, stretch, and cross the room to the window. You lean over the table that sits underneath and open the shutters.

The sky is light blue and cloudless. The shadows across the garden are long. Two men comb through hanging vines, and you watch them collect the debris into a basket. You can smell fresh manure, and you hear birds singing.

Beyond the men is a stone wall, and beyond the wall, the sea glistens in the morning sun.

The man sits up, blinks his eyes, rubs his arms. "Can you help me rise?" he asks.

"Of course."

You cross the room to stand in front of him. He swings his lower body around, letting his legs touch the floor. You extend your arms, and you both grasp the other's forearms. He pulls, you pull, and he stands up.

"Thank you, darling."

He hobbles to the table, grasps a pitcher, and pours from it into a large clay cup. He drinks it all without taking a breath.

He breathes hard for a minute. "Have you had your water?"

You nod, and he puts the cup down. He pokes through the various scrolls that lie on the table.

"Are you coming to the office today?" you ask. "The new overseer should arrive this afternoon."

"I'll work from here. If the caravan does come, send somebody to get me. We can welcome him in style."

"I will." You wrap a green silk robe around yourself. "Don't forget you have a lecture tonight."

He leans a hand on the table. "What would my school do without me?"

You give him a kiss. "They survived just fine when you were imprisoned. Some would say they even grew bigger."

He splutters a retort, and you smile as you walk out the door.

The air is hot. A man in a dark green toga stands in front of the doorway of the building across from the garden. When you reach him, his bow brings his forehead almost to his knees.

"Ave, Lillia of Cagliari."

"Salve, Marcus. Origen will work from home this morning."

"Noted."

"What is on today's agenda?" you ask.

"Mostly approvals. We received a flood of requests for funding from Rome."

You grimace. "Plague-related?"

He nods. "None require unanimous consent."

"How very un-exciting."

"It gets better this afternoon. The caravan from the east arrives. Piles of silks, spices, and tea."

"And our new overseer."

"Something we're all anticipating."

You follow Marcus into the building. You pass through a curtain, walk down a hall, and enter a large room. A table stands in the center, and it's covered with scrolls.

You let out a sigh and sit down with Marcus. Together you review the scrolls, rejecting most of them but approving a handful. You drip wax from a candle onto each approved scroll and press the seal on your ring into the hot wax.

Hours later, Marcus says, "That was the last one, Madame."

You massage your sore hands. "Now I know why Origen chose to work from home."

Marcus chuckles. "He's clever that way. Shall I ask him to come over now? The caravan will arrive shortly."

"I'll talk to him. He may need some persuading."

You both stand up. Marcus bows, and you walk out of the building, across the garden, and to the room where you awoke.

You open the door. Origen sits on a stool at the table by the window, his left side toward you. A woman wearing a white toga lined in dark green stands behind him, her right hand pointing to a scroll lying open in front of him. A lit candle held in a stone candlestick sits on the table.

The woman's left hand holds a dagger against Origen's lower back, causing his white tunic to dimple.

"Seal it. Now," she says.

The woman presses against the dagger, and Origen arches his back. A red spot appears on the tunic, just under the tip of the knife.

"Never," he gasps.

"Tabitha!" you scream. "What are you doing?"

A dark scowl crosses her face, "Your job, Lillia. The one you never completed."

"Stop this at once!" you yell.

Tabitha twists the dagger, and Origen lets out a groan. The red spot grows.

"Seal the order," she yells. "Or I'll kill her as well."

"Fine," Origen says. He pulls the scroll toward him and grasps the candlestick in his left hand, which he tilts to drip wax onto the scroll. He maneuvers his right hand to the puddle of wax, turning his hand palm side up.

Tabitha watches, a smile on her face.

Origen presses the back of his hand toward the wax, and he whirls to his left, smashing the stone candlestick into the side of Tabitha's head. She lets out a cry and pushes hard against the dagger.

Origen gasps. Tabitha stumbles. You dart across the room and grab her by the throat, dragging her down to the floor.

Your fingers squeeze tight around her neck, and you feel her tendons, her muscles, her windpipe, her bones under her skin. Tabitha shakes back and forth, her hands pounding your shoulders, her fingers clawing at your eyes. She glares at you, her mouth moving, but no breath escapes.

You hang on to her neck and squeeze tighter until her movements slow to a stop. Her eyes lose focus, and you keep squeezing.

Origen groans, and you see his body slide toward the floor.

You release Tabitha's neck and grab him by the shoulders, easing him down onto his side.

"Lillia. My love." He reaches out with his hand and cups your cheek. "My back. It's bad."

You look over his side and down to his lower back. The dagger is embedded to its hilt. His tunic is soaked in blood, more puddling on the floor.

"I'll call a physician."

He shakes his head. "The Delphians." He winces. "They finally got me."

"Why now? I thought they were happy."

"They wanted an alliance. Read the scroll."

You stand up, open the scroll, and scan it.

You kneel next to him again. "They must have felt this was their last chance before the new overseer arrived."

Origen lets out a groan. "Very soon you will be in charge."

You shake your head. "I just got you healthy again. You can't die now."

"You must promise me one thing." He coughs, his body tenses up, and he grimaces. "Make no alliances. It took me too long to figure it out, but I have learned that the true power of Psychen Euporos comes only from within."

You wipe the tears on your face. "I can't do this alone."

"You won't have to. The new overseer arrives today." He squeezes his eyes shut, and another groan escapes him.

After a minute he says, "You are proof that overseers will rise to the occasion. Trust them to do what's best for us. Trust them, and the organization will thrive. The world will improve." He grasps your hand. "Promise me you'll do this."

You nod and reach out and stroke his brow. "I promise, dear Origen."

He brings your pinky stub to his lips. "For luck. And for love."

You hold him tight in an embrace, even as his body shakes and his muscles go rigid. You hold him until he is silent and still.

You lay him down on his side and lie next to him until your own shakes subside.

You climb to your feet and—

Sixty-four

I yell for help. Ying tightens her arms and legs around me and I remember that I'm Zelly. Not Lillia. Origen may be dead and Tabitha too, but not Ying.

I had it all wrong. Again. Lillia loved Origen. She didn't rewrite history, and her arm-scratching wasn't from seducing him. It was from the stress of hiding their love affair from Tabitha.

"Oh, my God." I twist around to face Ying. "Lillia didn't kill Origen after all."

"She didn't," Ying says. "They stayed in love."

"I didn't know."

She puts her hand on my cheek. "Why would you let me vike there if you thought she killed him?"

Last week I wouldn't have wanted her to vike there. But I guess I'm learning. "Us both knowing the whole story lets us deal with it. That's better than assuming the worst about each other."

We stay nestled together, lost in our own thoughts.

At the end of his life, Origen soured on alliances. Has Ying connected this to her own dealings with BiggerGuns?

I wonder what came next in Lillia's life without Origen. Did she recover? Was the new overseer helpful? Did Psychen Euporos thrive?

These questions can be answered later.

Ying unwraps her legs from around me and puts on her pajamas.

"When I was growing up in China," she says, "my parents and teachers taught me that the way to make it in life is to find a successful example and replicate it. I did that with Origen before I even knew if he ultimately succeeded."

She's still thinking this through, so I stay quiet. I get dressed, and when I'm done, I switch on the light.

"What do you think we should do?" I ask her.

She says, "Origen's advice to Lillia was based on the wisdom he gained from his life experiences."

"That true power comes from within, not from alliances?"

She nods. "That and overseers rise to the occasion. We need to remember his hard-earned wisdom."

Yay. But I say nothing, knowing that I could easily ruin the moment.

Ying says, "I will start by rescinding my outstanding orders."

She walks out of the bedroom and into her office. When she gets to the desk, she raises it higher.

"Were you on my computer?" she asks.

I nod. "I saw your messages to Giovanni. That's how I knew you were in your bedroom."

She gives me a tiny smile. "Giovanni is an interesting person."

"He's a liar and a pervert." I fill her in on what happened in Idaho. When I tell her about his sleazy attempt to assault me, her eyes widen.

"He's done," she says. "I'll tell Adam."

"BiggerGuns?" I ask, like I don't know.

"Adam Monarch, their founder," she says. "He's ex-special forces, and he's tough as nails." She types for a minute. "I'm conferencing with him now."

I shift to the side so her web camera can't see me.

The computer beeps, a window pops up, and a man in his forties with close-cropped graying hair, a strong jaw, and plenty of bulk in the biceps peeking out from under his polo shirt, appears.

"Hi, Ying," he says. "What's up?"

"Hi, Adam. It's about Giovanni. He makes me uncomfortable, and I don't want to talk to him again. I don't want him in the organization, either. He's not welcome."

Adam leans forward and puts his elbows on his desk. "Can you give me more details?"

Ying shakes her head. "It's personal, and I'd rather not go into it. Just get rid of him."

"Sure thing. I'm in the middle of something, and I need to get back to it. Is there anything else?"

"There is. I want you to pause all investment actions, pending a full strategy review with you in the morning."

Adam stares at her. "You want to pause? Now?"

"Yes, please. Until we come to a new strategic agreement."

"I'm afraid that won't be possible."

Ying stares at him. "Of course it will be possible."

His image is still, unblinking.

"I'm sorry for being unclear in my answer." He glances at his watch. "As of approximately ten minutes ago, I am no longer in need of your approval. My team has acquired Valentina Nikolskaya, and after some persuasion, she has agreed to work with us."

How did they get Val?

He points into the camera, his finger large on Ying's screen. "Ouyang Ying, BiggerGuns considers you expendable. Thank you for your service and goodbye."

The calls disconnects and the window disappears.

Ying scrunches up her forehead and frowns. "Why would he—"

"We need to get out of here. Right now." Panic bubbles up in me, and I grab her arm. "As long as you're alive, Val will be limited to what she can approve."

I'm sure she can figure this out without me explaining it.

She races into the bedroom.

I call Scott.

"Sorry we're late," I say. "Ying and I are ready."

"Jeez, Zelly, we waited for as long as we could, but eventually I had to pull my parents out of there. We're almost to the parking lot."

"We kind of stirred up a hornet's nest," I say. "We need a way out."

"Let me get my parents safe, and I'll come up with something."

I'd love his help. But that would mean I'd have to withhold what I know about Val. I won't do that to him.

"No, Scott," I say. "You need to get Val back. BiggerGuns has grabbed her."

Silence. Then, "How do you know?"

I repeat what Adam told Ying about persuading Val to cooperate.

I hear nothing but his breathing for a few seconds.

"Zelly, I've got to find her," Scott says. "You'll have to manage on your own."

"Don't worry about us," I say.

Scott hangs up, and I shove back against the wall of anxiety that threatens to topple and crush me.

I step into the bedroom. Ying has lost the hair curlers, dressed in jeans and a white t-shirt, and is tying her shoes.

"We're out of time," I tell her.

Someone knocks on the office door.

"Don't answer it," I say.

She walks over to the door, staying to the side. "Who is it?"

"Security," a man's voice says. "Can we come in? There's an emergency."

"Sure, but I need to get dressed first. Just a minute,"

Ying stares at me, eyes wide.

I point at the bedroom window, and together we slide it open. I push out the screen, and it falls to the ground, two stories below.

I stick my head out, and I don't see any guards.

"We'll have to jump," I say. "Hang from your hands first. And bend your knees."

I boost her up over the sill and grip her arms as she balances on her waist. I help her hold onto the window frame. She dangles for a moment and drops to the ground.

I run back into the room and close and lock the bedroom door. I climb onto the windowsill, grab the frame, dangle, and release. I drop and hit the ground with a jarring thud, lose my balance, and fall onto my butt.

Ying helps me stand, and together we race toward the front of the building. We veer to the right before we reach the main entrance, and we run to the parking lot.

Scott and his parents stand in a shadowed area at the edge of the pavement. At their feet is the handcuffed and gagged body of a man in a gray guard's uniform. A white van is thirty feet away, parked under a light.

When we arrive, Scott says, "Simon and Archie are in the van."

"Did you find where they took Val?" I ask him.

His face is pale and his voice shakes. "Not yet. Sue says she dropped off Simon and Archie and left. A white SUV." He points to the guard at his feet. "I hoped this guy would know something. We're monitoring his radio, but nothing so far."

"We can ask the Uber driver, Boubacar," I say.

We use Scott's phone to request an XL ride. Sure enough, Boubacar and his white Escalade pop up, just two minutes away.

I tell Scott I'm going to check on Simon, and Ying and I walk to the van. Simon hops out and gives me and Ying long hugs.

"How are you feeling?" I ask him.

"Better, but you should see Mr. Morgan." He takes my hand and leads us around the van to the passenger side door.

Mr. Morgan smiles at us. "Miss Oliveira and Miss Ouyang. How nice it is to see both of you all grown up."

"Mr. Morgan, you're speaking," I say.

"I am speaking. And I am thinking as well." His eyes twinkle. "Master Green has been filling me in. You young ladies have caused quite an uproar."

Boubacar's white SUV pulls into the parking lot.

"It's a good uproar," I say. "But we've got to find Val. We can talk later."

When we reach Scott, I tell him, "The vike must have kick-started something in his brain."

Scott smiles, but it's strained.

"Did you hear anything on the radio?" I ask.

He shakes his head and points to the approaching car. "Hopefully, he knows what happened."

Boubacar tells us that after he and Val left the parking lot, they were pulled over by what he thought was a local policeman. Two guards in gray uniforms came to their windows, pointed guns, and drove away with Val handcuffed in their backseat.

"I followed them back to Soul Identity," he says. "They brought her inside through the front."

Scott says to me, "They'll torture her. I'm going in."

My mind races as I watch him jog toward the main entrance.

I run over to George and borrow back my modded eyeglasses. Returning to the unconscious guard, I press the reset button, hold open his eyes, and get a good look at them. I scrounge through his pockets and take his ID badge and Taser.

Then I chase after Scott.

Sixty-five

I catch up to Scott just ten feet from the front doors.

I tug on his shirt, and he whirls around.

"You're just going to charge in there?" I ask. "That's stupid. You need a plan."

"Zelly."

I put on the eyeglasses and hold up the ID badge. "Tell me you haven't replaced those vulnerable reader access points."

"You were able to hack them?"

"Yes, but it's hard coded to my eyes. I'm coming with you."

He nods.

Ying runs up, panting. "I've been here all week," she says. "I know their routines."

"You should stay here," I say. "We can't let them get you."

She puts her hands on her hips. "Don't try to stop me."

I hold up my arms. "Peace. So where would they have taken her?"

"Her office," she says. "Or mine. They need access to an authenticated reader device so Val can authorize the money transfers. She and I have the only two outside of the depositary."

"The third floor," Scott says. "There will be guards all over the place. Any ideas for getting up there?"

"Ying's window," I say. "That puts us right across the hall."

The three of us run around the building and gather by the screen that Ying and I pushed out. Her windowsill is at least fifteen feet above our heads.

The window is still open, just as we left it.

Scott stands close to the wall and crouches, reaching his arms back over his shoulders.

"Come and stand on my shoulders," he says to Ying.

Ying grasps his hands. She steps on the back of his legs, places a foot just above his waist, and gets a knee on one of his shoulders. She climbs to her feet, and Scott stands up straight. Ying grabs the second-floor windowsill with both hands.

Scott uses his left hand to hold onto Ying's left calf. He reaches his right hand over his shoulder. "Zelly, get on up there."

I try to climb like Ying did, but I lose my balance and fall. Ying falls, too. We try it again.

And again.

After two more tries, I stand on Scott's shoulders, behind Ying, my arms around her chest.

"I can't do this," I say.

"You can," Ying says. "Don't worry about hurting me. I have a good grip. Just climb."

I climb, and this time I'm able to throw one leg over her shoulder and bring myself up so I'm sitting.

"Hurry," Scott says with a grunt. "I can't hold for much longer."

I pull on Ying's arms and scrabble my way into a crouch, and I'm standing. I can just graze the third-floor windowsill with my fingertips.

"I'm too short."

"How close are you?" she asks.

"Two inches. I'm on my tiptoes."

She pulls one hand away from the windowsill and holds it up against the wall. "Step on my hand and jump. But I'm going to fall, so make it work."

I step onto her hand and jump, and I grab the windowsill with my right hand. I throw out my left hand and get a grip. I pull, and when I don't move, I let out a mighty groan and somehow force myself high enough that I can throw my elbow, my other arm, and one leg over the sill.

I roll myself the rest of the way into Ying's bedroom and spill onto the floor. This sends my modded eyeglasses flying, and I put them back on.

The door leading to the office is open. Nobody is there, so I close it. I pull the sheets off the bed and dangle one of them out the window. Ying is back on top of Scott's shoulders, and after she grabs the sheet, I pull her up and into her room.

I tie the sheets together, but when Scott grabs the end and tries to anchor his feet to the wall, the sudden weight pulls the contrived rope out of my hands. He tosses the sheets back up, and we try again, this time with Ying helping.

Together we pull as Scott walks up the wall, and we're all inside the bedroom, bent over, hands on our knees, trying to catch our breath.

"Whose crazy idea was that?" Scott says.

"Crazy?" I ask. "We're on the third floor, and nobody's been caught."

He straightens up. "Good point. Let's go." He walks into Ying's office. The door leading to the hallway is open, and he sticks his head out for a second.

I hold up the ID badge I removed from the guard. "This will get us into the office."

Scott holds out his hand for it, but I tap my eyeglasses. "They only work for me."

Val's door is opposite, a reader access point hanging from the wall next to it. I glance up and down the hallway, pull the Taser out of my pocket, and motion for Scott and Ying to follow me.

I wave the guard's badge, then double press the reset button on my modded eyeglasses and look at the reader's lenses, closing my right eye.

My tech had better work.

The door clicks, and Scott pushes it open and runs through, Ying and I right behind him.

Val stands at her desk, with Adam Monarch next to her. As Scott reaches them, a guard who must have been by the door uses a baton to wallop him on the back of his head.

Scott falls to the floor, and Val screams. I point the Taser at the guard's back. I pull the trigger and the darts fly into his gray uniform. But the guard turns around, unaffected. He must be wearing a bulletproof vest.

The guard sees the Taser and steps toward me, raising his baton.

Ying flies at him. She grabs his outstretched arm and flips him over her shoulder. He lands with a thud, and the baton clatters to the floor. I snatch it up—it's heavy—and I hit him on the forehead as hard as I can.

"Drop it now!" Adam's right arm wraps around Val's neck, and his left hand holds a combat knife to her throat, in the crack between his arm and her chin.

I stare at him as I stand back up. "Put down that knife."

He shakes his head. "I will slice her throat if you don't drop that baton right now. Do it!"

"If anything happens to Val, your money flow stops. Just put down the knife and walk out of here."

As he sneers at me, Ying edges around the desk toward Adam's back side. I step closer to him until I am just out of his reach.

Val yells and stomps her heel onto Adam's foot. Ying lunges and grabs at his wrists, and I lean in and swing the baton at his head.

Adam must have seen me, because he twists his body, and my baton strikes Val on her cheek with a sickening crunch. Adam pushes her at me, and as Val drops to the floor, he snakes his arm around Ying's waist and pokes the knife against her lower back.

Ying should have stayed outside.

"Forget what I told you before, Ying," Adam says. "You're not expendable. At least, not yet. I just received Valentina's blanket authorization. Yours will make it unanimous."

That means no more limits for BiggerGuns.

"Pull up the funding requests," he says. "Now."

Ying types for a second. "Here they are."

Adam leans over her shoulder and reads. "The one at the top. That's the blanket request. Open it up."

Ying clicks, and she catches my eye.

"Sixty-nine is definitely an old man's age," she says.

What is that supposed to mean?

Then I remember Origen saying this to Lillia in the morning. Before Tabitha killed him.

Ying is signaling for me to play along. But why? We both know how that story ended, and it wasn't a happily-ever-after tale for him and Lillia.

I shake my head at her. I am no longer interested in repeating the past. Ying should just authorize the request. That way we all survive.

I say to Adam, "Will you leave peacefully if she authorizes it?"

He jabs at the knife. Ying cries out, and the beginnings of a red spot forms on her t-shirt. "I'll cut her kidney in half if she doesn't."

Repeating history is the only shared context we have. Our only option.

I catch Ying's eye and say, "Sixty-nine is young enough for me."

A tear runs down Ying's cheek. She moves her mouse, and Adam leans forward again.

"Yes, that's the one," he says. "Authorize it."

Ying closes her eyes and remains still. She opens them and says in a clear voice, "Never."

Adam twists the knife, and Ying lets out a groan. The red spot increases its size.

"Authorize the request, now," he says. "Or I'll kill both you and your friend here."

"Fine," Ying says. She taps on the keyboard, and she pulls the reader closer with her left hand. She bends her head toward the reader.

Adam watches, a smile on his face.

Ying whirls to her left, smashing the reader into the side of Adam's head.

Adam stumbles, and I don't waste a second, because there's no way that I will let history repeat itself and lose Ying.

Screw the past.

I swing my baton at his head as hard as I can, and I hit his nose. Blood spurts out, and Adam lets go of Ying and the knife. He brings both hands up to his face.

I swing the baton again, and this time I hit his temple. He topples to the floor, landing on his side, and I hit him with the baton. Again and again.

He flips onto his back and raises his hands to block my blows, but I swing the baton at his crotch, and when his hands go down, I pound his nose, his eyes, his chin, until I can't make out his face.

Ying groans. She's slumped over the desk and slides toward the floor.

I drop the baton and grab her by the shoulders, easing her down onto her side.

"Did it work?" she asks.

I kick out at Adam's unmoving body, and it's like hitting a punching bag.

"It worked," I say.

She clenches her teeth. "Can you check my back?"

No, no, no. We just started patching things up.

I won't survive losing Ying.

I close my eyes for a moment before I look over her side and down to her lower back. The red spot is a little bigger, but there is no knife. I search the floor, and I find it lying next to her feet.

I lean forward and retrieve it. "Girlie, you're going to be fine."

"I'm not dying?"

When I show her the knife, she lets out a giddy laugh. "We're better than our predecessors."

"Origen and Lillia? We kick their butts."

Sixty-six

Six short months later. It's my first time back in Sterling.

After a speedy police investigation, I spent the rest of my time off in Rio, getting to know my cousin Bianca, taking long walks along the beach, defeating my newfound fear of boats, and coming to peace with the idea of Ying as an overseer while I wait my turn.

I never once opened my email, answered my phone, read my messages, or watched the news. I celebrated my eighteenth birthday alone.

When I walked the beaches, I didn't dwell on the past events. I didn't repress them, either. As the memories and emotions forced their way into my head, I examined them as if they had happened to somebody else. I tried my best to have self-compassion, to not beat myself up, and to let myself heal.

I didn't vike. I didn't even have the desire. I left the past where it belongs.

And I gorged myself on a diet of pão de queijo, churrasco, and brigadeiros.

My time in Brazil was perfect. Restorative. But I'm ready to see what I missed, ready to figure out the best way I can contribute to Soul Identity's success.

I walk into the conference room, and Ying, Simon, Scott, and Val greet me with warm smiles and embraces.

When Simon finally relaxes his bear hug, his face is plastered with a sheepish smile. "I've missed you more than I can say."

I reach up, at least an inch higher than before, to tousle his hair and straighten his bowtie.

As he leans close to whisper in my ear, I catch a whiff of cologne. "I can imagine my parents again!"

I whisper, "They come every night?"

He nods, his eyes shining, and I give him a big smile as I squeeze his shoulder.

I watch Ying putting away her book, Dale Carnegie's *How to Win Friends and Influence People*.

I take a minute to savor the sight of each of them.

"It feels like it's been forever," I say. "I'm ready to be put to work."

After we sit down, Val clears her throat. "What news have you heard?"

"Absolutely nothing."

"Then I'll start with the bad part." She takes my hand. "Zelly, Mr. Morgan's funeral was last Tuesday."

I open my mouth to say something. Anything.

Nothing comes out.

"Archie talked about you every day," Scott says. "You were his hero. He was so grateful that you gave him what he called his bonus time."

I feel a pain in my chest. Val hands me a tissue, and I swipe at the tears running down my face.

Ying slides a sealed envelope across the desk to me. "He left you a letter."

I examine the outside. It has *Giselle Oliveira* written in cursive by a shaky hand.

But I don't open it.

When the lump in my throat subsides, I say, "There had better be good news or I'm heading straight back to Rio."

"There's great news," Simon says. "Last month you and I officially became overseers!"

"Val insisted we do this," Ying says. "Mr. Morgan showed us how to use unanimous consent to change the age requirement. The new rule says overseers must be at least fourteen."

I glance at Val, my eyebrows raised.

"You were right." She shakes her head. "I was stuck in my fears. I'm so sorry, Zelly."

I ask, "That means the four of us now run Soul Identity?"

"Just the three of you," Val says. "Since Mr. Morgan passed, I'm no longer his trustee."

Wow. The three of us running Soul Identity was my dream. But it's funny how different the job looks after six months in Rio.

I clear my throat. "I'm not sure how to phrase this, but I don't want to be an overseer."

That gets their attention.

"Who are you and what have you done to our Zelly?" Simon asks.

I hold up my hands. "It's still me, Sy, but now with a little more self-awareness, a lot more trust in others, and a refusal to feel obligated by my past."

"Why don't you want to serve?" Ying asks.

"Someday I do. But only once I feel ready."

She nods.

I turn to Val. "Until then, would you please serve in my place, as my trustee?"

She stares at me, open-mouthed, for a few seconds. "I know I've improved over the past six months," she says, "but are you sure you want somebody with my kind of risk tolerance?"

"It's exactly what we need," I say.

She tilts her head. "You continue to impress me, Zelly. I'd be honored to be your trustee. Thank you."

Ying and Simon both break out into grins. Then Scott and Val exchange glances.

"Zelly, you should read Archie's letter," Scott says.

"Do you know what it says?"

"We all do," Simon says.

"Give me a minute." I turn to Ying, who looks fabulous in her tailored suit and silk top. "Are you a better overseer than your ancestor?"

She grins. "I'm kicking his butt."

"Girlie, you'll keep on kicking everybody's butt."

Then I look at Scott. "Did the factories pitch their proposals to you?"

"Yes, and I took the liberty to choose the best." He pulls a small black box out of his messenger bag and hands it to me. "This was the final prototype. The first batch arrives next week." He smiles. "And just so you know, I removed your hack against my reader access points."

I open the box and find a pair of horn-rimmed, stylish eyeglasses. I can barely see the camera lenses.

I smile. "They're gorgeous."

He points at the envelope. "Enough with the procrastinating. Read the letter."

I pull out the single page of cramped writing and read it out loud.

Dear Ms. Oliveira,

Simon says to call you Zelly, or at least Giselle. He claims I know you well enough from all the stories he told me that I am allowed to be informal. Alas, I am too old-fashioned to do so without your permission.

The bonus time you gave me has been a most precious gift. I was able to speak with your fellow overseers, reflect upon what I heard, and realize that you three, from your special generation, will be far more wise and far more capable than any previous set of overseers.

Because you rendered BiggerGuns leaderless, and because Mr. Monarch hadn't bothered with succession planning, I was able to purchase that company from his estate for a tiny fraction of its value. I consider that payback, something that Val's driver Boubacar calls the Jola Way, for what they tried to do to Soul Identity.

Once I purchased BiggerGuns, I canceled its military contracts, converted it into a non-profit, and funded it with most of my considerable wealth. Ying and Val also sold to me, at a good price, Soul Identity's advanced research teams, including the vike portal project. I transferred these teams into the new non-profit.

My last step was to replace its horrid name. Do you remember the story I told you, Simon, and Ying five years ago, right before my surgery? BiggerGuns is now known as Magic Garden Systems.

Magic Garden Systems has a broad mission—improve the world. Unlike Soul Identity, it does not bear the burden of its past. You, Ms. Oliveira, are its first managing director, and you shall remain so for as long as you wish. Scott and

Val sit on your board, as do your fellow overseers and my two great-granddaughters, Rose and Marie. You have a team of a thousand employees ready to do your bidding, backed by a huge operating fund.

Please, direct the company in any way you see fit. I am sorry I did not have the opportunity to spend more time with you. But from what I have learned, you will be outstanding.

This is my payback to you. I suppose I am also a believer in the Jola Way.

Please, think as big as you possibly can.

With all my gratitude,
Archibald Morgan

I look up from the letter. Four sets of eyes stare back at me.

I ask Simon, "What kinds of stories did you tell Mr. Morgan?"

"The ones about our adventures on the road and in the air. He especially loved how you outwitted Giovanni."

"I told him how you refused to leave me behind," Ying says. "And how you insisted that we inform ourselves with the truth about Origen and Lillia."

"I showed him your eyeglasses," Scott says. "And he literally took a pair with him to his grave."

"He believed in you, Zelly," Val says. "We all do."

Mr. Morgan's letter threatens to upend the peace I found in Rio. This morning, all I wanted was to support Val and Ying. I even said no to the overseer job.

Now I'm supposed to run a huge non-profit company?

The job is way too big for me. I won't have a large enough perspective, and I'll never remember to apply the most respectful interpretations. I'll get tripped up by my past, and when dealing with conflicts, I'll escalate myself into trouble instead of following the Jola Way.

In other words, Magic Garden Systems will fail if it's left in my hands.

But my people are gathered around me. We each bring wildly different histories and soul lines, and those are our greatest assets if we don't let the past dictate what we do. We can take the wisdom it offers and forge our own better future.

I can't run this company, but together we all can.

I choose to think as big as I possibly can.

Acknowledgments

Once upon a time, I had a bright idea—I would pivot to writing books for young adults, and that would introduce the Soul Identity world to a new set of readers. Now fast forward through seven years, twenty-eight drafts, and a crazy pandemic . . . Zelly's first story, *Oversight*, is in your hands.

Thank you for reading *Oversight*. Whether you've met Scott and Val in the *Soul Identity* books or this was your first exposure, I hope you enjoyed getting to know Zelly, Ying, and Simon as much as I enjoyed introducing them to you.

Thank you, Bianca Candida—the sparkle and warmth you showed your friends and family, along with your sharp intellect, was the perfect inspiration for Zelly. I hope you like how she turned out.

Through the darkest days of the quarantine, my wife Irina, my son Christopher, and my son-in-law Matt read each chapter as I wrote them. Your passion to the story, your insightful questions, and even your confusion gave me the power to keep going. Simon would never have flown that jet, Christopher, if it wasn't for your insistence.

Zelly's and Ying's cultural depths come from many readings and discussions with Glaucia Young and Hong Jia. You made them authentic and true to their backgrounds, and I'm grateful.

Throughout the novel, Zelly suffers from anxiety, jealousy, and the imposter syndrome. My twin daughters, Holly and

Alison, are clinical psychologists, and they ensured Zelly's actions, reactions, and techniques for working through her traumas were realistic and helpful. Thanks for giving your input during the lively discussions around our quarantine dinner table, where all your siblings participated, and where we all gained great life lessons.

A special thanks to these six early readers who helped me see new perspectives: my mother Arlene, my brother Jeff, my sister Kristin, Arunabh Trivedi, Hermineh Sanossian, and Gokcen Iskander.

Two editors made the story more succinct. Thank you, Kate Angelella, for your shaping, and Hannah VanVels Ausbury, for your polishing.

We authors may not like to admit it, but books do get judged by their covers and by their typesetting. Thank you, Zeeshan Alam and Andrew Tennant, for your work to make *Oversight* shine.

Finally, I am grateful, Rachel Cone-Gorham, for helping me market *Oversight*. Without your plan and suggestions, this reader would never have met Zelly.

About the Author

One of the world's experts at fighting cybercriminals and the co-founder of a growing internet safety company, Dennis Batchelder started writing novels with a 2006 New Year's resolution, vowing he wouldn't return from his 2-year overseas posting to India without a first draft in hand. *Oversight* is his fourth novel—following his best-selling *Soul Identity* series—and his debut for young adults.

Dennis lives in West Seattle with his wife, his mother-in-law, and his three youngest sons. He writes both on-scene and back home at his desk overlooking the Puget Sound.